A Slow Burn is a powerfully gripping story of a [illegible] peace after a horrible event rips her life to shreds. Mary DeMuth weaves a suspense that will keep you on the edge of your seat. Her characters and descriptions are captivating, bringing the story to life with the turn of every page.

Amy Clipston
Bestselling author of A Gift of Grace

Mary DeMuth is an author with a flawless sense of time and place. *A Slow Burn* is a thing of literary poignance and beauty, a brave story as only DeMuth can tell it, written in heart-wrenching, gorgeous prose.

Tosca Lee
Author of Christy Finalist Demon: A Memoir *and* Havah: The Story of Eve

In *A Slow Burn*, Mary E. DeMuth explores the depth and breadth of tragedy with deft sensitivity and raw honesty. She deals unflinchingly with murder, rape, adultery, drug abuse, and more, yet she weaves heartbreak and hope into the same tapestry. Her book will both rend your heart and then soothe it. A must-read for anyone who has hit the proverbial rock bottom and longs to turn around and look up.

Nicole Baart
Author of The Moment Between

A Slow Burn will linger with the reader long after the last page—a bit of us all in a novel filled with suspense and longing.

DiAnn Mills
Author of Breach of Trust, Sworn to Protect, *and* A Woman Called Sage

Mary DeMuth writes with clarity and grace about tragically flawed human beings and the God of second chances. This is another soul-stirring novel in a beautiful series by this talented author.

Kathleen Popa,
Author of The Feast of Saint Bertie

Mary DeMuth has intertwined artful writing, a powerfully imagined plot, and characters that are startlingly human. *A Slow Burn* brims with a prevailing grace that abundantly covers even the most devastating of human regrets. DeMuth's novels just keep getting better.

Tina Ann Forkner
Author of Ruby Among Us *and* Rose House

Mary DeMuth has continued the suspense of the Defiance Texas Trilogy in *A Slow Burn*. She continues to raise the stakes as another life is taken and secrets are exposed in this intense second installment. I can't wait for the third.

Sharon K. Souza
Author of Lying on Sunday *and* Every Good & Perfect Gift

With her consummate insight into the wounded human spirit, DeMuth prompts us to peel away our prejudices and find compassion for the unlovely. The story is a beacon of hope to the hopeless.

Rita Stella Galieh
Australian author and radio speaker

Inside the pages of Mary DeMuth's *A Slow Burn*, I have walked the streets of Defiance, Texas, with wholly knowable characters. I've felt the weight of their pain and cheered their small and monumental steps in grace. Above all, the story reflects the redemptive power of God's love. I didn't want it to end.

Patti Hill
Author of The Garden Gates series

Mary DeMuth raises the stakes in the search for Daisy's abductor. An inside look at loss, regret, and the meaning of second chances, *A Slow Burn* brings us closer to the truth and to the people who have been singed by it.

Bonnie Grove
A*uthor of* Talking to the Dead

Every man should read Mary E. DeMuth. Too many women shoulder burdens they should never have to carry. We have much to learn from her.

Austin Boyd
Author of the Mars Hill Classified Trilogy

Intense. Mournful. Gritty. Amazing. DeMuth weaves the intricate threads of this story so beautifully and tenderly that, without you realizing it, they've wrapped around your heart and touched the very depth of your soul. A masterpiece of the written word, *A Slow Burn* is a window of light into a dark world.

Kimberley Woodhouse
Author of Welcome Home! Our Family's Journey to Extreme Joy

A Slow Burn

BOOK TWO

MARY E. DeMUTH

ZONDERVAN.com/
AUTHORTRACKER
follow your favorite authors

We want to hear from you. Please send your comments about this book to us in care of zreview@zondervan.com. Thank you.

ZONDERVAN

A Slow Burn

This title is also available as a Zondervan ebook.
Visit www.zondervan.com/ebooks.

This title is also available in a Zondervan audio edition.
Visit www.zondervan.fm.

Requests for information should be addressed to:

Zondervan, *Grand Rapids, Michigan 49530*

Library of Congress Cataloging-in-Publication Data

DeMuth, Mary E., 1967-
Daisy chain : a novel / Mary E. DeMuth.
p. cm. — (Defiance Texas triology ; bk. 2)
ISBN 978-0-310-27837-5 (pbk.)
1. Texas—Fiction. I. Title.
PS3604.E48S57 2009
813'.6—dc22

2009015946

All Scripture quotations, unless otherwise indicated, are taken from the King James Version.

Any Internet addresses (websites, blogs, etc.) and telephone numbers printed in this book are offered as a resource. They are not intended in any way to be or imply an endorsement by Zondervan, nor does Zondervan vouch for the content of these sites and numbers for the life of this book.

Published in association with the literary agency of Alive Communications, Inc., 7680 Goddard Street, Suite 200, Colorado Springs, CO 80920. www.alivecommunications.com

Interior design by Christine Orejuela-Winkelman

Printed in the United States of America

---

09 10 11 12 13 14 15 • 23 22 21 20 19 18 17 16 15 14 13 12 11 10 9 8 7 6 5 4 3 2

To Wendie, whose regret has been washed by grace
and transformed into beautiful redemption.

He that covereth his sins shall not prosper:

but whoso confesseth and forsaketh *them* shall have mercy.

Proverbs 28:13

Who can save a child from a burning house without taking the risk of being hurt by the flames? Who can listen to a story of loneliness and despair without taking the risk of experiencing similar pains in his own heart and even losing his precious peace of mind? In short: Who can take away suffering without entering it?

Wounded Healer, Henri Nouwen

One

DEFIANCE, TEXAS, 1977

Worry had its way with Emory, enticing her to stay up late after her night shift, hoping against hope that her missing daughter, Daisy, would walk through the front door laughing and shouting and singing all at once. It made for groggy, sleep-sloppy mornings, where the only promise of coherence was a cup of joe followed by a tepid shower. Under the spray Emory shook hands with her tears, let them slip down her face, run down her chin and mingle with lukewarm creeks of shower water, racing in lines down her skin into the rusty drain circled by soap suds at her feet. Even then she listened. Turned off the nozzle three times when she thought she heard a noise.

But Daisy hadn't barged through the front door for two months now. Her unmade bed stayed that way, waiting for Daisy's warm thirteen-year-old body, bronzed from too much Texas sun, to collapse into it. Emory, dripping wet, stood in Daisy's doorway this morning—haunted it, really—and memorized the wrinkle of the sheets. Towel clutched around her as if the day gave a chill, she took five barefooted steps into her daughter's room, dropped the towel, and curled naked on Daisy's bed.

She didn't weep; that was for the shower. She didn't even pray. Preachers handled that. Every Defiance preacher prayed up a storm, she'd heard, but even their multitudes of prayers did nothing to undo Daisy's disappearance. Prayer didn't amount to much. No leads discovered. No kidnapper nabbed. No one but Daisy's dad under suspicion, and he was nowhere to be found. Pray? No, she moaned instead, a guttural anguish she pushed through her lungs, vibrating Daisy's bed. Two months without her only child, and all she could do was groan, hug her knees, and smell Daisy on the sheets, hoping this whole ordeal was a cruel nightmare and when she woke up, Daisy'd be standing over her, a sharp-witted look in her eyes and a sassy, "Mama, you're naked. Get yourself some clothes."

Daisy'd only found her near naked once. Or was it more? On the day Daisy went missing, Emory lay on the living-room floor half-nude and strung out. Emory remembered the shame, how it felt hot, simmering her face. She had noticed her attire: just a bra and panties, no real clothes in sight to cover herself, her body displayed like abstract art on the canvas of a hardwood floor.

"Mama," Daisy said, "I'm tired of taking care of you, you hear me?" Though Daisy's voice scolded, she grabbed a favorite quilt, the one she camouflaged their old couch with because she hated that ugly thing, and pulled it over cold toes, knees, belly, shoulders, and neck. "There, Mama. There. You sleep. I'm going to see Jed, okay? I'll be back for dinner."

Emory murmured a hung-over okay. She pulled the quilt around herself, closed her eyes, and slept away the afternoon, while Daisy played with her friend Jed Pepper, then disappeared into the Defiance dust under his neglectful care.

She stood, thirty years old but feeling arthritic all the same. She wrapped the towel around her and headed to her room, where a floor full of dirty clothes made up her wardrobe.

A knock startled her. Three stark raps against an aging door. "Just a minute," she hollered. She pulled on a ripped pair of Levis and a gauzy shirt. Emory caught her gaze in the full-length mirror; gaunt eyes stared back, the eyes of a bitter old woman.

Three more raps.

Halfway between her room and the front door, she knew.

She knew.

Emory stood in front of the door, the passageway Daisy was supposed to skip through, and tried to settle herself, but her heart hammered her ribcage. She took a deep breath, letting out a whisper of a moan. She opened the door. It creaked on its hinges as it opened onto her covered front porch.

Officer Spellman stood at her door, patrol hat in hands.

"Ma'am." He cocked his head, his eyes moist.

"No." She backed away two steps. Then again, "No."

"We found Daisy." He hesitated. "Actually, it was Jed Pepper who found her—in a clearing."

"No." Emory's gut wrenched sideways; her cold hands began to sweat.

"We've taken the body to Tyler. I need you to come with me to identify her."

Emory wilted into the doorframe, not caring a bit if it held her up or gave way and let her crash to the floor. Daisy. Her Daisy. Laughing, singing, skipping Daisy.

A body.

Nothing more.

The journey to Tyler in the back of a police car took ten years, or maybe ten minutes. She couldn't be sure. But she felt her body aging in the seat, the wrinkles forming around her frown, her eyes deteriorating in the light of this terrible day. She'd be an old woman by the time she reached Tyler. An old, childless woman.

"We're here," Officer Spellman said. He opened the car door for her. Opened the door to the hospital too.

A gentleman even in the face of death, she thought.

They wound through the hospital's underbelly, down stark corridors. Heels—hers and his—clicked a cadence she'd never forget, one that would accompany her nightmares from here on out.

Another door opened.

Then another.

She filled out forms. In triplicate. Answered questions no mama should ever have to answer. Officer Spellman sat in an antiseptic chair, hat in hands, eyes to the floor.

A man in a white coat said, "Right this way, Mrs. Chance."

"It's Ms." Emory didn't look up.

"My mistake," he said. "We won't know her exact time of death until the autopsy's done. I'd wait on ordering the gravestone just yet, until we pinpoint it."

"Gravestone," she croaked to the sterile air.

"She's right in here." The nameless man opened another door.

Emory felt her heartbeat in her neck; put her hand there, as if to calm it back down to its proper rhythm. In front of a pale green wall was a gurney with a white sheet stretched over a body. Her little girl.

The last time Daisy'd had a sheet over her head, Halloween did its haunting. Though past trick-or-treating age, she'd insisted on being a ghost, taking young Sissy Pepper around their Defiance neighborhood. "To protect her," she said.

"And what kind of ghost can protect a little girl?" Emory had asked.

"My kind." She tugged at the sheet pulled taut over her head. Two phantom eyes darkened with black-tinted Crisco looked through two crudely cut holes in the nearly white sheet. Around Daisy's neck Emory tied a ratty string, giving her head a jack-o-lantern look—just like the picture in *Family Circle*'s Halloween issue. Daisy flapped her arms, sheet billowing in stark contrast to the porch's night. "I can even scare away the boogie man."

The man pulled back the sheet to the body's chest, but Emory wouldn't look. Not yet. She turned away, pretending interest in the wall color. She inhaled. Swallowed bile. Shook her head as if that would keep the tears away somehow. She turned. Grabbed her stomach. Smelled death. Then saw her, open eyes to sunken eyes.

Daisy.

Her blonde hair browned by clods of dirt. Emory wanted to comb them away, give her hair a good brushing, though she'd never bothered when Daisy was alive. Daisy's eyes, closed lids over caved-in sockets, emanated death. Her mouth turned uncharacteristically down, a frown etched into Daisy's face for eternity.

"Ma'am? Is this your daughter?"

She looked at the man. "She was."

"I'll slip out. Give you a few moments."

Emory watched Daisy. But Daisy didn't move. Didn't sing. Didn't holler. Didn't run. Didn't scat. Didn't pick the dirt out of her hair. She lay there. That was all.

Emory stepped closer.

Dark marks circled Daisy's neck—the same place that cord circled her ghost costume. Was she choked? Were her last breaths stolen from her by hands too strong?

"Daisy, it's Mama. Your mama." She suspended her hand inches above Daisy's pale shoulder, afraid to touch it. "Who did this to you, baby?"

Daisy didn't tell.

Emory knew who bore part of the blame, felt it way down inside. If Daisy's eyes were open, they'd look right into Emory's soul, spotlighting guilt, the guilt she kept pushing down with the same ferocity she tamed her nausea.

She touched Daisy's shoulder. So cold. So hard. So unlike Daisy.

Yet so much like herself it made Emory shudder.

Two

The squad car hummed along the road toward Defiance. Officer Spellman cleared his throat. "Do you have close family nearby?"

"What's that supposed to mean?" She heard the edge in her voice but didn't care. Why'd this officer have to be so nosy?

"Nothing. Just that funerals, well, they cost—"

"I buried my mama. I think I know."

Emory found herself on the front porch of her freshly painted house, the memory of touching Daisy's cold shoulder chilling her. The officer drove away. A stray cat meowed at her feet, nuzzling in and out around her ankles. She kicked it away. She fumbled with her keys, let them clank to the porch floor. There, propped up against the front door was a gift wrapped in comics.

She guessed it came from Jed. According to Officer Spellman, Jed found Daisy in an open field, her hand crooked to the sky like she was pointing at God, begging him to rescue her. Only he hadn't.

She fetched the gift, grasped her keys from the porch floor, then unlocked the door. The stray skittered inside, but she didn't bother to chase it. It was the couch that held her there—the sorry paisley mess Daisy hated. The quilt covering it had slipped off once again, but Emory didn't have the heart to right it. That was Daisy's job.

She dropped the keys on the coffee table, then examined the package, turning it over in her hands. It was the size of a large photo album, only lighter. No card attached. Still standing, Emory ripped it open. A black cross-stitch bordered in red and orange roses stared back at her. It read: " 'I will punish you according to the fruit of your doings, saith the Lord: and I will kindle a fire in the forest thereof, and it shall devour all things round about it.' Jeremiah 21:14." Emory dropped the framed piece. It clattered on the floor. She ran to the door, flung it open. No one there.

Heart pounding, she grabbed the sickening declaration and threw it in the hall closet. She slammed the door so hard the house shook against her force. Emory slid down the wall, grabbed her knees, and held herself. The cat slunk alongside her, purring, but Emory didn't acknowledge it. Didn't scat it away or touch it. When she closed her eyes, all she could see were Daisy's empty sockets staring at nothing, not even her.

Three

Hixon believed God was in the habit of sending signs his way. Which is why when he saw his cancer-ridden friend Muriel's letter on the floor by his feet, he knew it was meant for his eyes today. She slept with a pen crooked in her gnarled hand, a smile etched into her dying face. While her chest rose in rhythm to his breathing, he bent low and picked up Muriel's testament—words from her pen straight to Hixon's heart.

He read:

> By now I'm with the good Lord, taking dancing lessons. I'll be learning the rumba and the cha cha, most likely. And maybe I've even met your mama by now. Here's my guess: if she's here, she's whole. I don't know much about heaven and regrets. The Bible says that God wipes away all those tears we cried, so maybe the regret is there at first, but it fades real fast the more we dance for Jesus on streets of gold. I hope that's the case because I have regrets aplenty—like your mama probably did. Maybe even like you. Or like Miss Emory's wrestling, though she won't be showing her struggles to a soul. (She might not even let herself know she's wrestling.)
>
> I have one request. Don't get all cranky on me now. Realize you're reading this simple note while I'm healthy and happy in heaven—kind of like a living and dying wish

all wrapped together. What I'd really love you to do is take God seriously and finally ask Miss Emory to marry you.

Hixon placed the letter back at his feet and stepped away from the blessedly breathing bald woman. He retreated to his kitchen table, one of the places he had it out with the Almighty, and pointed a finger ceilingward. "Lord," he whispered, "what do you mean by sending me this letter today?"

The faded kitchen walls creaked, but God didn't answer back with words this time.

"I get it. I understand. You want me to marry Missy—only she doesn't even know she's Missy to me. And just to be sure I'd listen, you sent your words through a dying saint to get my attention. It was a nice touch to breeze the letter to the floor."

If he strained enough, he could hear the Almighty laughing. But this was no laughing matter. Emory Chance was not a woman to be wooed. She wasn't even a woman to be talked to—particularly now. Why was it that God called him to do such a crazy thing? Hixon swallowed, realizing afresh that he served the God who saw his swallowing, his wallowing, his whining. The memory of Muriel's letter stinging his conscience, Hixon sighed another okay to the God who sees. And then he went in search of winter flowers. Because wasn't that the way to win a girl? He didn't write the words of a poet. His singing voice was meant for the Almighty alone. And he didn't exactly have money to spend on perfume. But he could find flowers. He hoped that would be enough.

He stood on Missy's porch, a short bouquet of pansies in hand, she on the other side of the screen door, clutching its handle. She, with her red-rimmed eyes and tight-lipped grief. He would not be able to hold her yet, to press out the grief.

"You can leave the flowers on the porch." She spoke the words in such a matter-of-fact way, as if Hixon were the milkman and she were merely conducting a business transaction. "You been here recently?" He heard fear behind those words, couldn't make sense of them.

"No, not until now."

"You sure?"

"Yes," he said. "Why?"

She looked away. "No reason. Just wondering."

Hixon put the flowers on a small table next to her porch swing. "Missy, I'm— "

"Don't say it. I'm sick of those words: 'I'm sorry,' " she hissed. "Sorry? Like you have anything to be sorry about. Life stinks. Death happens. Don't be sorry."

"But I am. Sorry for your sake." Hixon took a step closer.

She let go of the screen door, the barrier between them, and stepped farther back into her house. "I don't need your pity."

Hixon put his hands in the air. "I don't mean to pity you. Just offer my condolences. And my help. Is there anything you need? I can pray for you."

She touched the screen's handle again, inching a hint closer. "One thing."

"Anything."

"I can't abide Reverend Hap Pepper preaching my Daisy's funeral, you know? Would you do it?"

Hixon looked at his feet. He smiled, but then thought the better of it, placing a hand over his mouth. He wiped that smile away, then looked into Missy's eyes. "Of course. It would be my privilege."

She nodded and shut the front door, leaving Hixon with a remnant of hope, a lump in his throat, and a mess of flowers next to her porch swing. She hadn't even noticed he'd called her Missy.

He walked down the stairs, remembering the last time he'd spent at this house after Daisy went missing. How he and a haunted Jed Pepper scraped away peeling paint, primed it, and made the house preen. So much like Missy, a shock of beauty, startling in its brightness. And yet, no one really knew what went on inside the newly painted house, nor did Hixon know what lit her from the inside. He'd looked in her eyes, craning his neck just so, only to find her curtaining the windows of her heart. Sometimes her beauty alone was enough to sustain him for days, weeks. And sometimes a wry smile from her pink lips was simply a tantalizing enticement to something he'd never know—Missy's soul.

Hixon tried to whistle his way home, but his lips were too dry to keep any long notes. With each step on Defiance's cracked and buckled sidewalks, his thankfulness to preach Daisy's funeral—the privilege of being asked—waffled into dread. What if he didn't remember Daisy proper? He pictured himself in a pressed suit—his only one—standing before Daisy's small coffin, unable to speak. He saw Hap Pepper smiling his way to the pulpit, gently pushing Hixon aside, determined to preach about the girl he barely knew. Hixon prayed as he walked down Love Street, asking Jesus to please give him love-tinged words, the right words, words to make Daisy smile from heaven and give Miss Emory the gift of a life remembered perfectly.

He turned onto Elm and headed home. Behind closed curtains, Muriel would be waiting for him—his adopted mama. She'd be heaving in cancerous breaths, talking about Jesus between each rasp. It wouldn't be long before he preached another funeral, his second in one year. In one life.

The front door creaked as he pushed it open. Muriel lay propped up in a hospital bed, eyeing him. He noticed the letter now clutched in her hands. She smiled, winked, then placed the letter in an envelope and sealed it. Though dark circles bagged underneath, her eyes still danced, her mouth upturned like praise. "Did she say yes?" she asked.

Hixon sighed as he closed the door. He adjusted to the darkness of the room. Light gave Muriel headaches something fierce.

"Don't you think it's a little early to be courting?"

"Never too early."

"She asked me to preach Daisy's funeral." Hixon held Muriel's hand. "What should I do?"

"What your heart tells you to do," Muriel rasped.

"I told her I'd do it. I'm just afraid is all. I'm worried I'll freeze up with sadness." He squeezed her hand and let it go.

"That poor girl."

"I still can't believe she's gone." Hixon went to the window, pushed away the drapes for just a moment, to remind himself that the world continued on as usual in the bright daylight.

"Not poor *Daisy*. She's laughing in heaven, son." Muriel took a breath, let it out. She smiled. "I meant poor Miss Emory. Your future wife."

Hixon turned. In the light of the opened drape, he noticed Muriel's gray lips inclined toward the ceiling, a laugh nearly escaping. "Quit your teasing," he said.

"I'm not teasing. Just stating fact."

"Some things are better left unsaid."

Muriel coughed, then cleared her throat. "You told me Jesus ordered you to marry her."

"I know. But maybe I was wrong. Maybe it's my crazy mind thinking impossible things."

"Impossible things are God's business." She coughed so weakly Hixon rushed again to her bedside. He lifted a cup of lukewarm tea to her mouth, but she shook her head. "No. I'm fine. Sit me up more."

He adjusted her pillows, propping her as best he could.

"You'll marry her, son. But it won't be the way you imagine it." She looked at Hixon then, eyes full of the world's sadness. "She may break your heart—she's so broken herself."

"I understand broken folks," he said.

"I know. I know." Muriel closed, then opened her eyes, her eyelids a theater curtain that closed on a tragedy then opened to a comedy. She smiled, but even if she hadn't, he'd have known she was smiling by the dance in her eyes. "And she'll understand someday. It's my prayer, Hixon. You know that, right?"

He nodded. He remembered her letter, how she'd made everything clear in blue and white.

"Preach hope at that funeral, you hear me? Daisy's gone to wide fields where her Creator lives. Life can't get any better than that."

Hixon nodded. She was right. Always right.

"Hixon, look at me."

He obeyed her. Ever since she adopted him as her own son, he'd done everything he could to accommodate her, taking her into his home, doing everything the doctors said and then some. "Ma'am?"

"You need to do it." Air stumbled over the rasp deep in her lungs.

"Maybe it's time to rest."

Muriel closed her eyes; even that small movement seemed to weary her. She moaned, breathing air that sounded like soup as it passed through her lungs. Gurgling in. Gurgling out. She didn't bother with wearing her red wig anymore. Even so, Hixon knew her head got cold, so he'd given her his black stocking cap to warm her shiny head. It slipped off.

Hixon gently fitted it back. He sighed. How much longer? The news of Jed's finding Daisy's body leeched the breath from Muriel, while at the same time reigniting one last flicker for another dream. She'd had one dying wish fulfilled—to paint a mural on the wall of the rendering plant—and she and Hixon and Jed Pepper had accomplished that, but that hadn't been enough. No, one more thing, she'd told him. One last way to make her mark on Defiance, Texas—an eternal mark, she'd said.

"It's time," she said.

"But the wall, it's all that's needed. The whole town loves it.

It's a testament to your kindness, to God's beauty. Can't that be enough?"

Muriel opened clear eyes. "No," she said. "Not enough." She inhaled, then exhaled. "The Lord said— "

"I know what the Lord said. But what if you can't do it?"

Muriel's eyes looked beyond him to a spot on his wall where a cross he'd fashioned from scrap metal hung crooked. She pulled in another labored breath. "Jesus." She smiled.

Hixon turned to look at the cross. No Jesus. But he may as well have stood right there, smiling his shiny Jesus eyes on Muriel in Hixon's shadowy living room. What with the way she beamed, it may have been so. Or maybe she was so close to seeing him in the next life, he'd chosen to appear to her in this life, like a heavenly concierge service. "What is it?"

"He's not finished," she breathed, "with me yet."

Yet? Hixon didn't like that word. It proved there'd be an ending. Though he'd mourned his mama's death, something inside him knew grieving Muriel would snuff him clear out, flatten him like roadkill, leaving little opportunity for resurrection. He looked at Muriel, her eyes still shining, and nodded.

Four

On days like today, Emory road her bike to work. It's not that the old car wouldn't crank to life. It would. But the sun-bleached pavement cast a spell over Emory, drawing her away from floor pedals toward bike pedals. Besides, pumping her legs might just push away the grief—something she intended to hide when she got to Little Myrtle's Café. So she pushed the pedals faster on Love Street's bumpy sidewalk, dodging live oak tree roots as she passed low-slung fifties ranch homes. Her breath came quickly.

Emory veered right onto Elm, then pedaled past Hixon's home, wondering again why a handyman would have such a crooked, broken house. The windows weren't plumb in their casings. The porch had an incline a marble would love. The front door, now grayed wood, held only splinters of brown to prove its former color. She shuddered every time she spied Hixon's attempt at taxidermy. He called the squirrel sitting as sentinel over his front porch railing "Chippy." Stiff as a brick, Chippy didn't gather any acorns this fall. Never would again.

Only four blocks to go while the sun shone on shedding trees, their twiggy shadows crossing the sidewalk like pick up sticks. Big Earl had called as soon as he found out about Daisy's body, told Emory to take a few days off, but she wouldn't. She needed money for the funeral and her rent, which was now past due, according to a kind but pointed letter from her landlord, Clyde Van Tassell. Besides all that money mess, she needed the café's distraction—the bustling of patrons in and out, the clinking of coffee mugs, and Big Earl's big voice booming orders from the kitchen. Even so, nearing Little Myrtle's, she wondered how she could paint on an indifferent face, knowing the customers would surely bring Daisy up, shoot sympathetic looks her way.

She parked her bike out back, next to the fermenting dumpster that the city of Defiance emptied only twice a month. With gallons of food scraps, rendered bacon, rotting cabbage and corn, the wait staff and cooks called it the City Dump. She opened the back door. It creaked closed. From the peg near the entrance, she grabbed her apron and tied it behind her.

"You really should be home," a voice said from behind her. Big Earl.

She turned around. There he was, Mr. Concerned. "You need me."

He wiped sweat from his brow, then placed fat arms around his even fatter middle. His white cook's apron held years of grease and stains. "You're right, darling. I need you. But I'm worried about you too."

"Rent doesn't pay itself, Big Earl. Besides, funerals cost a lot of money."

He shook his head. Emory saw tears in his eyes—something Big Earl didn't bother to mop up with greasy hands. "Don't I know it. My Myrtle's cost a fortune. But I'd give all the money her café made in twenty years to have her next to me right now."

Emory patted his forearm. "I know."

He sniffed. "You'll be the first I let go off shift today, okay?"

"Don't do me any favors."

Earl turned, facing the bulletin board in the kitchen. He pointed to his collection of postcards—all of Tahiti—adorned with palm trees, beaches, sunsets. "We were going to go there," he said. "But we never did. Life shrinks before your eyes; before you know it, your dreams are gone."

Emory had swallowed a dream or two when Daisy died. There wouldn't ever be that trip to the Tyler zoo now, though the place wasn't as exotic as Tahiti. "I hear you, Big Earl." She patted him on the shoulder, felt the sweat seeping through his T-shirt.

She pushed through the kitchen door that swung into the checkerboard-floored dining room. Candy winked at her with sad eyes, then trotted toward her. "I'm so sorry," she said. "That poor baby. How are you doing, sweetie?"

"Good as can be expected." Emory looked beyond Candy's perfectly pressed uniform to see which booths needed attention. She counted how many sugar decanters were half mast and reminded herself to fill the Heinz bottles.

Thanks to Aqua Net, Candy's blonde hair barely moved when she shook her head. "And she was all you had left in the world." She smacked Doublemint gum, her cigarette substitute between breaks.

"I need to get to that two-top." Emory pushed past Candy toward a familiar duo sitting at table seven next to the ancient jukebox belting Elvis.

"Hello, gorgeous!" Angus Day stood, his perfect smile stretching what seemed beyond his cheeks. He'd pulled his long brown hair into a ponytail.

For a moment she wondered how he'd looked with a Vietnam-style buzz cut. Would he be as beautiful then? Or just like every other part-time rendering plant worker? "Today's not the day to be calling me that. Now sit down."

Angus obliged. "I'm surprised to see you here."

Curly Sanders, wearing a white T-shirt and a pair of ancient Levis, nodded his full head of brown ringlets. "Me too."

"A girl's gotta work. Pay bills." She swallowed, then pulled out her order pad, though she already knew what Angus wanted.

Emory avoided his eyes, the number 650 dancing in her mind. How much she owed him. For all that dope. "Order?"

Curly laughed. "Shucks, Em. You know what we want." He drummed his fingers on the Formica table, a goofy look on his face.

"Sometimes a little variety helps a person. Ever thought of ordering a salad? Big Earl makes a mean chef salad, you know."

"Salads are for rabbits," Angus said. "Give me chicken-fried steak, or give me death!"

Other patrons looked at the twosome, rubbernecking their way. "Shh," Emory said. "Everyone's looking." She wondered how much pot the two had smoked on their way to Little Myrtle's.

"Why don't you come over after your shift?" Curly pulled two fingers together and placed them at his mouth and sucked in an imaginary joint. "We can forget the world together."

Angus punched him. "Stop it, Curly. She ain't gonna date you. Ever. She loves me. Right, baby?"

"Whatever you say, Angus." Emory scribbled "2 CFS" on her pad and tried to leave. Angus caught her arm.

"We have some business to settle, don't we?"

The money she'd been saving for Daisy's college fund sat secure in a plastic baggie in her rice jar way up high in her yellow cabinets, to the left of the sink. It wasn't much of nothing, but it was enough to cover Daisy's funeral now. Had she known she'd been thrifting away money for death, maybe she'd have blown it on clothes or beer or...

But in a way, she hadn't saved a thing. She'd just racked up debt in marijuana equal to Daisy's death fund. "I have some money, but—"

"Great." Angus smiled again.

Emory didn't return the favor. "It's for Daisy's funeral, Angus. All I have." She looked behind her. Through the rectangular opening toward the kitchen, she saw Big Earl eyeing her, his large face behind the spinning wheel of orders. His expression said, Get to the next table. "I need to take other orders."

"Suit yourself." He gave her the up-and-down leer, settling his eyes on her chest. "There are other ways to pay."

"You'll have your money," she said. "Come by the house tonight and fetch it." She walked away, a nervous flutter in her chest. Funerals didn't pay for themselves.

A triple knock, Angus's signature greeting, came just as he barged in. "I'm here," he said. His hair, no longer ponytailed, fell in waves beyond his shoulders.

"So you are. Where's Curly?"

"I told him to get lost."

"How nice of you." She pulled down the jar of rice, lifted its lid, then poured the little white grains onto the countertop until the baggie showed itself.

"That where you stash your stuff too?" Angus's hands shook—proof that dope wasn't his only drug of choice. Meth had been his latest conquest—jittering an already fidgety man to near epilepsy.

"None of your business."

Angus stepped so close to her, she smelled his chicken-fried breath. She backed up, but the counter prevented her escape. He put a strong hand behind her neck, his other at her waist and pulled her close. His hair tickled her face.

"You'll have your money."

"It's not just the money, and you know it. You intoxicate me. I want you."

"Wanting and getting are two different things, Angus."

"Don't lie to me." He took her hand, pulled her into the living room. In a swift moment, he dance-twirled her in front of the couch, then brought her to himself. He held her chin in his hand, kept her pressed against him with his other hand in the small of her back. "You want me too. Don't you?" He bent near, pulling her chin to his mouth. In one smooth motion, he kissed her way down deep, fireworks exploding in her head.

To be wanted. To be loved. It felt so good. She gave herself to him, spending her soul for several kissing minutes only to open her eyes briefly and see Daisy's face staring at her from the mantel. She pulled away.

"What? Do I frighten you?"

"Daisy," she said.

Angus whipped around. "It's just a picture."

"Angus, I can't. It's not right."

He turned back to her, but she retreated to the couch, a hand covering her eyes. "Since when are you so concerned with right?"

She said nothing. She stood again and went into the kitchen, fetched the bag of money, and handed it to Angus. "Here's your money," she said. "I won't be needing anything more from you."

Angus smiled. He put both hands on her hips and slid them down.

She backed up. "No!"

"I like a little fight."

"You've chosen the wrong woman and the wrong time, Angus Day."

He stepped back, sadness in his eyes. From the mantel, he touched Daisy's picture. "She had pretty eyes."

"Let go of her."

"Why?"

"Just let go of her."

He placed the picture back on the mantel then shot his shaky hands in the air. "Sorry! I give up."

"Just take the money and leave."

He took it. "You'll be calling me again. I promise you that. You may be able to resist my charms, but let me tell you this, Emory Chance. You won't be able to say good-bye to Mary

Jane. She's your friend. She's been *our* friend these many years. And now that you lost your little Daisy with her pretty eyes, you're going to need to spend a lot more time with Mary Jane." He shook the baggie in the air.

"Good-bye," she told him.

"Later, alligator."

Five

The morning sky mocked Emory, a thin line of pink across the horizon, like God was throwing a baby shower for all of Defiance. Only this was no day for new life. Not funeral day. She pulled her car into the funeral home's parking lot and killed the engine. Her hands trembled on the steering wheel. She exhaled her worry, fogging the windshield, but the turmoil stayed inside. What she wouldn't give for an inhale of Mary Jane about now.

The metal table held a body covered in a pink blanket. Bare white walls, ivory cabinets, and a stark window made the table stand out like a June bug on sun-whitened concrete. Only this June bug didn't move. Emory hugged herself. The plastic department store bag she was holding dropped to the floor. She didn't bother to pick it up.

Officer Spellman stood next to Mr. Jeremiah Ellington, the funeral director. Neither looked at the bag, nor did they look into her eyes. They were three silent people staring at paper-white walls.

"Mrs. Chance?" Officer Spellman pulled out a small notebook.

"Ms."

"Sorry." He pointed to three plastic chairs the color of mud. "Sit?"

She picked up the bag, nodded, and sat heavily on the far left chair. It squeaked under her slight weight, sounding like a shoe scuff on linoleum or maybe a kitten's mew.

Mr. Ellington left the room, motioning silently that he'd return in a moment.

"Her body wasn't badly decomposed, Ms. Chance."

He said this as if it were important news, though Emory couldn't figure out why. "What do you mean?"

"Just that her death happened a day or so prior to Jed Pepper's finding her. Not months earlier when she went missing."

Hearing Jed's name made her swear. If he had protected her, Daisy wouldn't have been taken. She looked at Officer Spellman. "What? You're saying someone had her all that time? Before he killed her?"

"Yes."

"Oh, God." She wrapped her arms around her stomach, trying to push down her nausea. All she could see was Daisy crouched in the corner of a shack, spiders crafting webs above her. And standing over Daisy was a man with a pipe and a sneer.

The officer put a leaden hand on her shoulder. "I'm sorry," he said.

She jerked away. "Have you found anything? A hideout?"

"No ma'am. That's the mystery of it all. We have nothing. We collected samples from the scene, from Daisy, but so far nothing conclusive."

Emory looked at the lump on the table, her eyes filling with tears. She should've been there to protect Daisy. Should've been in her right mind when Daisy left for the day. Someone took her child, ripped her away like a Band-Aid from congealed blood, and then did unspeakable ... No, she couldn't think about it. Wouldn't.

"Ms. Chance, I need to tell you something."

"Oh, no. Please, nothing more."

Officer Spellman stood. He held his chin in his right hand. "The coroner checked Daisy for signs of sexual assault."

"Please—"

"And found no evidence of it."

Emory stood. "You're sure?"

He nodded. "And none of her injuries appeared to be older than the date of her death. You can safely assume that she was probably not abused during the entire duration of her captivity."

Captivity. Emory rolled the word around her mind. Her daughter held captive.

Mr. Ellington stepped back into the room, a sympathetic look etched into his face. He nodded to Officer Spellman.

The officer nodded back, as if he'd done this procedure before, accompanying someone to a funeral home to fill in awful details, only to leave again when the job was done. "I need to go, Ms. Chance." He stuck his hand out to her.

She held it, then released. "Thanks."

"I don't want you to worry. I'll keep you posted if we learn anything else." He turned on his black-heeled shoes and left the room, his footsteps clipping fast down the funeral home's hallway.

Mr. Ellington cleared his throat. "We'll transport Daisy to church in the coffin you picked out," he said. "You won't need to fret about a thing. Then we'll take her to the cemetery. We handle it all, Ms. Chance."

"Thank you," she heard herself say. "I brought her clothes." She reached down, grabbed the plastic bag, and thrust it Mr. Ellington's way. "Her favorite outfit."

He opened the bag, pulled out a pair of jeans, a T-shirt, underwear, an undershirt, socks, and a pair of shoes. He set each item in order on a metal table. "She doesn't have dresses?"

"She had them. But she didn't like them much."

"Perhaps you'd like to make a different choice."

Emory fought to control her voice. "Sir, I mean no disrespect, but wouldn't you think a child's mama would know what she'd want to wear forever? I'm telling you this: Daisy would want to wear her jeans."

"If the casket's open, others will see what she's wearing."

Emory turned away. She looked out the window at the swaying trees, wishing there'd be one she could climb forever, one so high she could stretch her arm to heaven and nab Daisy back to earth. Daisy'd settle this matter, now wouldn't she?

"Ma'am?"

Emory turned. "I have no intention of parading my girl in front of the entire town. The casket will be closed. And she'll wear jeans. Understood?"

Mr. Ellington nodded. "Of course." He looked away from Emory, his eyes resting above her head. "There is the matter of payment."

Emory looked at her hands. Her payment had been freed from the rice jar and was now safely inside Angus's wallet. Daisy's college-turned-funeral fund morphed into drug money. Emory wanted to throw up. "It's, well— "

Mr. Ellington cleared his throat. "It's always awkward in these kinds of situations, isn't it?"

Emory nodded. Indeed.

"You see, there's been a change."

"You're not telling me it's going to cost more?" Emory heard her voice rise, heard the panic strangling out.

"Well, yes, but— "

"Sir, with all due respect, when a man quotes me a price, it's the price." She saw Angus, then, in her mind. He handed her a baggie of green freedom, quick to add its cost—twenty-five dollars. The price. *He* never raised it.

Mr. Ellington directed her to sit down. He sat next to her, his hands pressed together like prayer between thin knees. Daisy loomed in front of them both. "How do I say this?"

The smell of rubbing alcohol and peroxide stung Emory's

eyes. "Just say it." She searched her mind for people who might owe her money, for family she could turn to (there were none), for ways to bring in extra income. She could have a paper route. Deliver pizza. Sell magazines door-to-door. She could. But even coulds couldn't erase the guilt that permanent-markered her soul. She'd smoked away her daughter's funeral money. Had Daisy been alive, no doubt Emory would've done the same thing to her college fund. What kind of mother—

"It seems the flowers— "

"I didn't order flowers." There, it had been a mistake. A simple mistake. At least she wouldn't owe more.

"—were ordered by someone who wishes to remain anonymous."

"And I have to pay for them?"

Mr. Ellington sighed. "Ms. Chance, let me finish. Please."

"I'm sorry." She rubbed her temples, then looked into the painfully kind eyes of Mr. Ellington.

"Everything's been paid in full. And some extras were added. All donated by a person who wishes to remain unknown."

"Paid in full?" What?

"Someone has taken kindly to you, Ms. Chance." He stood. From his black suit pocket, underneath his lapel, he pulled a small white envelope. "Instructions were to give this to you today."

She took the envelope, worry and fear mingling in her mind as she did it. She hated pity. Hated charity too. Who would she be beholden to? And how long would it take to pay the person back?

"I'll give you a few moments alone before we prepare the body for the funeral." Mr. Ellington clicked the door shut behind him.

She held the envelope in her hands. Just a simple white envelope, no markings, no address. Nothing. She opened it. A single sheet of lined stationery paper—the kind you got for fifty cents on a pad at the dime store—held five lines of neat penmanship:

> Sometimes people need mercy—like a pardon for a crime.
>
> Sometimes people need some grace—like an extravagant gift for folks who don't feel they deserve it.
>
> This is a mixture of both, Emory Chance.
>
> Mercy and grace on a day such as this.

She turned it over, but no signature danced on the paper. Just printed words about mercy and grace, and not a clue to who'd sent it her way. She folded it back into the envelope and placed it in her purse. She'd worry about it another day.

Emory stood, arms crossed over herself. Daisy's table was a good five feet away, but she couldn't walk closer. Now would've been a good time for supportive parents, for a father to hold her up as she wept, a mother to shush her wails, stroke her hair and tell her everything would be all right. But those kinds of parents lived in storybooks, she knew. They didn't live and breathe and love in Emory's life. They didn't pay funeral bills. They might've existed once, but Emory couldn't remember that far back. And what she did remember brought more tears, not comfort.

She pulled in air, then let it out. She picked a hangnail until it bled, all while Daisy slept on a metal table—her last bed.

How could she say good-bye forever?

Part of her wanted to run out of there, never saying good-bye. Would that make Daisy's death unreal? Another part wanted to rush the table, pull Daisy to her chest and fill her daughter's collapsed lungs with her warm breath. She settled for standing five feet away while a sterile clock ticked away minutes.

She walked to the table, then lifted the blanket. She gasped. Daisy lay there, eyes closed, her skin like paper. They'd washed the mud from her hair, but they had parted it on the wrong side and clipped it in a way that would have made Daisy fume.

Emory willed Daisy a backbone to sit straight up and, with a slap in her voice, scold those stupid funeral home people for being so dense. Anyone with half a brain knew she didn't part her hair that way.

But Daisy's hand didn't flinch. Her mouth didn't twitch into a rebuke.

Emory placed her thin hand over Daisy's. No matter how hard she squeezed, her warmth had no effect on Daisy's temperature. So very cold. Daisy's hand iced Emory's, seeping cold water into her bloodstream.

"Hey, kid." Her voice bounced off the white walls. "Hey."

She pulled her hand away and looked at Daisy's face. A hint of blush decorated Daisy's cheeks—a strange attempt to color her, Emory thought. She looked like a nearly blank paint-by-numbers piece, with splatters of #6 rose placed strategically in one place on the canvas. Strange how a brush stroke attempted but miserably failed to pretend life. No amount of paint or blush would do Daisy's dead face justice. Only life would. Life pulsing through her veins, giving fuel to her many words, her legs that longed to run, her strong arms that could never fling around Emory's waist again.

Emory turned away, a memory assaulting her.

Seven-year-old Daisy. Towheaded, with two askew ponytails bouncing in the sunshine. The backyard of their home was awash in partiers, twenty-somethings like Emory with ripped jeans, tie-dyed shirts, and sweet smelling "cigarettes" dangling from smiling lips. Daisy ran to Emory, who had just sucked joy from a smoldering joint. She blew smoke heavenward. "What'cha need, kid?"

Daisy didn't say anything—quite unusual for her. She simply pulled Emory's arms around herself. "Hug me, Mama. Please?"

But Emory needed another drag, so she pushed her daughter's spindly arms away, emptied the joint of its remaining weed, and threw it to the ground. A small flame lit the dried grass. Daisy jumped. "A fire!"

"Put it out yourself," Emory heard herself yell. She wasn't wearing shoes, but Daisy was.

Daisy hopped and jumped on the fire, obliterating it beneath her soles. "My shoes! They're black on the bottom. Make them better!"

Emory remembered laughing, remembered how ridiculous Daisy's request seemed at the time. Her mind floated above her body, looking down at Daisy, who held her black-soled shoes to the sky. "Fix 'em!"

Emory watched from atop a tree canopy while she grabbed the shoes and hurled them across the yard, hitting Curly Sanders in the shin. He swore, then laughed, his hair shaking in the effort. Emory laughed too. All while Daisy chased the dust, looking for her shoes.

The white walls, sterile table, pink blanket, and Daisy's made-up face swirled back to her now. How she'd do anything to remake that scene. To welcome Daisy's plea by holding her tight for minutes, hours. To fling away joints instead of Daisy's hopes. To favor her daughter more than the next high. The thoughts seared her inside, burned like the fire from a spent joint on hay-dry grass.

All at once nausea hit like a tornado, roaring through her stomach. She grabbed her mouth, then ran out of the room, leaving Daisy once again while she retched her regrets into the antiseptic bowl of a funeral home toilet. When she splashed water on her face, she caught a glimpse of her eyes in the mirror. Such hollow, terrible eyes. Eyes allowed to see the world Daisy's had been shut to. Eyes that didn't watch a girl prone to wander. Eyes that traced the outline of her dead daughter just minutes ago.

When she returned to say good-bye, Daisy'd been wheeled away. The pile of clothes, gone. Maybe it was as it should be, she thought. Maybe she didn't deserve to say a proper good-bye.

Six

Daisy had been so cold, so terribly cold. Emory knew the only way to warm her daughter was to drape the quilt from their paisley couch like a flag over Daisy's coffin, smack dab in the middle of Hap Pepper's kingdom—in front of his pulpit. In truth, Daisy was a war veteran, fighting a terrible battle to the death, leaving her mama a war widow of a kind.

Sprays of pink roses from two large vases flanked Daisy's coffin—flowers Emory didn't pay for. Pews flanked either side of a long, central aisle—ready for sinners and saints alike. The wooden cross loomed above Daisy on the wall, lit by fluorescents from behind. A large sign to the left of the cross boasted the offering numbers and the hymns from last Sunday, but they were simply numbers to her. What did hymn 44 have to say? Why did hymn 356 end the service? Only Hap Pepper would know these things, he and his obedient congregation. Of course, that meant that Daisy would understand the numbers, now wouldn't she? Emory touched the pew beneath her, feeling the worn velvet fabric. Had Daisy been right here once?

Hixon stood behind Daisy's blanketed coffin, his hands on Hap Pepper's pulpit, but his words sounded like the distant song of doves, or the cry of a baby three rooms away—indistinct but full of ragged mourning.

She fingered the daisy chain Sissy Pepper had woven for her.

It felt like a choke hold around her neck. But she kept it there, the bottom loop of the chain covering her heart. The only thing she held was a piece of notebook paper, creased into fourths.

She looked over at Hap Pepper, the man who piloted this church and seemed to wrap the entire town around his pinkie finger. His grim face looked the same whether he attended a funeral or preached salvation or fixed cabinetry. Ouisie, his wife, resembled Emory—a woman whose thoughts lived far away from Defiance. Her eyes held more tears than Emory ever cried.

She didn't give Jed the satisfaction of a look, he who knew Emory's secrets—the boy who last saw Daisy alive and left her. He could not be forgiven. Especially not today.

Hixon spoke from above Daisy's coffin. He wore a sixties-era suit, and he held the podium like he was meant to be there. Although she understood his sermon perfectly, it filtered back to her as random words, not strung together in sentences like you'd see in *Huck Finn*, but simply words in a dictionary. She tried to concentrate, to pull something good from Hixon's chocolate voice, but her mind blanked itself. And as he talked with tears in his eyes, she made a note to thank him later.

Hixon left the podium and walked down three stairs on red carpeting. He stood before her, then put a strong arm around her shoulders. She didn't resist. With his free hand, he motioned her to speak. She unfolded the paper and cleared her throat. "A mother lives with grief every day of her life," she read, her voice shaky. "Grief that her baby is growing up and won't need her anymore. Grief over mistakes. Grief that time can't be bought back." She sniffed, then fought a tear. "I'm going to miss my Daisy. Going to miss her smile. Her laughter. Her—" She whispered to Hixon, "I can't." He kept his arm around her shoulders while she heaved in sobs, her soul tortured by a quilt-covered coffin cradling the girl she'd never hold again, while the fluorescents behind the cross sputtered, flickered, and died.

Seven

Hixon kicked the dirt of the graveyard, not so anyone would notice, but to ground himself there. He hated that dust metaphor, that we all came from dust and would return there once again. Muriel's heaven-eyes pricked his memory as folks arrived to say their final good-byes to Daisy Marie Chance. Soon Defiance would bid farewell to Muriel too.

Hixon caught fourteen-year-old Jed Pepper's gaze, something he hadn't been able to do at the church. But Jed immediately looked away. It pained Hixon to see Jed like this. They'd grown close over Daisy's disappearance, but no matter what Hixon said or did, Jed seemed to curl his guilt inward. He'd left Daisy at Crooked Creek Church, then Daisy went missing. So Jed blamed himself—a terrible formula for an angry life.

But when Missy death-marched across the graveyard barefooted in the cold, Hixon's heart thrummed his ribcage. Frail, whispery, she seemed to haunt the space around her, though he felt for sure if a stiff Defiance wind kicked up its heels, it'd blow her clear to Louisiana. Maybe that's what she wanted. That being the case, he'd have to follow her on that wind, watch a spindly armed tree tangle her up like an out-of-control kite, and gently woo her back to the grass below. And to him.

Hixon said a prayer and committed Daisy to heaven and the earth, her quilt-covered coffin pitched above a great gnawing mouth of red dirt, ready to be lowered. One by one people came to pay their respects, each dropping a single white and yellow daisy on the top. Nature's litter, he thought.

When Sissy Pepper stood next to Daisy's coffin, she cried and cried and cried some more. Her mama put a pale arm around her, holding her up, but it seemed to Hixon that it could've been the other way around. Or maybe they both kept each other from falling over. Sissy sniffed in another sob. She pulled a daisy chain necklace from around her neck, held it high so the sun could shine on it, then wreathed the coffin with its blossoms, wetting it with more tears.

A long silence passed.

Missy drifted to Daisy's side. From around her neck, she took the garland of daisies Sissy had woven for her. Without a tear staining her paper-white face, she lined it on top of everyone else's flowers, her own exclamation point of grief. A now-childless woman burying her daughter, crowning her with frail daisies. It choked Hixon to watch.

From above, a vulture swooped downward, its leathery wings flapping slow and steady in the windless sky. The crowd followed Hixon's gaze, spying that bird along with him. It circled above Daisy's flower-strewn coffin three times, then lifted heavenward, disappearing behind a thicket of Defiance pines, never to be seen again. Hixon's heart flew with it into the great unknown—that wilderness place called Missy's affections. He glanced over at her, hoping to catch her eyes, but she'd turned by now, walking barefooted on cool grass toward some great unknown while clods of red dirt pelted and dirtied Daisy's quilt and flowers as her body was lowered to sleep for the last time.

But Missy didn't stay to watch.

Eight

When they lowered Daisy's casket into Defiance dirt, Emory half wanted to crawl on top of the coffin and cling to it for dear life. She knew a part of her, the good part, was buried with Daisy, leaving her with memories, some hazy, some as bright as the Texas sun in winter, all that cut into her without mercy. Truth was she never watched the lowering. Never quite said good-bye. Just turned on her feet and disappeared while Daisy sank into the earth.

Every time Emory closed her eyelids, Daisy's lifeless eyes fixed on her paper-thin soul, boring into the guilt she dared not feel. Since Daisy's burial, she'd coped at night by reading *The Adventures of Huckleberry Finn*, *The Scarlet Letter*, and *Leaves of Grass*, her curious adventure into the classics of American literature. The librarian slid slick-backed books across the smooth wooden counter, almost like a drug pusher, but with this drug Emory's mind filled with words, not shadows or regret. At night, those books not only helped her escape the dark places of her mind, but they rescued her from Daisy's eyes.

Today Emory rubbed her temples. She pulled on a pair of jeans, a T-shirt, and her ratty gray sweatshirt, cursing the bra that splayed on the floor like a seductive woman. She kicked it, but it didn't fly. "Stupid, stupid thing," she said.

She stumbled toward the empty kitchen, turned on the

stove, and waited for the teakettle to whistle. She thought she'd cleansed the house of Daisy reminders—with the exception of one item—but she kept running into tiny shards of her murdered daughter in the strangest places. An unmatched sock mysteriously appearing in the dryer. A gum wrapper peeking out from underneath the fridge. A hair clip her newly named cat, Mary Jane, found, then batted around the linoleum floor as if to taunt her. Emory hated the guilt she felt after kicking the poor cat across the room. The once-friendly Mary Jane now scaredy-cat walked around her. Not even a cat could forgive her.

She poured hot water into a cracked mug and stirred instant coffee crystals to life. Sitting at the fifties-era chrome table in the sunlit nook, steam curling to the peeling ceiling, Emory willed her daughter to life just this once, hoping Daisy'd walk through the back door, singing John Denver songs, smacking gum. But Daisy's voice choked and died on a hill behind the forest while empty blue eyes reflected the sky above, her corn-silk hair splayed out like wheat bent over after a storm. That terrible picture of Daisy's last minutes jarred Emory at happenstance moments, and almost always shocked her into the reality of Daisy's empty room. Daisy was gone. That was all there was to say, really. Gone.

Her voice.

Her eyes.

Her laughter.

All gone.

Emory stood, her body creaking like a grandma's, although her mirror told her she was still a spring chicken. The sun caught dust as it angled its morning hello through her windows. Daisy used to say sunlight made the dust dance, but no matter what Emory could do, she couldn't chase away the sun. She closed the faded curtains, but the drafty kitchen windows billowed the curtains slightly apart, letting the sun illuminate the dust once again. Some memories couldn't be erased.

She pulled on her shoes and walked out the back door. She didn't lock it. Everything that really mattered had already been stolen, as if God had reached down and placed a gray mark on Emory's forehead—in his Ash Wednesday way—and decided to unbless her.

She turned right on Love then left on Hemlock, her usual route away from town, crossing over Hope Avenue until Hemlock made a sharp right, becoming Faith Drive, the road flanked by a forest to the left. If she looked just beyond the treetops, she'd see the crest of the short bluff where Daisy had been found. Every morning she kept her eyes straight ahead, shoving the memories down. Her lungs hurt from the sting of the November air, and her worn-out socks threatened to blister her feet. Still, she walked.

She spied the familiar opening in the pine forest and jutted left into its mouth. A few well-placed steps through the bramble of roots and fallen leaves brought her to the edge of Swan Field—her own private pasture. She frequented it right after Daisy died. It'd become her place away from the eyes of every Defiance citizen, where she could think, holler, or sit, arms outstretched to the sky, begging God to give Daisy back. Surely he had no need of the girl.

As the sun spotlighted her shadow to the earth, she remembered hearing an overloud preacher on the radio. He droned on about the Trinity, how God, three in one, was the first love story, that he didn't need anything but the love among himself. It made her wonder why God felt the need to make folks. If he was so happy in his own little party with himself, why spoil it? He certainly spoiled his harmony when he made Emory, when he marked her for sadness and trials by crisscrossing her palms with trouble lines.

She stood in the field, railing against God. But God, the Silent One, didn't answer back. Not one almighty word. He gave her a daughter like a fragile, beautiful gift, then he took her away. An Indian-giver God.

When God didn't answer back, leastways not in the way she figured he would (Hixon always told her to expect God to speak, that crazy man), she sank to the ground, let her face brush the red earth. No ashes, no sackcloth—but both, in an East Texas sort of way. The earth gritted between white hands, her thrift-store clothes eating dust for breakfast.

Only Emory didn't repent of anything; instead she nursed her grief, feeling the great injustice of it all. She reminded herself she was a good mother to Daisy, considering. She wasn't wicked. Not as wicked as her parents were. Daisy, she didn't know how good she had it.

Nine

Hixon watched Missy there, rocking on her porch swing, her eyes looking past East Texas clear to Baton Rouge. She didn't see him at her picket gate, didn't lift her head in welcome.

Hixon swallowed. That was his wife on that low-slung porch, at least according to the Almighty. At first the declaration from the heavens caught him openmouthed. Missy? She hated him. She hated everyone.

But as he painted her peeling house white, covering up all those imperfections, Hixon fell in love with Missy somehow. He saw snapshots of her vulnerability that made him want to protect her. And he grew to understand her gruffness was a big, fat show she put on because she was afraid. Maybe it was her fear that kindled his love. Because she was so much like him, though they lived different lives. He, a black man in the south, raised by a white mama, in love with the palest, bitterest woman in Defiance—a surefire formula for marital bliss. But that was the way of Jesus, always paradoxing Hixon's life, giving him impossible tasks just to prove he is in charge and can do miracles despite heated objections. Funny thing was Hixon's objections lessened the more he fell for her.

Besides Jesus, only two people knew Hixon's Missy plans: Muriel and Jed Pepper, who was pretty young to understand the ways of a man and a woman.

Other than that, not a soul knew. Certainly not the vacant woman rocking back and forth, with an emptiness he aimed to change. Hixon creaked open the gate. Missy's head didn't turn, though he detected a slight shift in her shoulders. A hesitant crook of her neck.

"Good morning."

She said nothing, didn't offer him a seat, but he walked up her steps anyway—a lamb to the slaughter, as they say.

"You're looking healthy today," he heard himself say.

She jerked her head away from his gaze, locking her eyes on the old tree out front. "Jed lost his shoe there, didn't he?"

Hixon swallowed. It'd been their conversation since the funeral—the endless going over of the details of Daisy's death. "Yes."

"His left shoe. Like Daisy's."

Hixon reclined against the porch railing. "Yes, while we were painting, but—"

"He should've told the police right then, don't you think?"

"Jed was scared. You forget he's just a boy."

Missy shifted her weight in the swing. She pulled something from her pocket, then lifted her hair into the air and ponytailed it. "Boys should be held accountable like men. Should carry the weight of their folly on their shoulders. 'Specially if they obstruct justice."

"Those are high words."

"They're the truth."

"The truth can be slippery, you know. You forget that Jed left Daisy in the church because his daddy demanded him home. And that he ran back as soon as he could. All he wanted to do was protect his best friend, and he feels awful about how it all turned out, Missy."

"Don't call me that." She pulled a cigarette from her jeans, grabbed a lighter next to the porch swing, and lit it fast, pulling smoke into her lungs, eyes closed.

"Don't call you what?" Hixon fidgeted with his hands. This was not going the way he'd hoped. How could he romance a woman like this?

"Missy."

"But that's your name. Miss Emory. Miss E."

"No, I'm plain, undecorated Emory."

"Emory." He said it as if he'd never said it before, which he hadn't, divorced from Miss like that.

She pulled in another drag of smoke, blew it out his direction. "Don't you have a job you need to go to?"

Hixon looked away from cold eyes—the kind of eyes that knew exactly the right place to cut a man down to size. "I'm a handyman," he said.

She didn't answer back. She smoked her poor cigarette to stubby death, reddening the filter with her lipstick. Lipstick that would probably never touch his lips. Hixon stood. "Never mind." So much for courting. He walked down her porch steps, his feet like cloddy weights with each descent, her eyes boring into his back, he knew.

"Wait."

Hixon turned.

No affection lived behind her eyes, but a hint of something was there. "Thanks," she said.

"Thanks for what?"

"For the funeral. Daisy would've said you did a fine job, Hixon."

He felt a tear forming in his left eye. Such healing words, those. Though the compliment wasn't technically from Missy, it would sustain him. "You're—she's welcome." He looked at his feet when he hit her cement walkway, all helter-skelter and uneven from years of neglect and from wear and tear by previous renters. "Your walkway needs fixin'," he said.

"So it does. But I doubt Clyde will stoop to fix it. He's not keen on keeping up his rentals, as you know. Besides, I'm not exactly his favorite tenant."

"I'll be back tomorrow to fix it."

"Suit yourself."

He nodded, then turned away, placing his feet on uneven cement cobbles, wondering if demolishing and re-cementing a walkway was a painfully correct picture of Hixon's insane task of winning Missy's heart.

Could be. But first he'd have to crack through all that cement.

Ten

I never wanted kids, Emmy." Mama said her words through stained teeth. "Never a one." Mama pinched Emmy's chin between workwoman hands. "But you forced your way here. Just had to be born."

Emmy wanted to free herself from Mama's grip but couldn't. In the trying, Mama's fingers took on strength. Tears sprang from wet eyes.

"You disobeyed me from the moment you came out, you know that? I figured, at least I could have me a son if I had to raise a kid, but no. You came out hollering, all pink and girly. That's why you have your name, you know."

"My name?"

"Emory. It's a man's name. When you weren't one, I didn't care to find you a new name, so I kept you Emory."

"I have a boy's name?"

"Don't go bellyaching now." Mama let go, then looked away. "You know I can't stand bellyaching."

"I'm sorry, Mama. Is that why you call me Emmy instead?"

She didn't answer right away. Instead, she took Emmy's hand in her own and turned it over, palm up. "I'm going to give you a warning—something to heed, child. My mama didn't care a lick about me. Didn't warn me like I'm going to warn you." She traced a dirty finger down Emmy's palm. "See here? Shows me your lifeline is long. But this one." She pointed to another patchwork of crisscrossed palm lines. "This shows you it'll be tough going. Troubles. Heartaches. Death aplenty."

Mama's eyes looked wet. She looked away, then turned on bare feet, her housedress soiled from days of wear, and walked down the porch steps, pounding wide feet through a dirt-packed yard. She faced Emmy. The sun behind Mama's head made her look like a wiry-haired angel, but in doing so, it darkened Mama's face. "I would've liked to've been warned."

Defiance didn't think about death much, must not have had trouble lines on its palm, because the sun shone on aging streets, blessing the days with 80 degrees—good porch swing weather. Emory watched Hixon as his sweat-slicked back sledgehammered her walkway. Seeing him there was a curiosity to her, and though she wished he'd scat, part of her needed him, cracking the cement, toiling under a peek-a-boo autumn sun.

In a way, Emory envied him. At least he could take out his frustrations on something. The first few weeks after Daisy'd been buried, Emory attacked her house in like manner, but it never made her feel any better. Closet doors kicked in. Flooring pulled. A sink fixture wrenched free and thrown through a window, now taped up. Maybe it was that Hixon's demolition had a purpose while hers was simply destruction. Hard to tell.

But even through all that kicking, she didn't destroy the cross-stitch. This morning she resurrected it from the closet, admired it again, and hung it above her mantel on a nail still stuck in the plaster. It comforted her, in a way. At the very least, it indicated that her life had meaning. She did bad things; God punished, devouring Daisy. A very convenient system, she thought. Though taking her life had crossed her mind at least five times since Daisy's death, remembering that cross-stitch with its orange and red flowers kept her from going through with suicide. Her duty was to live out the rest of her life as payment for her sins. It seemed right.

She battled between needing to pay for her sins and denying them altogether—two different views slapped together in her life like peanut butter hugging jelly between slices of store-brand bread. Most parts of most days, she preferred to believe life was cruel, God its crazy instigator, punishing her for nothing in particular. Wasn't sin made up by preachers? Seemed so. To keep folks pressed firmly under their fingers, like mosquitoes crushed under a thumbprint.

Swaying on her porch swing, she watched Hixon bend, break, lift, sweat—toiling in his steady way, producing something while battling grief. At least that's how she saw it. What had she produced of value in this world? When had she demolished, then rebuilt something to splendor? Daisy was her only masterpiece, and even then Emory could hardly take the credit for Daisy's flamboyance, her zest for life, her ease in making friends. With Daisy under the earth, Emory clawed at life with her hands, scratching out a blank existence, wishing upon wish that she could keep from seeing Daisy sunken-eyed on those metal tables.

The phone rang. She excused herself from Hixon's work. He nodded her way. She answered the phone inside.

Nothing. Just breathing in and out—a rasp of a whisper.

"Hello?" Emory placed her free hand on her stomach. A crank phone call?

"Emory," the voice whispered.

"Yes. Is this some sort of joke?"

"Need Hixon. Please. It's Muriel."

She felt terrible the moment Muriel's name spilled out. "I'm so sorry. I'll get—"

"Send him home."

"I will."

"And." A cough rankled the line. Emory dropped the handset to the phone. She ran outside.

"Hixon!"

He looked up, alarm on his face. "What is it?"

"That was Muriel. She said to come home. Now!"

In one fluid motion, Hixon stood, then ran down the block, his feet slapping the sidewalk. If panic had a cadence, Hixon's feet pounded it.

She'd admired him for taking care of Muriel, now in the last throes of cancer. Liked how he'd sacrificed for her—something that sparked longing in her, though she didn't know what for. She couldn't remember the last time someone looked after her—other than when Hixon and Jed painted her house.

She sat on the porch swing a long time, her eyes tracing Hixon's handiwork in the broken-up sidewalk. She counted the upheaval, felt guilty for all his labor. The phone rang, startling Emory. She ran inside and picked it up.

"Missy, it's Hixon."

"What is it?"

"Muriel said she tried to tell you something."

Emory remembered Muriel's raspy "and," how she hung up before Muriel spoke again. "I'm sorry. I thought it best to get you."

"You were right in doing it, but here's what she was going to say."

"What is that?"

"Muriel wants you here. She wants to tell you something."

"I ... I don't know."

"Listen to me." Hixon's voice gained teeth. "There's no time for excuses. Time's about up." The dial tone hummed in her ear.

She shook her head, then looked out the window at her torn-up sidewalk. Hixon had given that to her—his gift. The least she could do was this one small thing, right? But every step through the door, down the steps, around the walkway and through the picketed gate made her stomach flutter. Though she'd seen Daisy dead, she'd never watched a person die. Why did death haunt her everywhere she planted herself? Try as she might to blink it away, all she could see as she walked toward Hixon's house was Mama's face.

Eleven

Emory knocked on Hixon's door. She'd been here twice, both times to visit Muriel at the dying woman's request. Though only two meetings made for their relationship, Muriel called her friend. She'd learned Muriel's story in bursts and flurries—how she'd been married to a hard, religious man, what happened when she met Jesus, what she felt the day she heard "cancer." But mostly Muriel spent her words praising Hixon—her surrogate son, she called him. And when she felt spunky, she donned a blazing red wig—which made Emory smile despite telling herself not to. It was never nice to smile when someone was dying.

A priest answered the door. He nodded to Emory, sadness in his eyes. He stepped outside, turned, and said good-bye to Hixon. "She's a beautiful one."

"Thanks, Father Tipper." Hixon's voice sounded pinched. He motioned to Emory. "Right this way." He took her hand and led her to Muriel's bedside. Emory shook his hand away.

"Why was the priest here?" she whispered.

"Last rites," Hixon said.

Emory wished she hadn't asked.

"Not dead yet," she heard Muriel rasp, as though a hint of laughter still lived behind those lips. Muriel's bed now faced the living room windows. Before, the curtains had been drawn and clothes-pinned together. Now they flapped happily inward as the opened windows let in wafts of Defiance breeze. Muriel's glassy eyes seemed to fix at a point far beyond the panes. Her head glazed bald and shiny.

Emory sat in the chair next to Muriel. She fiddled with her hands.

Muriel took her gaze away from the outdoors, fixed her eyes on Emory, and smiled. A gurgle of spit ran through the crack in her smile down her left cheek, dampening the pillow. Hixon wiped it.

Muriel lifted her right arm. "Blessing," she said.

"You need to bend down," Hixon told Emory. "She wants to bless you."

"I don't need blessings." Emory didn't bend. Muriel's arm wavered in the filtered light of the room, then dropped to her side again, as if thankful for relief.

On his knees now, Hixon faced Emory, placing both of his hands on her shoulders. "This is a holy moment. I don't care how stubborn you are or how much better you think you might be. You will bless a dying woman if you'll simply bend nearer. A blessing isn't something to fear. Please."

Emory shot a fire of a look Hixon's way, then regretted it. He stood, then melted away. Even so, she bent.

Muriel lifted her arm again, but it fell. "Help," she said.

Hixon lifted Muriel's arm so her hand was inches from Emory's forehead. "Bend closer so she can touch you," he said.

She did. Muriel's bent hand touched her forehead. It felt cold there, and for a moment, Emory wanted to run out of the house to the safety of her own. Feeling the touch of someone so near death made her wonder what Daisy had thought as death choked her breath. Did she scream for her mama?

With Muriel's hand touching her forehead, Emory suddenly saw her daughter choking, a strong arm clenched around Daisy's neck. She could smell alcohol, taste grit in her mouth while she watched Daisy struggle for breath. A gray-green tattoo of a serpent snaked across the arm choking away Daisy's life. It flexed. Daisy fought. It flexed again, this time the tail of the snake wriggling, writhing on the arm. "Mama!" Daisy screamed. Then nothing.

Emory jerked away.

Hixon placed Muriel's hand on the bed. "What's wrong?"

"I think I saw Daisy's killer. Just now. When Muriel was touching me."

"What did he look like?"

"A snake tattoo," she said. "On his arm."

Hixon bent near Muriel. "Did you hear that?"

She nodded. "I'm sorry," she said.

"Don't be sorry," Hixon said. "You can't help what Emory saw."

"I wanted ... to ... give ... a ... blessing."

Emory heard the rattle between each word, saw a tear wet Muriel's cheek. This time Emory wiped it away. "I should be going."

"No!" Muriel's voice sounded terribly alive, the command not matching her frailty.

Hixon looked at Emory, a plea in his eyes. "Stay," he said.

So she stayed. Hixon once again lifted Muriel's hand to touch Emory's forehead.

Muriel sucked in a phlegmy breath, let it out. "Fire," she whispered. "This one's gonna get fire."

Emory remembered the mantel-preening cross-stitch. Yes, fire. That made sense.

"It's not what you think," Muriel said, though this time soft as butterfly wings on a petal. "Fire of life." She took a breath. "Matthew 3:11." She pulled her hand away from Emory and pointed to her nightstand. "Read," she said.

Hixon grabbed the Bible.

"The last bit." Muriel coughed.

Hixon looked right at Emory, his eyes burning into her. He

cleared his throat. "It says, 'He shall baptize you with the Holy Ghost, and with fire.'"

"Let it be," Muriel said. "Give me your hand."

Emory offered it. A silent understanding passed between them, she could feel it. A warmth of kinship between two palms. All at once, Emory understood Hixon's affection for Muriel, understood why he fussed over her. It was mama love, something she had longed for—but never quite tasted—her entire life. Something she scraped at. She longed to give pieces of that mama love to Daisy but couldn't. It felt like warm acceptance, cheerleading, and hope all at once—coursing through the palm of a dying woman.

Emory moaned. "Please don't die, Muriel." She didn't boohoo her tears, hadn't ever really done that—not even when Daisy died. But she let them flow unhindered down her cheeks. One simple hand touching her crisscrossed palm turned the key to her tears, and she didn't bother to lock them back up.

"A time for death." Muriel squeezed her hand, held it tight.

Emory heard Hixon gasp. She looked at him while tears wet her skin.

"You're crying." He said it as if it were a miracle. Maybe it was.

But as her eyes held the wonder of his brown eyes, Muriel's firm hold on her hand and heart let go, grip to release. Just like that.

"No," Emory heard herself say.

Hixon pressed his finger into Muriel's neck, then sighed. "She's alive. Still alive."

Emory stood. She wiped tears from her face with the back of her sleeve. "I can't be here," she said. "Not when someone dies."

Hixon nodded. But in that moment, with the breeze shifting dust through the room, she saw anguish in his eyes. Emory wondered briefly if she and Hixon were friends, if his eyes were pulling her to stay with him to keep vigil. Like companions would do. She looked away, straightened herself, and walked out the door, leaving Hixon to bide his time with death. Alone.

She ran home, ignoring the town folk who probably peeped at her from their windows. She ran around the sidewalk upheaval Hixon had bent over just hours before. She swung open the screen door, then the front door. Calm, she told herself. Calm. She spied the picture of Daisy on the mantel.

"Mama's trying to be good. I promise you that. But today's just too much. I saw your killer's arm but not his face. I nearly saw another person die."

She'd made little vows since Daisy went to heaven. No drinking in the mornings. Fewer cigarettes than before. No more dope. All promises she'd broken time and time again, while Daisy looked down on her from the mantel over the fireplace. Her picture never changed. That smile. That mischievous look. Always scolding Emory for her lack of self-control. She picked up Daisy, then placed her face down on the mantel. From behind *War and Peace* on the bookshelf flanking the mantel, she pulled out a rusted Folger's can, the plastic lid scratched with lines of wear and tear. In a determined rush, she pinched the dried weed into a rolling paper, rolled it thinner than a pencil, and licked its edge, a smudge of her lipstick making a pink smear where her lips graced it.

In a moment, her salvation was alight. Emory sat on her quiltless couch, laid her head on its paisley back and sucked in fiery sweetness. Then again. And again. Until she forgot about death, forgot about guilt, forgot about her daughter's choking, forgot about Hixon's pleading eyes. When Mary Jane jumped onto her lap and purred, Emory let her be, stroking the silky fur while smoke took her away once again.

Twelve

Hixon felt Missy's departure in his chest. He remembered how casually he'd held her hand until she shrugged his away. In those few short moments, Hixon realized her hand fit perfectly in his, and he wanted to hold it the rest of his life. Dear Jesus, please. Make it so, he prayed.

He sat next to Muriel, her rhythmic breathing a comfort. She was just tired was all. Nothing more. She had given her blessing, but it took a lot out of her, he knew. When Jesus slipped out of a person, it took some effort. So now it was time for Muriel to nap, to meet with Jesus in her sleep, to wake up again refreshed. Holding her hand, he prayed resurrection into her. He spoke death to the cancer and life to her heart and mind. He willed her to open her eyes, but they stayed shut while her breaths slipped in and out over thin lips.

Muriel stirred, then opened her eyes. "She gone?"

Hixon nodded.

"You promise ... to carry out ... my plan?"

"Yes, of course. But that will be a long— "

"No, not long."

"Don't talk that way. Please don't talk that way."

"It's truth, Hixon."

"No." Hixon hoped declaring the word outright would put a halt to the inevitable. Like a heroic shout at the forces of darkness. If he said no, they'd have to let go of Muriel, opening icy talons in release.

Muriel responded with a cry—so deep from within her Hixon wondered if her lungs came out with the grief. "Can't stop it," she garbled.

He stroked her hatless head. "Don't fret, Muriel. It's not your time."

"It is," she said between barely open lips, a hush of words. "I love you."

Each word crashed into his heart. He knew her love. Knew it like the back of his wrists. But hearing the words for the last time? Excruciating. Would he ever hear them again? Would another soul love him as Muriel had?

Muriel opened her eyes just a moment and caught his. He placed his warm hand over her bony one.

"Psalm." She coughed, her lungs shuddering.

Hixon sat her up straighter, then wiped mucus from her nose and chin with a white hankie. He opened the Bible and started reading. "The Lord is my shepherd; I shall not want."

Muriel's choke-coughing quieted down.

"He maketh me to lie down in green pastures: he leadeth me beside the still waters."

Her cool hand wrapped around his and squeezed. "Yes," she said.

He put down the Bible.

She let out a long, liquid breath, opened her eyes again. She inhaled the word *Jesus* and blew him out into the fresh air of the room—her gaze beyond Hixon, through the windows, to life beyond Defiance, Texas. Wind rushed through the curtains all at once, but she didn't take it into her lungs.

Hixon touched her neck. No steady beat. He held her hand as the heat from her body spilled out from her, like her soul was taking its own sweet time leaving him behind. He shuddered.

Muriel died with her eyes toward the sky, Jesus on her lips, a smile on her face.

"Oh, God, Muriel," he said to the silent room. His words sounded like someone else's—an announcer's on a radio far, far away. Echoing. Empty of life. He looked into Muriel's smiling face, but he couldn't smile in return. Clouds of anguish hovered over him, threatening rain, but his face stayed dry, his eyes too. Gone. His surrogate mama. Gone to be with Jesus. Hixon stood, paced the room, fidgeted with his hands. "God," he said to the room. "Why? Why her? Why now?"

The drapes fluttered in reply.

He turned to look at Muriel, leaning back on that hospital bed, her face toward the breeze. And he saw her move. He lunged toward her, only to realize the wind had ruffled a sleeve, nothing more.

"So it's good-bye then," he choked. He knelt beside Muriel's bed, placed her hand on his forehead, and wept. "Bless me, Muriel. Bless me now. You blessed Emory, but she'll never take it in like I would. Never appreciate your blessing. But I'm your son. Oh, God, bless me."

Muriel didn't bless him. Didn't say a word. Didn't move her hand or make a face.

Death paralyzed saints and sinners alike.

Thirteen

Muriel had dictated a funeral list to Hixon weeks ago, and he intended to tick off each item one by one—anything to make her smile down on him from heaven. He arranged for a private burial in the same cemetery where Daisy had been put to rest, gathered what few flowers he could find, and rented out the Defiance community center. Muriel felt a Catholic funeral would run off her old friends, so she opted for neutrality, the priest having his say while her coffin sat above the ground before the guests congregated in the community center later.

Only Hixon, Ouisie, Jed, and Sissy Pepper came to that service. Missy had been invited, of course, but she told Hixon she couldn't see another coffin. Just too soon, she'd said. Muriel invited Hap Pepper, too, her gracious act.

"I'm sorry," Hap said when Hixon gave the invitation over the phone.

"She specifically asked for you."

"It's Saturday," Hap said, as if that were supposed to settle the matter, like he was the preacher with the final word on doctrines and baptism and what to do on Saturdays.

"And what about Saturday?"

Hap sighed like he was explaining something complicated to an idiot. "Sermon preparation. Besides I'm sending my wife and kids, letting them go."

Hixon thanked him and hung up. There was no telling Hap Pepper what to do, particularly pertaining to church things. If he had a sermon to prepare, so be it. So help him, God.

"Just as well Hap's not here," Ouisie said, her eyes tired. Hixon knew she meant every word.

Father Tipper stood above the coffin, performing what he'd told Hixon was the rite of committal. As he spoke ancient words, quoting the gospels and familiar texts, Hixon remembered the first time he'd taken food to Muriel when she'd become a widow.

He'd heard through the Defiance grapevine how the small church that congregated at Chuck and Muriel's had gone its own way, leaving her alone on all that acreage. Hixon fixed greens, a few slices of honey ham, some cornbread, and a whole cherry pie he'd made himself. He placed the food in a box, then put the box on the seat next to him, driving tree-lined roads until he found her place.

She'd angled a gun his way when he approached her porch. He put his hands in the air. "I don't mean no harm, ma'am."

"How would I know that?" Muriel said.

"Because I brought pie."

"Pie?"

"Pie. It's in the car. If you'll put that thing down, I'll have a chance to fetch it. As it is now, everything's just getting cold in my car. You hungry?"

Muriel lowered the shotgun, then placed it on the porch swing. "Maybe," she said.

He took the box to the porch, setting it on a small metal table next to a lawn chair that had seen better days. Half the nylon bands had worn terribly thin, and rust tickled every square inch of metal.

"Have a seat," she said.

He looked at the chair again. "I'll stand, thanks." But she looked so upset that he cautiously settled himself into the chair.

It promptly gave way underneath him, bending and breaking until he landed on his backside.

Muriel roared laughter then. Couldn't seem to stop herself. She found a wooden stool and placed it in front of Hixon. "I'm Muriel." She extended an arm his way and helped him to his feet. "And you are?"

"Hixon."

And that was how it began—a broken chair, a laugh, a hand up, and two names exchanged. And a home-cooked meal shared between strangers.

"She's feasting on the supper of the Lamb," Father Tipper said.

Feasting, yes, but without me, Hixon thought.

Father Tipper led them in the Lord's Prayer. When they said, "Give us this day our daily bread," Hixon let the tears out.

On the porch that day, in the genesis of their friendship, Muriel had said, "Hixon, this cornbread is the bread of God. More than daily bread, it's his grace. Not just sustenance, but perfect flavor too. Isn't that just like God? He gives us what we need, then surprises us with flavor."

Hixon looked at her then, marveled at her countenance. "I'm not sure what to say, Miss Muriel."

"It's a compliment, son. Plain as day. Say thanks."

So he did, but he wished he'd said more.

Father Tipper prayed over the small congregation while Hixon wiped his eyes. Sissy wept. Jed stood straight and tall, not a tear in sight. Ouisie placed her arms around both, her eyes moist.

"Muriel has requested we sing 'Morning Has Broken,'" Father Tipper said.

So they did, five voices cracking under the Defiance sky. When the workers lowered Muriel into the earth, Hixon whispered, "Good-bye."

Later that day, at the community center, Hixon rushed

around making everything just so. He'd commissioned Jemma Dockery to bake sweet potato pies and Ouisie to make a big bowl of sherbet punch—both Muriel's favorites. Jed hung streamers in pink, yellow, and white from the center's rafters, while Sissy Pepper tidied up the place. Hixon placed chairs in a circle, according to Muriel's wishes.

Hixon expected a hundred or so, but only a couple dozen folks meandered through the hall, looking sheepish. Ouisie, mascara permanently smeared, handed each a program, mimeographed at Hixon's own expense. The tall stack piled neatly by the door mocked him. Where were Muriel's friends?

Jed sidled up next to him. "Streamers are done," he said. "Now what?"

"I guess we wait."

"Where's Miss Emory?" Jed looked older. More world-weary at fourteen than some folks in their fifties. Losing his best friend must've done it to him. Made him harder too. At least that was Hixon's observation.

"She doesn't like to be called that, Jed. She told me so. It's just Emory."

"Mama would kick me under a table if I didn't say Miss. You know that."

Hixon battled an intruding thought—that at least Jed had a mama—but decided to keep his mouth shut about it. Jed didn't need his grief right now. Jed had his own bucket load. And Hixon hadn't done much lately to help Jed empty it.

Missy walked in the door, her face pale as a cloud. She wore a charcoal gray dress, nearly to her ankles, and a shiny black bracelet around one wrist. Her hair was pulled high on her head, a braided ponytail bobbing down, like a show horse's tail. Hixon crossed the room toward her. He told himself to breathe.

"You came," he said.

"Yes." Emory looked beyond him, to the streamers.

Ouisie handed her a program and placed a long arm around

her. "We haven't spent much time together lately. Let's remedy that."

Missy nodded, tears glassing her eyes. Ouisie walked her to a chair, settling her there like any good mama should, leaving Hixon alone with the programs and a heart that bled in every way.

With half the chairs still empty, Hixon stepped into the center of the circle. He cleared his throat. "Folks, seems it's time to remember Muriel. This is her doing—the pies, the chairs, the punch. She wanted a celebration, not a dirge, she told me. Would you turn your programs over?" A ruffle of papers filled the silence. "Let's sing 'When the Saints Go Marching In.'"

Ouisie Pepper sat at the piano and played an intro. All at once, everyone stood and sang the song, though it seemed slower than normal. And no matter what Hixon did to try to be joyful, he couldn't crack a smile. Muriel marched into those streets of glory, leaving him on a trail of his own tears. He wiped a few, sniffed the rest in.

During the third verse, a door opened in the back of the room. A man stood, shadowed in the darkness of the entryway, bare arms across his chest. Missy, closer to the intrusion, turned around. She gasped, then ran toward the man. He crashed out the back door.

Hixon careened through the circle of chairs, chasing after Missy.

When he blinked in the November sunlight, he didn't see her. Or the stranger. Just an empty street and the echo of birds overhead. "Emory!" he hollered. But his voice carried down the street and no further.

Fourteen

Emory felt a rush of cold air while saints marched in, Defiance voices singing in a circle. She turned. In the opened door, a man stood just out of the light. He pulled muscular arms across himself, and one arm had something snaked across it. Without thinking, she gasped, then ran toward the man. He left in a rush.

Now outside, she heard footsteps to her left. She followed the noise, but couldn't run fast. In one fluid motion, she ripped off her heels and threw them to the ground. Barefooted, she sprinted toward the man. In a hiccup of a moment, she spied him running down Love Street—her street—a white T-shirt above gray pants.

He darted left through her picket gate and bounded up the stairs into her house. The front door stood open. She must have forgotten to lock it. Should she go in? Stay outside? She remembered how real the vision felt when Muriel touched her, how Daisy choked under the muscled arm of a man with a snake tattoo. Her legs wanted to stand still, but she forced them to move.

"I'll find you!" she shouted. The house was eerily silent, like a tomb. "You hear me? I swear I'll kill you, whoever you are."

Emory ran into the kitchen. The back door stood open. She took off through the doorway. In the backyard now, she spun around, looking frantically for the intruder. She ran around the house. Nothing.

Emory barged through the front door again. Shaking, she

caught her breath in the living room, then noticed the closet door ajar. For a pregnant moment, she did nothing, rooted to the floor in deep terror. Should she look? Maybe it was nothing. Or maybe it wasn't.

Emory took quiet steps to the closet. She ducked under the doorjamb. All at once, something jumped at her with a screech. She screamed. Heart throbbing, pulse racing, she saw something streak by. Mary Jane meowed, and Emory clutched her chest, calling herself a scaredy cat. She even tried to laugh. But the room felt peculiar; there was something out of place that she couldn't quite determine in the flux of the moment. What was it?

She scanned the bare living room. Yes, there was her couch, her chair, the fireplace, the mantel.

Emory froze. Daisy's picture. Gone.

A violent rap pounded the door. Emory jumped, catching her breath.

"It's Hixon."

She siphoned out a breath and unlocked the door. "Thank God you're here."

"What's wrong?" He reached an arm out Emory's way, but she retreated to the couch. "Who was that in the back of the community center?"

"Daisy's killer," she heard herself say. She was convinced of it.

"We need to call the police," Hixon said.

Emory nodded. But she wasn't so sure the police could save her from the likes of a stranger who stole the only thing precious to her.

Hixon placed his hand on her shoulder. She let it rest there, fighting her instinct to wriggle it away. Her heartbeat slowed under his touch, and for a brief moment she thanked God for sending her this man who was bent on protecting her. She placed her hand over his for a hesitant second. "Thank you," she said.

She'd chased one evil man only to be protected by a noble one. With Daisy's picture under the tattooed man's spell, she hated to admit she needed Hixon. She almost told him so.

Fifteen

Officer Spellman sat on the hideous couch, jotting down notes while Emory gave him every detail two or three times.

"And you're sure this man wasn't Daisy's father."

"Of course I'm sure. Wouldn't I know that?"

"We still have the warrant out for his arrest."

She sighed. "Yes, I realize that. But perhaps you're after the wrong man. Someone broke into my house."

"You said the door was unlocked."

"Yes. Unlocked. But he intruded. And he stayed long enough to mess with stuff before he left. If you ask me, it seems mighty suspicious."

Officer Spellman stood. "Do you know anyone who might be angry with you? Have you crossed anyone?"

Hixon coughed. Emory shot him her knock-it-off look. She knew she wasn't exactly popular in this town, but for crying out loud, she just lost her kid. Folks should give her a break.

"Snubbed anyone?"

She immediately thought of Angus, his passionate kisses, the way he looked at Daisy's picture like she intruded on his fun. No, Angus wouldn't do such a thing, would he? Besides, he had no tatto, and she was pretty sure the man she saw had short hair.

"No, I can't think of anyone."

Officer Spellman rubbed his head. "This whole thing is strange. We'll certainly investigate it. In the meantime, you need to look into buying some better locks, okay?"

Hixon piped up, "I'll be happy to install some, Officer."

"Good." He looked at Emory. "We'll patrol this block for the next several nights, keeping you safe. You call me any time, you understand? Here's my card." He extended a white card her way.

She took it. "Your name's Hank?" She placed the card on the coffee table.

"Yes, Hank Spellman. Feel free to call me that if you prefer." He cocked his head.

"Thanks, Officer Spellman," she said. Calling him Hank didn't seem right.

"Bye." He closed the door behind him.

Hixon stood. "I best be finding those locks."

"But what about Muriel's memorial?"

He looked away. "Well, it wasn't exactly what I had in mind, but I think she'd understand." His words sounded small, his voice tired.

"I'm sorry I ran out like that." She sat on the couch, held her hands on her lap.

Hixon looked into her eyes. "It's okay." He stood. "I'll run and get those locks."

"Let me pay you for them." She stood.

"It's all right. My treat. A little bit of grace in a terrible day."

That word triggered something in Emory. "Hixon?"

"Yeah?"

"Did you pay for Daisy's funeral?"

Hixon smiled. "I couldn't even pay for Muriel's. Wish I could've. That would've been mighty nice. Did someone pay for it?"

"Yes," she told him. "But I don't know who."

Hixon put his hand on the doorknob and tilted his head as if to say good-bye when a triple knock rattled the door. Angus pushed the door open. Hixon tripped backward, then caught himself.

"Gee, man. I'm sorry." Angus put his hands up in surrender.

Hixon looked at Emory.

"This is Hixon, Angus. He's my friend."

"Friend." Angus extended his hand again. "She could use a few of those."

Hixon took it, shook it quickly and withdrew his hand. "Everyone needs friends, is what I always say." The two exchanged a long, hard look.

Angus turned to Emory. "What's with the fuzz coming around? I saw the squad car."

"It's nothing. They check on me every so often, fill me in on Daisy's investigation." Emory didn't meet his eyes.

"Well, I best be going," Hixon said. "Nice to meet you, Angus." He nodded Angus's way, then looked at Emory with a strange longing in his eyes. "I'll be back to fix the door."

She nodded. "He's a great handyman."

Her words, meant to fill the awkward silence in the room, seemed to strike Hixon as if she slapped him. Shoulders down, eyes to the floorboards, he mumbled "handyman," and left the house. She heard each of his steps down the front porch.

"Fits him—handyman," Angus said.

"Why so?"

"He just seems a little rough around the edges, the kind of guy with dirt under his nails, wouldn't you say?"

"Just cut it out." Emory sat on the couch. "What do you need?"

Whistling "Lucy in the Sky with Diamonds," he shook a nearly empty baggie, a few small pills dancing in the bottom. "They're free. I promise. No strings attached."

"Knock it off, will you? I'm down to dope, nothing else. And after that, I'm finished."

He sat next to her on the couch, his thigh touching hers. He ran a hand through her hair. She let him. "Em, you know I care about you, right?"

She nodded.

"These are little pills that help you take a trip. Go somewhere other than Defiance. To stop remembering Daisy." He shook the bag in front of her. "You know I wouldn't give you anything bad, right? I'm here to help."

"Help?"

"That's me. Mr. Help." He pressed the baggie into her hand and stood. "I guess you could call me your *personal* handyman."

Sixteen

Emory held the bag a long time. She pulled out one pill, examined it between two fingers. Such a small pill. Surely it wouldn't have much effect. Knowing Angus, it was probably a sugar pill, meant to mess with her head. He'd done it before, rolling mint leaves into a joint, telling her it was a new import from Mexico. He called it spicy. When she inhaled, she tasted mint tea. He rolled onto the living room floor then, laughing.

Daisy was four years old when Angus balled himself into laughter on the hardwood. After midnight, she came into the living room, dragging a ratty blanket behind her. Eyes heavy lidded from sleep, she padded over to Emory. She crawled over Angus like he was a rock in her path, which made him giggle all the more. The haze of mint smoke sent Daisy into spasms of coughing. She curled into Emory's lap, a girl-child lapdog who smelled of sweat. Emory ran her long fingers through Daisy's snarled hair.

"It's so loud, Mommy."

"I know, baby. Angus was just leaving."

Angus sat up. He gave Emory a grizzled look, then painted on a smile for Daisy. "I'll be quiet, I promise. I was just playing a trick on your mommy."

"Tricking's not nice," Daisy said.

"I think it's time you left, anyway." Emory shot her gaze to the door. "Daisy needs her sleep."

Angus stood. "So she does." He slammed the door, rattling the front room.

"I'm scared, Mama," Daisy said.

"Ol' Angus? Oh, he's nothing to worry about. More like a puppy than a mean dog, sweetie. Close your eyes now."

Daisy did. She felt hot against Emory's skin. Slow, steady breathing settled into her, the coughs a distant memory. Emory hefted the blonde-headed bundle, shuffled across the living room to Daisy's room, and laid Daisy down on her bed. She pulled the covers to her daughter's chin, smoothed them just so. "I won't be far," she whispered. Then she tiptoed away, grabbed her bong, and ran out the door, looking for Angus. Always searching for Angus.

Emory shook her head free of the memory. Daisy hadn't been hurt. She slept the sleep of dreams, been chipper and spry the next morning. Daisy's awakening every day had been Emory's reminder of the kind of love she longed for. That no matter how many cocktails of drugs she tried, no matter how many bottles of beer, Daisy's waking brought new dawn, a clean slate to live the day on. Her wonder at butterflies in the yard. The chase of lightning bugs on muggy evenings. The laugh she gave freely to anyone in earshot. The stuffed animals she named and threw tea parties for. The forts she built from blankets and sheets. The way she took Emory's hand, her little fingers curling around Emory's sadness. Daisy had been pure grace. But Emory didn't taste the grace often enough. Didn't relish it like she should have. Never would now.

And now every time she remembered Daisy, all she wanted to do was forget. Because she'd tasted grace, having it taken clear away made her crazy for the longing. As Emory brought the pill to her mouth, a knock came at the door. In a flurry, she dropped the pill back into the bag and shoved it between her couch cushions. "Just a moment."

She opened the door to Ouisie Pepper. "I'm sorry to barge

in like this, but, well, you left Muriel's service in such a rush. I was worried is all."

Emory knew it was the right thing to invite her in, but one thought of the peculiar plastic bag shoved in the couch changed her mind. "I'm fine. Just spooked. You want to join me for lemonade on the porch?"

"Sure I do."

"Wait here, I'll get us some glasses."

She walked past the couch, wondering what trip she might've gone on, worrying what would've happened had Ouisie come just a few minutes later. She filled glasses with lemonade and sighed. From a tattooed man to Hixon to Angus to terrible memories to a little white pill to lemonade on the porch—a strange string of events. She hoped Ouisie wouldn't stay long. There were things hidden that Ouisie needn't know about, pricks of conscience Emory had kept dull by drinking or forgetting clear out. No use in spending long periods of time with the woman.

"Here we are." Emory placed two sweating glasses between them.

Ouisie took a long drink of lemonade and let out an ahh. "Nothing like ice cold lemonade, even in November, wouldn't you say?"

"It's powdered."

"Even so, it's perfect. Thanks." Ouisie sat back, ran a thin hand through her hair.

She was beautiful, Emory thought. The way a mama should look. A tenderness in her eyes, neat clothes, a good laugh. Though she knew living with Hap Pepper must've stifled Ouisie's joy, whenever Ouisie was free of him, she glowed. A glow Emory never seemed to manage. "How did the memorial service end?"

"Quickly." Ouisie laughed. "After Hixon rushed out, we finished our verse and cleaned up the place. Simple as that." There was a long pause as they both sipped their lemonade and gazed out across the street, not speaking. Finally Ouisie placed both hands on her knees as if she were pushing to get up, but then she looked at Emory, her eyes wet. "Jed's worried about you."

"Jed's worried about me? Why?"

"I don't know. He just is. He doesn't say it outright, but I can tell. A mama can always tell." She took another drink, then concentrated on the sidewalk beyond Emory's fence. "The thing is..." She sighed. "The thing is I think he needs your forgiveness."

"My forgiveness?" True, she'd blamed him, even snubbed him, treated him harshly, but he was a Pepper like his father. Surely, he could take it. The plain fact was Jed saw Daisy alive last. He left her. And in his absence, the tattooed man stole her.

"Forgiveness takes time to settle in our souls. Lord knows I have a daily battle with it. But just consider it, will you? Daisy's death has been a chain around that boy, and one of the links has been you holding a grudge."

Emory stood. "I haven't held a grudge." The words didn't sound convincing, she knew.

Ouisie rose slowly. "Then prove it by forgiving him. That's all I ask. Or at least consider it. I best go get supper ready. Hap likes his food on time and hot."

"That he does," Emory said, the words leaving her mouth before she thought.

Ouisie turned her head, cocked it to the side. Her eyes narrowed. "And how would you know that?"

"Jed told me," she said, "while he was painting my house. Had to skedaddle whenever suppertime came, on account of his dad liking a hot meal on time." Something needled inside her, poking into her conscience, then lacerating it altogether. "Maybe it's Hap who's to blame. Hap with his demanding ways. Your Jed wouldn't have left my Daisy had it not been for that man's stomach and his holler. Ever consider that?"

"I've considered many things, Emory. I'm tired of the considering. Sometimes folks get lives they have to live, whether by choice or consequence. I'm living mine." She started down the stairs, then turned. "Are you?"

Seventeen

Redemption. Redemption. Redemption. The word toggled through Hixon's head as he finished Missy's front walkway, then fixed her rickety doors with deadbolts, messing with every thought of her. He'd experienced God's great redeeming when he finally gave up trying to walk through life without pain. But his had not been an easy story, tied up neatly with a carefree smile. He'd journeyed to hell on the back of a mama who didn't want him, all to find redemption. He looked at his wrists. Raised pink lines intersected over each other like crucifixion marks, only he had been the one doing the crucifying. He wondered if Missy had such marks. Wondered if she'd tried to end her life before. Finishing the front lock, he wondered how exactly God's healing took place. So many doubts clouded his head every time he saw her. Sure, God stooped to pick him up, stopped him short of bleeding to death when life felt too big to live. But would he stoop again? For her? Could a heart get too far away from God's long reach?

Missy came from the kitchen, two icy glasses in her hands. "Want some tea?"

Hixon nodded.

"Why don't you have a seat?" She pointed to the couch.

"Don't mind if I do."

She handed him the tea. As he reached for it, his fingers

touched hers for a second. He saw in her eyes a hint of longing, on her cheeks a slight blush. The glass slid from his hand, spilling everything on the couch, then rolling off and crashing to the floor. "I'm so sorry."

"No problem," she said. "I'll get something to wipe it up." She left for the kitchen, humming a tune Hixon didn't recognize.

On his hands and knees, he picked up pieces of glass. He tossed them into the kitchen garbage. She handed him a towel, and he took it, this time not touching her. He blotted the couch cushions, letting the cloth absorb the tea. His hand slipped between the cushions where it met something slick. He tugged it free. A baggie with white pills stared back at him. "What are these?"

Missy snatched it from him. "Oh, thank God." She averted her eyes from his, but in the movement away, he could see panic. "They're Mary Jane's—my cat's—epilepsy pills."

"In a baggie?" By the look on Missy's face, Hixon knew these pills were not for a cat—unless the cat liked getting high, that is.

Missy stood. "I think it's time you leave."

"But your back door."

"Maybe another day. I've got to get ready for work. The rent's overdue."

Hixon stood, paced across the room to the rhythm of redemption, redemption, redemption. He turned to face her. Sure, the Almighty said he was destined to marry this woman. He'd obliged the good Lord by keeping his mouth shut when he saw things, by letting Missy have a long, long leash. He'd worried that if he started messing with her version of the truth, she'd haul off and hit him and their chances at romance would be cut off. But this? This couldn't be swept under a rug. And he was tired of guarding his words. "You know what?"

"What?" He heard the coarseness in her voice, the harsh rattle that came from a smoker's throat.

"You know I care about you, right? I mean, I wouldn't be fixing your sidewalk and putting on locks if I didn't."

"So you say."

"Sometimes the pain's so great nothing will mask it. Not even little white pills."

"What're you saying? You calling me an addict?"

"I'm not calling you anything." He looked at his wrists, then pointed to them. "You see this?"

She looked the other way.

He moved toward her, placed his wrists eye level so she'd have to see them. "These lines here are proof that nothing can take care of pain. Believe me, I tried everything, hoping to forget my awful life. Women. Drugs. Parties. I even became a recluse—anything to escape. But the pain kept chasing me, hunting me down."

She stepped back. "I know about your wrists, Hixon. You forget Defiance is a small town."

He backed away, put his hand on the door he'd just fixed minutes ago—at a fleeting moment when they'd been happy, before he opened his big mouth. "Nobody truly knows someone else's grief. Even those who think they do can't really know." He felt tears in his eyes right then. He wiped them with his right hand, his slit-wrist scars face out toward Missy.

Missy stood there, her irises bluer than the sky, and pulled up her sleeves. "I understand." She pointed to identical raised welts lining both wrists. "You're not the only one low on hope."

"I'm sorry. I didn't know."

"Well now you do. So don't go high-and-mightying me about pain and escape." She looked at the baggie. "Sometimes folks just need a little help."

"Please don't take them. It's only a quick fix."

"I didn't have one."

"But you kept them. Sooner or later, you will. When the grief's too much. Only Jesus— "

"Don't go talking to me about Jesus. I don't want to talk about him. Not at all. He's as helpless as you are, Hixon. Where was his might when Jed left my Daisy? Doesn't Jed know Jesus? Couldn't Jesus have told him to stay? Where was his rescuing arm you Christians are so sure about?"

"I thought you *were* a Christian."

"You said it. Were. I don't know what I am anymore. Maybe I'll reconsider if you answer me this: Where was Jesus when my Daisy was choked to death?"

"I can't answer that."

"Of course you can't. Jesus is no better than drugs. He's the same, or maybe even worse. Churchgoers sing a few songs and raise a few hands to prove their trust. Me? I sing my songs and Jesus doesn't whistle along. Doesn't even help me escape."

She shook now, whether from anger or sadness, he couldn't tell. He wanted to take a warm coat, lined with rabbit fur, and wrap it around her, to change her trembling to peace. But he couldn't. She'd have to shiver alone in that desperate place all by herself. She'd have to want to reach for that coat. But he knew the agony of that rock-bottom place, knew its fickle geography, knew its sadness. If he could spare her that, maybe she'd see he was on her side. "Maybe you should let me dispose of those pills."

"I can take care of myself. I don't need anyone telling me what to do, what not to do. I certainly don't need a poor excuse for a handyman loitering around here all high and mighty, acting like he's got life and Jesus all figured out." She wiggled the bag in her hand, then left the room in a huff.

He heard the toilet flush. She came out, her eyes wild. "See? I can redeem *myself*. I don't need some anemic Jesus to take care of me. I can say no all by myself. I don't even need an escape."

Hixon shook his head, then opened the door. Late afternoon sunlight flooded into the room, silvering Missy's hair. Angel's hair, he thought. If only angels could be redeemed.

Eighteen

Mama?" Daisy'd called from her room, five months before she went missing.

Emory found her sitting on her bed, her face pale. "What is it?" Emory fussed with her uniform, tried to fasten the back proper but couldn't seem to do it.

"Here, let me help you." Daisy hooked the eye at the back of Emory's neck. "I don't feel right."

"Are you sick?"

"It's, well— "

Emory, mellowed by a hit of pot earlier, sighed. "I don't have time for you to be sick, darlin'. I've missed enough work already."

"Did you ever feel like you weren't ready?" Daisy's eyes seemed bigger in her face, the shape of which had changed from girly round to thin and long—like a woman's.

"Weren't ready for what?"

Daisy didn't say a thing. She sat on the corner of her bed looking all at once like a scared five-year-old, a baby with the cares of the world on too-thin shoulders. She shrugged. A tear journeyed down her cheek.

Emory took a deep breath, then looked at her watch. Not much time before her shift started. She put an arm around her daughter. This was something she told herself to do, not the result of motherly instinct that those parenting articles lied to her about. No, she didn't get a dose of it when Daisy screamed into her arms. The only thing that kept Emory from giving up completely on motherhood was that stubborn voice inside her telling her to do things different. To hug when she didn't want to. To soften her voice when she felt like hollering. More times than Emory could count, though, the strangling voice of her mother boomed from Emory's mouth—a monster that she tried desperately to keep locked away.

Daisy settled into Emory's feeble embrace, seeming to soak it up like a wilted flower under a watering can. She wrinkled her nose. "Mama, you promised." Daisy'd filled every ashtray in the house with water once, her way of extinguishing Emory's joints, but Emory caught on, emptying them in front of Daisy, a look of defiance in her eyes.

"It's just a little—to get me through the day. It makes me happier. A nicer mama."

"I'd rather have *you*, Mama. All there. Please stop smoking that stuff. It makes you spacey."

Anger bit Emory, and she recoiled inside, smarting. "Someday you'll understand what it means to carry the weight of life on you, Daisy. Someday you'll understand what it's like to be afraid or alone. Someday you'll understand what it's like to not be able to pay the bills. Someday you'll give your mama a break for trying to cope, being a single mother and all. Someday— "

"I'm afraid of someday."

Emory took a breath, told herself to calm down and stop taking things personal. It wasn't Daisy's fault she was a lonely single mom trying to put food on the table. None of it was her fault. "Don't be afraid. I'm sorry. You know how I get sometimes. My mouth runs off and says things it shouldn't."

Daisy snuggled closer.

Though Emory wanted to shift away, she told herself to squeeze Daisy harder, to be the mama she needed.

"I don't want to become a woman just yet," Daisy said, barely a whisper.

The words resonated through Daisy's room, boomeranging off walls, and settling into Emory's torn heart. A woman? Her little Daisy? Daisy, swinging on the tire out back, toes touching the clouds, laughing, spinning, giggling to the rhythm of the rocking motion of the swing? She saw her skipping through a meadow, two pigtails bouncing to the rhythm of her gait. Daisy picking whitened dandelions in bunches, just to blow their heads toward heaven. Her little girl. Swinging. Toddling. Gathering flowers. No. It wasn't time to take the next step. There was still too much childhood Daisy hadn't experienced. Still so much to make up to Daisy. Why was there never enough time? Emory ripped her embrace away like peeling a scab from a knee. She stood above Daisy. "Don't be in any hurry to grow up, you hear me?"

"That's not what I—"

"I mean it. You're my little girl. Soon enough you'll be making out and drinking and Lord knows what trouble you'll get into."

"I don't want to do those things, Mama. That's what I'm trying to say. I'm scared." She pulled her arms around herself, then grimaced. She held her stomach.

"Come on, Daisy. What in God's green earth brought this on all of a sudden?" There it was, her mother's voice. Loud. Fiery. Downright mean. "You've been making out with that Jed boy, haven't you?"

Daisy wilted under that voice, her tears coming in streams, then rivers, though she didn't heave in and out in a sobbing mess. Just tears. And lots of them. "No, Mama, nothing like that. He's my friend. Nothing more." Her voice cracked.

"I've warned you about boys, Daisy. Especially that boy. Knowing his daddy, he can't be trusted."

"You don't know Jed. You never even talk to him. But that's not— "

"I have to work." Emory told herself to soften her voice, but no matter what kind of pep talk she gave herself inside the confines of her head, her mouth betrayed her. "No visiting Jed today. And when I come home, this room better be clean."

Daisy's room had been clean. Spotless, in fact. Her bed perfectly made, not a wrinkle to be seen. But when Emory noticed several maxi-pads missing from under the bathroom sink, she chose to forget.

Though one voice inside her told her to ask Daisy about the missing pads, three other voices fought for dominance. Her mother's that said, "You had to learn on your own too, and it didn't do you no harm." Her own that cracked, "If you acknowledge her passage into womanhood, you'll have to face the fact that she's not a kid anymore and you can't win back those years of crummy parenting." And Mary Jane's, that sweet-smelling weed, that hazed, "It'll take too much effort to talk about this—just relax and pretend it didn't happen."

She heeded all three, ignoring the one, preferring to buy extra maxi-pads each month rather than sitting on Daisy's bed, wrapping mama arms around her, and shepherding her into womanhood.

All this memory backhanded Emory as she stood now above Daisy's bed, adorned with the stain that darkned the mattress pad in its middle. She left Daisy's room, a bowling ball in her stomach. In the bathroom she spied the baggie on top of the toilet. She meant to flush it down, to show Hixon it had no bewitching power over her. Really. But at the last minute, she rescued the bag from the swirling bowl.

Nineteen

Emory opened the still-wet bag, holding a white pill between thumb and finger. It's just a small pill, she thought. And what would Daisy care now? Emory quieted her resolve to stay away from drugs—her flimsy promise to keep clean for the sake of Daisy's memory. Such a tiny round pill. Surely, nothing would happen. Probably just a minuscule dose of sugar and nothing more. She could use a little sugar right about now.

Someone knocked on the door. Just ten minutes had passed since she swallowed the pill, and nothing. Just sugar. That Angus—always a joker. Though this time, she'd been hoping for a memorable, happy trip.

Emory opened the door, expecting Angus. He always seemed to know when she went off the wagon and took a hit or a pill or a swig. But it wasn't Angus. It was a pot-holder-bearing old lady with a casserole in front of her.

"Hello. May I help you?"

"M'name's Ethrea. Ethrea Ree. I live next door to the Peppers."

Emory tried to focus, but the woman's face blurred terribly. Saliva slicked Emory's throat. All at once she wanted to blow her nose. Or sing. Or holler. Or. She shook her head. "Daisy told me about you," she said, though she felt like she floated above them both, watching herself and this Ree lady talk back and forth.

"I brought you a casserole."

"Okay."

"It's tuna." She handed Emory the warm dish, potholder underneath.

"Thanks." Emory took a big whiff of the casserole. It smelled like everything good baked into a dish. "This smells amazing. Wow. It's so beautiful too. And surprising. And completely, um, surprising. Did I tell you it smelled good?"

Ethrea Ree nodded. "Sure enough. I best be going. Just put the dish and the hot pad on your porch when you're done, and I'll fetch it later."

Holding the food in one hand, Emory waved with the other. "We should become friends, you know that? I need an old lady to be my friend. I just lost one, you know. Muriel. She was trying to be my very best friend, but then she had to up and die. That's not very nice, you know."

Ethrea Ree said nothing in response. She walked briskly down Hixon's walkway, opened and shut the gate, and kept her head down as she left Emory's block. Still, Emory called out. "It was mighty nice of you to share your supper with me. You're a nice lady. Why are you leaving?"

But no one answered back. Emory shut her door and set the casserole on the fireplace mantel for safekeeping. She sat on the couch, wondering why she was wearing her uniform. She didn't work tonight, right? Silly her. She stripped off the uniform, let it lay on the floor like a paper doll's clothes. Then she laid on top of them, her arms splayed wide. "I'm a doll. These are my clothes," she told the ceiling.

Her jaw burned, then clenched. The ceiling became a child's merry-go-round spinning and spinning and spinning. Emory worried, briefly, if her stomach would keep its contents, but then she didn't bother to think anything more about it. If it emptied, she could eat tuna casserole.

For a flash of a moment, she remembered the happy white pill, how it slid down her throat so easily, how she'd waited for something to take hold, but not experienced a thing. Oh, but now the trip was starting. Boy, was it! Emory laughed. She grabbed her sides, rolling around on top of her clothes like a child being tickled. Just as quickly the tears came like a tornado, rushing, whirling, demon tears that threw her off-kilter. The world's sadness pummeled her. Dying babies. Angry mamas. Ugly outfits. Country music. Broken fingernails. It all seemed terribly sad.

How long she cried, she didn't know because suddenly everything became hilarious again. So wickedly funny. Mary Jane the cat walked over her. She walked *over* Emory. Little pink paws over Emory's stomach. Who would think a cat could be a comedian? Or was it better said: comedienne? She didn't know. Didn't care. Emory jumped to her feet, energized beyond belief. She could run one of those marathons maybe. Or ride her bike to the next town just to see what was there today. Maybe she'd meet another friend and they could ride together. Or she could ride past a farm and buy it, just like that. Because she had the will to do it all.

She looked at her watch. It said 11:15, which didn't make sense because it was just 5:32. So many hours between. What happened? She looked for the casserole on the mantel, but it was gone. Then she saw the empty rectangular dish on the couch. Had it been good? She felt her stomach. It felt full. It looked full. It probably was full. Mary Jane sat smiling next to the casserole, lipping her licks. No, wait. Licking her lips. Did she eat it?

Emory sat next to Mary Jane, stroking her soft fur. Goose bumps tickled her arms as she noticed she was only wearing a bra and panties. How did that happen? Did that Ethrea Ree lady see her like this? Hard to tell.

Daisy walked in from her bedroom. "Mama, that whole thing about my death. It was wrong. Can't you see? I'm alive!"

Emory ran to Daisy, pulled her close. Sniffed the top of her head, which smelled a lot like tuna casserole. No matter. Daisy was alive. It'd been some tomfoolery by that Officer Spellman character. He wanted to have Daisy, wanted his own daughter, so he spun the whole kidnapping and murder tale. He did seem buddy-buddy with that funeral guy, didn't he? The way they nodded at each other?

Daisy pulled away from Emory's hug. She looked her mama in the eyes. "That's right, Mama. I've been living with Officer Spellman. He's very nice. You know why?"

"Why, darlin'?"

"Because he doesn't do drugs, Mama. He's clean. And sober. And he doesn't raise his voice like you did. And he never leaves me by myself."

Emory sat on the floor, the wood planks like slivers on her bare legs. Daisy joined her there but didn't seem to grimace.

"I was a good mama to you."

"You were."

"You need to come home to me."

"I don't think so. Not this time. I'm happy where I am. Safe too. It's awful pretty here. We sing songs." Daisy winked at Emory. She stood. A hula-hoop materialized around Daisy's middle—hot pink. Daisy whirled it around herself, the little balls inside making a swish with each rotation. "I have toys there, plenty of them."

"But you're too old for toys."

"Not anymore, Mama. Where I am I'm never too old for anything. I can play whatever I want." With that, the hula-hoop disappeared in a mist. "I have a present for you."

"I like presents." Emory smiled, then clapped her hands. "Presents! Presents! Presents!"

"Just one, Mama. One present." She pulled a daisy necklace

from behind her back. "It's the one you put on my coffin. I snatched it away while you weren't looking. I thought you might need it to remember me by."

Emory laughed. "Yes, I need this. You are right." She pulled it over her head, let the wilting daisies flower her neck. They didn't smell, but Emory could nearly taste the scent garlanding her. "Thanks, Daisy." She reached toward her daughter, to touch Daisy's slender shoulders again, but this time her hand fell through the air.

Daisy smiled. "It's that kind of thing, my visit. I'm here sometimes, but I'm not here other times." She pointed to the wood floor, pressed her finger into it until it absorbed her hand, then pulled it out.

Emory tried to do the same, but cracked a nail in the effort. "Why can't I touch you anymore?"

"You had your chances a hundred thousand times, but you didn't take any of them."

Emory felt the weight of Daisy's words in the chain around her neck—a prisoner's iron chain, too heavy for her to bear. She tried to take it off, but the weight was too much. "Take it off, Daisy."

"That's your burden. You'll have to wear it the rest of your life. I'm sorry, but that's the way things are. Like that cross-stitch. You owe for what you've done. And you don't get free until you pay the very last cent. Officer Spellman says you owe a million trillion dollars." Daisy reached out to touch Emory's cheek, which was now wet from crying, but Emory felt nothing. Not even the breeze of her hand whirring by.

She tried to heft the chain from around her neck, pulling, pushing, clawing, but it wouldn't budge.

"I have to go now," Daisy said. "I need to grow up. To become a woman, you know. Or maybe you don't know because you wouldn't listen when I tried to tell you, Mama. It's that way with you, isn't it? Telling yourself it doesn't matter if you ignore me. Telling yourself you were a good mama. Now, here's the funny question: if you were such a good mama, why don't you get to see me grow up into a woman?"

Emory couldn't answer. Wouldn't. She shook her head. As she did, Daisy's face blurred into dots, like a dying TV screen. A buzzing hiss pelted her. She cupped her ears, telling the hissing to stop, but it continued, louder, louder, louder until Emory cried out, "Enough!"

Her word silenced the noise, thank God. But it also silenced Daisy's voice. Where she'd sat, nothing was. Nothing but one single daisy, white petals wilted on the wood floor. When Emory tried to pick it up, it disintegrated.

Twenty

Drumbeats pounded like a bass drum in an old rock and roll band. Thump. Thump. Thump. So persistent. So loud. Emory clamped hands over her ears, but the drumbeat continued. She opened her eyes, then surveyed her blurry living room. Everything that seemed Technicolor last night had hazed into dreamy pastels. Yet that beat kept its drumming, kept pounding her temples.

She swore as she sat up, her back against the couch. All at once she realized her clothes were splayed on the floor, not on her, and the drumbeat was a persistent knock on the door.

"Just a minute," she hollered, ducking out of the window's sight and dashing to her dark bedroom. What time was it? She looked at her watch. Six. No wonder it was dark. Who in the world would come by at six in the morning? The gall! As she stood in the center of her bedroom, the walls moved toward and away from her like waves on the Gulf shore. Her stomach rollicked with the shifting plaster. The knock came again, this time with a voice. "Miss Emory? You okay?" Officer Spellman. Hysteria throttled her voice. He took Daisy, right? Wasn't that what Daisy told her last night while she swung a pink hula-hoop around her hips? Emory threw on jeans and an old T-shirt from the floor and marched into the living room, her head still dizzy, the room still hazy, determined to get to the bottom of the officer's evil plan.

She opened the door despite her fear. Officer Spellman stood there, hat in hands, no Daisy in sight. Emory found her voice. "Just where is she?"

"Excuse me?"

"Daisy."

"Ma'am?"

"You took her, didn't you?"

Officer Spellman backed up, his eyes concerned. "Yes, ma'am. We took her to Tyler, but then brought her back here. You saw her in the funeral home. She's in the cemetery down yonder." He pointed.

"Interesting."

"Listen, I came to— "

"To deceive me?"

"Did I wake you up?"

Emory rubbed her temples. "Yes. It's pretty rude to wake a girl at six in the morning."

"It's not morning."

"Why, heck it's not. My watch says six. That's a little early, don't you think?"

"Ms. Chance, I'm going to give you the benefit of the doubt right now, figuring your grief's made you crazy. It's six at night, ma'am."

"What?" She looked at her watch again. "But my watch says six."

"Yes, you're right. But it's suppertime, not breakfast." He motioned inside. "Can I come in?"

She backed away, letting him pass. At that moment she noticed the living room in shambles. A chair overturned. Her clothes on the floor. Potato chips everywhere.

"Ma'am. Has someone else been here?"

"I have no idea," she heard herself say. Had someone? Why was the chair lying on the ground like that? Who did that? Who threw potato chips on the floor? And what happened to an entire day of her life?

"How can you have no idea? Either someone else did this or you did." He picked up the chair. "Have you been drinking, Ms. Chance?"

"No!" She gathered her clothes from the floor. "Absolutely not!"

"Don't you work nights at Little Myrtle's?"

Emory felt the world spinning, like her feet were planted on it while it circled around and around. Last night she was scheduled to work. Tonight too. But she hadn't. "Oh, God, I forgot!"

Officer Spellman bent over the couch. "Smells like tuna." He picked up an empty casserole container. "You make this?"

Did she? When had she ever baked a casserole? Daisy used to pine for them, but Emory wouldn't oblige her. Hated those things. Especially when they called for crushed saltines. "I don't think so," she finally answered.

"Someone's been here, Ms. Chance. And from the looks of your face, I'd say they knocked you around pretty good. I should take you to the hospital."

"What?"

"Look for yourself." He pointed to the mirror near the entrance.

She did. A bruised, battered woman with a shiny black eye and a scrape along her right cheekbone stared back at Emory. Her lip, scabbed over, looked like it had bled a river.

Officer Spellman put an arm around her shoulders. The confusion over his taking Daisy melted quickly into her need to be protected, just this once. There'd be time enough for investigating. Right now she needed to clear her head and remember what happened to her.

"Sit," he said. He removed the casserole dish and placed it in the kitchen, then returned. He sat on the now-righted chair. "Listen. I came here to tell you something important. Now it seems my news takes on even more importance. I need you to focus. Can you do that for me?"

Emory nodded.

"They found Daisy's dad. He's just returned from Mexico."

Emory sucked air from the room but still couldn't breathe. They found David. "You're kidding me."

"No, I'm not. But I'm afraid that doesn't make things any easier. He's been cleared, Ms. Chance. Clean alibi. Which means—"

"Daisy's killer is still out there." She heard her voice say the words, but it sounded so far away, an echo of a voice. "I never did think David had it in him." She remembered the tattooed man pilfering her house, stealing Daisy's picture. She knew then David couldn't be that man, wouldn't have done something so mysterious and rash.

"I'll need to dust for fingerprints here. In case the suspect came back through here. You sure you don't remember anything?"

A memory fluttered back in. The old woman. What was her name? "Yes, someone came by last night with a tuna casserole. That old neighbor of the Peppers'. Something Ree."

"Ethrea Ree?"

"Yes, that's it."

"Did you eat the casserole?"

"It's the last thing I remember."

Officer Spellman made a note on a small notepad. He pulled out his radio. "Spellman here. Can you run Carpenter up here to dust? I'm at Emory Chance's. Might've been a breaking and entering. Most likely an assault." A static-filled voice answered back. He pushed another button and answered, "Affirmative."

Emory tried to focus on Officer Spellman's mouth, how it produced such confident words. No wonder Daisy loved him best. No wonder she was in a better place. Or was she? Hadn't she buried Daisy? Emory remembered the daisy chain she'd dropped like a desperate prayer on Daisy's flower-strewn coffin, remembered the emptiness the gesture gave her. She remembered Daisy's dead eyes. She couldn't recall Officer Spellman's face among the mourners. But she remembered him in the funeral home, telling her about the time of death. Death. Yes, Daisy was dead, wasn't she? Her head pounded with the memory, louder than the drums earlier. She closed her eyes, felt herself falling, then landing on something soft. All she wanted to do was sleep and dream Daisy alive, forget all this nonsense about death and intruders. She'd never been so tired in her life.

Twenty-One

Here's your mail, ma'am." The man's voice jerked her awake from a dreamless black sleep.

"What?" She rubbed her eyes, found herself on the couch, her clothes wrinkled, the taste of aluminum on her tongue.

The officer, not Officer Spellman, handed her two white envelopes. "Your mail. I saw it when I was dusting for fingerprints. I'm about done now, so I'll be going. I hope you feel better."

"Thanks." Emory took the mail, then dropped it on the couch. She noticed the officer's gray eyes, the way his dark hair, cropped short, wreathed his head. Kind eyes, she thought. Kind but distant.

He gathered his things into a black duffle bag, nodded her way, and let himself out, leaving her alone with a groggy head and the pleasant memory of his face.

The phone rang. She let it ring four times, trying to think who would call her. A phone call was a rare thing these days with Daisy gone. No Jed calling. But the phone continued its pestering, so she answered it with an annoyed hello.

"Where have you been?" Big Earl sounded ticked and concerned all at once.

Emory looked at her watch: 7:30. Past her shift by an hour now. "Oh Earl! I'm so sorry. I think I'm sick."

"You think you're sick? Then why didn't you bother to call

me last night? Poor Candy pulled the weight of all the tables for you. And it looks like she'll do it again tonight."

Emory's hunger, something she hadn't paid any mind to, returned with a growl. How long had it been since she ate? And if she lost this job, how would she afford to buy food or pay the rent? "I don't know what happened. Honest. I fell asleep is all and didn't wake up until about an hour ago. Then I fell asleep again."

"There have been rumors, Emory. You need me to remind you of them?"

"No," she whispered. No doubt Angus told all of Defiance about her tiny addiction to weed.

Big Earl sighed. "Listen, it's not in me to fire a woman who just lost her kid. But I have a business to run, you understand?"

"I understand. I'll jump in the car and be there in a minute."

"Don't bother. It's a slow night. But make sure you're here tomorrow. There've been a few ladies by lately asking after your job. Eager ladies needing cash. Don't disappoint me, you hear?"

"I won't." She hung up, then slouched back onto the couch. She noticed two envelopes then. One from her landlord Clyde Van Tassell, a hairball of a man with a sniveling manner, and another envelope she didn't recognize. She opened Clyde's, scanned the words and sentences that amounted to two delinquent payments. He wrote of mercy, of Daisy's loss, but reminded her he was a businessman after all. The rent past and present was due. Very due. She crumpled the letter and threw it across the living room at Mary Jane, who screeched away.

She picked up the other envelope. Her name, typed with a space between each letter, stared back at her:

E m o r y C h a n c e

6273 Love Street

Defiance, TX

No zip code. No return address. No other distinguishing marks other than a postmark from Burl, Texas, and yesterday's date. She turned it over, sliding a finger between flap and top. It came open easily. Inside was a folded piece of notebook paper that'd been torn from a spiral binder. Centered on the page was a typed note:

> God of the Second Chance,
>
> You make everyone whole. You put people back together.
>
> Would you please mend Emory Chance?
>
> And stitch together her frayed soul?
>
> She's trying to sew herself back up, but I'm afraid she's knotting herself instead.
>
> Please, God of the Resurrection. Hear this prayer. Amen.

She turned the paper over, but nothing else was written there. No signature. No handwritten note of explanation. She read the words again, wondering who could've written them. She knew no one in Burl other than Curly Sanders. She'd been there one spring to see the dogwood trees in bloom, but other than that, she'd never been.

The prayer didn't sound like Hixon. He was always Jesus this and Jesus that. Besides, with the way he wore Jesus on his sleeve, he'd just up and pray for her. Or at least try.

Ouisie, she knew, hated typing. And Jed hated *her*—surely he wouldn't type such a thing.

Emory wouldn't put it past Hap Pepper, but, then, why in the world would he, of all people, wish her mended? Hadn't he told her she was in the business of tearing things up?

Part of her wanted to throw the note away, or burn it with her lighter. Another part worried. Was this a mean joke written by the tattooed man? But why all the kindness, then? And all that talk about sewing and stitching made her wonder if the cross-stitch had something to do with who sent it.

Should she tell Officer Spellman? Instead, she stuffed all

those questions way down deep, in that same place she filed painful memories about Daisy and her. She folded the paper, placed it in the envelope, and slipped it between the pages of *Huckleberry Finn* for safekeeping.

In the bathroom, she splashed water on her face, spying herself in the mirror. "You gonna be homeless, Emmy Chance? You better shape up, or you will be." Her mother's words—from twenty-five years ago. It startled her to hear them come from her own mouth—the same lilt, the same harsh tone, every bit the same amount of hatred that woman could muster. Mama had crouched to look into Emmy's eyes then, and Emmy obliged her by giving Mama full attention, while slackened pieces of her soul spilled out with every second she held Mama's gaze. She could nearly feel herself slip out, and Mama's hatred slip in.

"It's up to you and me to make our way, you hear me? And if you can't pull your weight by helping me out when I'm gone working, we're gonna end up on the streets. You understand?"

Emmy nodded. Oh, she understood. Mama meant for her to wash things—dishes, clothes, floors, toilets—to spit-shine clean. And if she didn't? Well, homelessness lurked around the corner, like a closet monster preying upon an unsuspecting child. How Mama equated Emmy's ability to clean and homelessness she never could piece together. But in her five-year-old mind, it made perfect sense.

So she cleaned. And worried. And even though she did everything right, they ended up evicted. Shaken back to the present, Emory spied the baggie—still several pills left. Last night came back to her—the feel of the pill on her tongue. The disappointment that nothing would happen to take her out of her life. The spinning room. The old lady and her tuna casserole. Daisy. Then blackness.

Officer Spellman was right when he suspected someone had forced entry into her home and thrown chairs and chips and fits.

But when they analyzed those fingerprints, she knew the only ones they would find were her own. An intruder in her own life.

She pinched the baggie over the toilet, sick of its hold over her. She dropped it in and reached for the silver handle. She felt its coolness on her hand. She meant to flush those pills. Really, she did. But she held the handle instead, hesitating, hesitating, while the bag floated in the stained bowl below. She knelt before the porcelain and fished out the baggie for the second time. She held it to herself, breath coming in spurts, her heart pounding for more.

Whoever sent that prayer was right. She was a mess. But God wasn't in the business of mending Emory Chance; this she knew. He hadn't paid any mind when Mama said those things. He hadn't stooped from heaven to save Daisy. And he certainly wasn't going to stitch her back together. That was the job of the little pills. And no one could take those away from her.

Not even her.

Twenty-Two

Hixon told himself to stop bothering with complicated thoughts of Missy. Wasn't that the way of God? To quit fretting and plotting and scheming and let the good Lord do his thing? Even so, he let a prayer slip from his lips. "God, show me what to do next to win her. Give me a sign, please." He picked himself up out of bed, put on a fresh shirt, and made his way to the kitchen.

He had his cup of coffee with Jesus, asking him to carry all that grief. While instant coffee steam rose like worship to the light fixture, Hixon remembered a time when his coffee with the Almighty had been interrupted by a son.

He could picture the boy even today, how his wild eyes hid behind too-long hair, how he couldn't keep still while Hixon read the Word to him. How much like Jed the boy was. And how quickly he disappeared.

He took a last drink, willing the boy back to the table. Instead of face-to-face talking, he settled for another prayer, hoping the God in heaven, who saw every face, would touch the boy's today.

Church wasn't the same without a companion.

He'd been singing and worshipping without her for quite some time, but now it felt different—like he had a vacuum in his heart sucking out all the good stuff, only dust and clattering cockroaches remaining. The moment she breathed her last, Hixon mourned her prayers, felt their absence in his chest. He wished himself more Catholic then, just so there'd be no interruption to Muriel's prayers. She prayed for him in sweltering Defiance; certainly the air'd be different in heaven, and her prayers would catapult to God on a sweet breeze. Oh, let it be true, he prayed. Loneliness threatened to smother him without those prayers.

Mounting the steps to Hap Pepper's church, he felt the strange weight of folks' stares as he did every Sunday. The looks that said, "I am a good Christian person, so I know I'm supposed to love a black man, but it's pretty hard, and I resent you forcing me to do so by sitting in the pew nearby." Suspicion lived behind those eyes. Prejudice too. Even so, he entered the church, his head high, his chest full of air, ready to sing songs to Jesus. After all, he'd been raised by a white mama, learned life under her disinterested care. Truth was, he felt normal here, a black man with a white mama's heart, ever spanning the widening gap between two worlds he longed for acceptance in. With one black foot in the white world, another in the black, Hixon teetered in the middle, his center of gravity tilting him this way then that.

Sissy Pepper ran to him. She wrapped spindly arms around his middle. "Hey, Hixon."

He bent near her, brown eyes to blue eyes. He loved those eyes, brimming with expectation. "Hey, yourself. How are you?"

She looked behind her at the pulpit, the cross. Her voice got smaller. "Okay."

"I wish you could sit by me today. Do you think your daddy would mind?"

"No, he wouldn't mind. Not today at least. I'll ask Mama." She walked away, her yellow dress swishing down the church's center aisle as she did. Hixon wondered if Missy had swished that way when she was little, if she had endeared herself to grandfathers, if she'd sung songs to the heavens like Sissy Pepper. What did it matter if she had? The little girl Missy used to be got swallowed up by the monster called life, and she seemed happy to reside in its belly, away from anyone trying to love her. Hixon shook his head to free it of the thought and prayed again that God would give him the wherewithal to see beyond all Missy's walls, to climb them, and to rescue the girl behind.

Sissy returned. She slipped a thin hand into his and led him toward the front of the church on the left bank of pews—the pew behind Ouisie and Jed. Ouisie laughed, her hair bouncing. She turned Hixon's way. "Hap's itinerant preaching today, off to Burl to give a word from God. Today we're hearing Big Earl Jenkins. Should be interesting."

"You're right on that account," Hixon said.

Jed turned. "You okay, Hixon?"

Hixon nodded. "It hurts." The organ bellowed its signal for everyone to stand. Jed and Ouisie turned around to face the front. Hixon filled his lungs again, wishing that just this once God would pull back the curtain separating heaven and earth so Hixon could get a look at Muriel with hair and health and joy, and show her he was all right, considering. But the stained ceiling of the church didn't blur and give way to the blue sky. Didn't bother with such an effort. And the lungs that once filled deflated at this thought: I won't see that woman until I breathe my last breath. Hixon hung his head while "It Is Well" murmured and moaned over him. It was not well with his soul. His best friend was gone from the dust-gritted streets of Defiance, Texas. Her smile no longer lit his mood. Her cackle-laughter had ceased. Her stories had been silenced by the sovereign shush of God. And now he didn't have one person he could talk to about Missy. Not a soul.

He mouthed hymns, not daring to elevate his voice. If he did, he'd cry, sure as day. So he formed his lips around words like *God's faithfulness* or *Jesus' love* or *the Spirit hovering*. He believed what he mouthed, but he didn't feel any of it way down deep. Maybe that was how Job felt after everyone and everything was stripped away. Hixon, he'd like to meet old Job. Ask him a few questions or maybe just commiserate a bit, shoot the sad breeze while they drank bitter lemonade and nursed their festering sores.

Big Earl waddled toward the pulpit. He hefted himself, one thick leg over another, to the platform. It seemed higher because of Big Earl's sweaty effort. Before he opened a tattered black Bible, he mopped a damp forehead with the back of his hand. He laughed. And laughed again, his belly shaking like Santa's. The congregation laughed alongside him, even Hixon, despite his Job-wandering sadness. Big Earl Jenkins cast that kind of giddy spell over folks when he preached. Hap Pepper ranted and raved and angered while he admonished the sheep. Maybe Big Earl was his laughing antidote. Or maybe it was watching the man sweat and guffaw that brought comedy to the pews. Hard to say, but good to experience.

"Ever think about the humor of Jesus?" Big Earl asked. In his peripheral vision, Hixon caught a few folks shaking their heads. Truth was he hadn't thought much about a smiling Jesus, certainly not a joke-telling one. Jesus was all about sorrow, grief, wearing others' sin clothes, bearing the devil's schemes on his bloody back. Hard to think of him telling knock-knocks to the disciples.

"Well, I'm here today to teach you about his effervescent joy!" Big Earl laughed again. Hixon could count the man's teeth if he wanted to. He wondered if Muriel was counting, too, from her seat way up high. Perfectly white. Perfectly spaced. Dentures did that to a man, Hixon knew. And with all that smiling and laughing, Big Earl sure seemed to want folks to notice his square pearls.

"The Bible says that for the joy set before Jesus, he endured the cross. Ever think that way, folks? That there is immense, over-the-top joy awaiting you in glory? And in that anticipation, if you picture it just right, you can endure any sort of hardship because you know. You know. You know that what's happening today in Defiance, Texas, can't compare to the hip-hop-happy joy that awaits you on dancing streets of gold." He mopped his head again, this time with a white-as-his-teeth handkerchief. "I got me some problems, congregation. Got me plenty. M'heart's going out on me. Doctor tells me I'm too fat."

Hixon heard a gasp from behind him. He caught a whiff of his own gasp too. Folks at this church weren't accustomed to a preacher's dirty laundry flapping in the breeze for all to see—even if the preacher made his living cooking french dips and patty melts. But here was Big Earl airing his skivvies on a clothesline right down the center of church. Hixon sat forward. Sissy too.

"It's not like it's any big secret." He laughed.

So did a bustle of churchgoers behind Hixon. Sissy giggled.

"So here's the thing. I'm going to die someday. Probably because I make way too many fried pies and purple hulled peas and brisket and fried chicken and okra and baked beans and ... well, you get the idea. Not only do I make them, I eat them. So I'm fat." He grabbed his belly with both hands and jiggled himself. Hixon wondered what exactly Ouisie would report back to Hap.

"The service was dignified," he imaged her saying. Hixon laughed at the thought.

"I'm in love too," Big Earl said. "With Jesus Christ." He looked around the room, then stepped away from the pulpit and waddled down the steps, leaving the microphone behind.

"What if he tumbles down?" Sissy whispered.

Hixon prayed it wouldn't happen, though Big Earl did teeter a bit on that last step.

"I am flat out enamored with the Man. I say that with a capital M. Man. God and Man married in one person: Jesus. It's a hoot and a haven to me." He leveled an amused gaze at Hixon.

Hixon squirmed. Sissy took his hand again and looked his way, those blue eyes piercing through him.

Big Earl cleared a rheumy throat. "Like you, Hixon. I know you're enamored with Jesus too. Here's what you need to know. The devil's out to sift you like barley, but you need to keep your laughter on, you hear me? The sifting'll be bad. It'll feel like it's unto death. You do what God's called you to do—the thing only you can do. You keep your wits. You keep loving Jesus even as all that chaff is being burned away. You keep your head. You keep your heart. You keep laughing, all right?"

Hixon shifted in his seat just slightly, but he felt all at once that Jesus lived behind Big Earl's eyes, warning and wooing him all at once. Yes, he nodded. This was God's sign. To him. To hold Missy in a lighthearted way, to let go of the seriousness.

He shook his head, smiling.

Sissy smiled too. "Jesus loves you, Hixon. Doesn't he?" She squeezed his hand.

Big Earl took her free hand in his.

Hixon wondered if Big Earl's hand felt hot and wet in Sissy's.

Big Earl looked into Sissy Pepper's blinking eyes. "You're right, little one. Jesus loves Hixon. There'll be many times when he doesn't right know if Jesus even sees what's happening all around, but Hixon here will trust. I know it. He will trust in Jesus' love even if he can't see it. Do you understand?"

Sissy said yes, her voice like a bell ringing to summon folks to church.

Big Earl ruffled her hair, then looked again at Hixon. "You love her," he said. "Even when it feels like coals on bare feet. You know what I'm talking about."

Hixon nodded. It had never been hard to love Sissy Pepper, or even Ouisie for that matter. But Big-Earl-with-Jesus-eyes was talking about Missy Chance. In that moment, Hixon knew he would do anything to make her smile and laugh like Big Earl. Even if it meant risking his life.

Twenty-Three

When a knock came, Emory forced open crusted eyes, threw on some jeans, harnessed her hair in a ponytail, and flung open the front door.

Officer Spellman stood at the door, his hat in his hands. "Sorry to intrude, but I need to tell you something."

"You could've called."

"Your phone's off the hook or something. Otherwise I would have."

She spied the phone in the corner, its handset off the body. "Well, you're here now, so what is it?"

"Some news."

"Great. Who else could die?"

"It's not that. David Carter wants to see you. He's in Burl."

Emory shook the sleep from her brain and said, "Why can't he come my way?"

"I don't know," Officer Spellman replied. "But he was very specific on the phone that you were to drive to see him. Here's his address and phone number." He handed her a small piece of notebook paper, nodded, and left.

She read the paper several times. Fifty-three miles stretched between Defiance and Burl. A long ribbon of road for Emory, with far too much time to think while each mile marker sped by. She could live alone with her thoughts in the confines of her clapboard house, but riding in the car with Defiance rolling behind worried her. She knew her thoughts would scatter, then focus, bringing her back to guilt.

What if David sent those prayers? That would be messy, she thought—David, the man of few morals and even lesser dedication sending typewritten prayers from Burl, Texas?

And what if the police were wrong? What if David Carter, deadbeat, was David Carter, murderer? Would she be safe? Had he taken his daughter's life as some sort of grudge against her? But then she remembered his eyes, how she lost herself in them, how kind they seemed. Murderers didn't have eyes like that, did they?

But what really pricked her was undecorated grief. Though David kept Daisy at arm's length—shoot, at county's length—all her life, he'd surely bring her up and want to talk about her now that she was gone. Maybe he had regrets the size of Texas. Or maybe he didn't, and Emory would have to shoulder another grief—getting pregnant by a sociopath. No matter what transpired between them, Daisy would come up.

Another knock startled her from her imaginings. Before she stood to answer, Angus barged through, a wide smile on his face. "You take a trip lately?"

Emory shook her head. "I flushed 'em."

"What?" He threw himself on her rocking chair, arms and legs lanky and askew.

"I told you; I'm finished."

He swore. "Em, you know how much those little darlings cost me?"

She crossed her arms in front of her chest like a shield. "You shouldn't give gifts expecting something in return," she said. "Something an old aunt taught me. Otherwise you're giving with wrong motives."

"Oh, listen to the high and mighty one. Don't think I don't know your little secrets."

Emory's heart quickened. What secrets? She steadied herself, told herself to be cool, collected. "Everyone has secrets. Even you."

"Well I know one of them, anyway." He stood, then jangled motorcycle keys in the air. "I hear you're supposed to go on a visit to Burl."

Now it was Emory's turn to swear. "I just learned the news ten minutes ago, and you tell me you know my business too? This town is too small."

"I make it my business to know things about you." He sat next to her, placed his warm hand on her thigh. "I like you. Have for years now."

She looked at his hand settled on her leg like a red hotel on Boardwalk, meant to be there. She tornadoed it away with a flurry of her palm. "Let's not go down that road, Angus."

He stood. Jangled those keys again. "Hey, you can't blame a man for trying. Besides, I have something you need. A ride. Free, too. I'll take you to Burl if you'd like. I'll even make myself scarce when I drop you off. I've got business there with Curly, anyway."

"Business." She felt her mouth bend into a smile. Though she tried to flatten her lips, she couldn't. Angus had that way about him.

"Come on, Em. Let's go. No time like the present. The world is our oyster. You can kill two birds— "

"Quit cliché-ing me. All right, I'll go."

They revved down the streets of Defiance, her blonde hair ripping through the air on a nearly December day. If only her worries could fly free as her hair in the wind. But worries didn't often oblige her the way she'd like. As they growled closer to Burl, her hair whipped around her, stinging her face.

When Angus parked the motorcycle and dismounted, she

threw a still-buzzing leg over the seat and stood, her head throbbing with the effort.

"This here's the address." He pointed to a ranch house sitting on the corner of two country roads—isolated by pine trees, brown grasses, and swatches of red dirt. Another house, probably a football field away, stood empty, broken windows for eyes. The wind howled through pine branches. Emory pulled her light jacket around her.

"Let me walk you to the door." Angus placed a hand on her lower back and guided her there. He knocked on an over-wide door, then smiled down on her. She didn't return his grin. How could she?

The door opened slowly. Emory gasped.

Twenty-Four

Surprised you, didn't I?" David grinned two feet below her, anchored to a wheelchair, his right hand pushing a black and metallic lever that motored him forward. His feet lollygagged their own way, askew and unmoving, housed by running shoes that would never touch pavement again.

"I'll leave you be. I'll be back in three hours, okay?" Angus kissed the top of Emory's head, something she'd normally shoo him away for, but this time she nodded and let his motorcycle roar him away.

"Another man, I see." David's voice seemed deeper. Maybe it was because she was used to hearing him mouth to ear, not mouth to belly button. Or maybe because whatever it was that did this to him changed everything about him.

"Just my ride."

He backed his chair away from the wide doorway, then motioned her in with a slight bow of the head. "I bet you didn't expect this."

"No."

"Come sit down." He motored left into a living room floored with orange indoor-outdoor carpeting. A fireplace decorated the far corner of the room, faced with red river rock—a staple in those parts.

She sat on a sad-looking plaid couch, the cushion sinking

around her, holding her hostage. Her tongue seemed to feel the same claustrophobia, unable to unfurl and say pleasantries. Not even, "Interesting weather we're having." Mute, she sat on the couch and counted the spokes on David's wheelchair.

"You look good," he told her. Now that they faced each other, a familiar shyness returned, the kind that had niggled its way into her soul the first time they met. He took charge way back when. A man to be reckoned with, to be sure. Even wheelchair-bound, he stirred the same feelings in her.

"Thanks." She looked at her hands, noticing dirt under her fingernails. She'd never be one of those Cinderella-obsessed girls who pined over perfectly matched nails. But noticing the dirt shamed her. She placed her hands under her legs, while a grandfather clock older than Burl ticktocked in the corner.

"You don't say much."

"What's there to say? You asked me to come."

"I wanted to tell you straight out: I didn't kill Daisy. I was in Mexico, getting special treatments for this." He pointed at his legs.

She looked away. "I know." Somehow she had known it even when the police slapped up wanted posters around Defiance, David's face somber in an empty-eyed black-and-white picture. She knew. But it didn't make things any better.

"How did it all happen, Emory? I mean, I read the papers and all. Chatted with my share of police officers. But I want to hear it straight from the horse's mouth."

"I'm no horse."

"That I know. Have always known it. Though you remind me of that horse in that song. Wildfire, was it? Running free? Leaving her loved ones behind?"

She tried to pierce him with her eyes, hoping to wither him. "I'm not the one who did the leaving, now, am I?"

He simply smiled back. "That's right on. But you still remind me of Wildfire."

"Suit yourself."

"So what happened?" He motored closer, his knees nearly touching hers. She wished for a coffee table between them before realizing things like crowded furniture would get in his way.

"She spent that day with Jed, her best friend."

"A boy?"

"Don't look at me that way, David. You have no right in the world to raise your eyebrows that way. She and Jed were like biscuits and gravy, stuck together since way before when."

"Sorry. It just seems strange that a young lady— "

"A young lady? Since when did you ever talk like that?"

"Always quick to criticize, aren't you? Let's just say things've changed since I last saw you. Can we let it lie at that? I'll tell you the story if you want, but right now I need to know what happened to our daughter."

"*Our* daughter? Interesting word choice."

"If it'll make you spill the story, I'll play your game. What happened to *your* daughter, Emory?"

"They went to a broken-down church out in Old Defiance —their hideout. I don't know what they did there, other than talk. Daisy, she liked to talk, and Jed, he listened, so they made for good friends, I suppose." She removed her hands, dirty fingernails exposed, permitting her palms to gesture at will. "Jed, he comes to my house later that evening. I'd made supper for Daisy, and it burned me up that it was getting cold on the plate. He's carrying her shoe and asks if he can see her."

"He has her shoe?"

"Yeah. It didn't take long for us to discover neither of us had seen her for a couple of hours. I called the police. They searched for weeks, months even. Turned up nothing. Until Jed found her half-buried under a pile of dirt out in a field." Just saying it so controlled and matter of fact made her insides shudder. It was as if she were telling David, Daisy's living, breathing, crippled father, the recipe for sweet potato pie, step by step.

"And they don't know who did it."

"No. They were hoping it was you. Now everyone with a kid is on edge, and no one has a clue who did this or why." In some ways it felt good to give voice to the fears of the citizens of Defiance. Like a mile marker on the road, it showed reality, declared it out loud. Daisy died. No one knew who did it.

"I'm sorry." David's eyes, the eyes she addicted herself to, filled with tears that spilled down ruddy cheeks. "I'm so sorry."

She felt tears form. She pulled them in, steadied her mind. "You should be," she whispered.

He looked at her, a hint of sass in his eyes, the same fire she had once known. Once loved. "Something I've learned over the past few years," he said, "is that folks often blame others when they're trying desperately not to blame themselves. A fancy thing psychiatrists call projection, I hear."

Emory clenched a fist. She considered what kind of woman could barely hold back from punching a man in a wheelchair. Oh, how she wanted to. She could picture her fist hitting his face, him not lifting a finger to stop it. She relaxed her hand, but her anger stayed fisted. "I'm not the villain here, David. There's never any glory for a single mother. None. I'll remind you, if you'd like, how hard it was to keep food on the table and clothes on a girl who grew like a weed. She needed parents, but she only got one in the deal. Me. And I did my best." She felt the strength in her throat, how her words turned up louder and louder. She shot him a don't-you-dare look. "At least I did my duty, David."

"Duty? Didn't you love her?"

Emory stood, towered over him. She could see David's hair thinning on top, one hand resting on a thin leg. "I don't have to take this."

"Sit down. Last I checked your boyfriend wasn't coming around for a while."

She sat, but she wanted to get out of there. "He's not my boyfriend."

"If it makes you happy to say it, go right ahead." David laughed like he'd done in the past—always one to laugh at his own jokes.

"He's not—"

"I don't really care. You know that? I should. But I can't. I've been entwined with your crazy world before, caught up in that web. I don't have the energy to do it anymore." He caressed the black lever with his right hand. "Being struck down has its way about it—helping a man see his life as he should. I'm nursing some hefty regrets, Emory. If you'll promise not to interrupt, I'll give you the whole story."

She sat back. Something about the way he said those last words settled her down, like he was a kindly horse trainer muttering soothing words to a wild stallion who gentled himself with every one of the trainer's sentences. She felt so comfortable that she started picking the dirt from her nails. She looked at David. "Sure, tell me what happened."

"It started the day I got so drunk I didn't know my name. I called for you, but you didn't come. Something much worse did."

Twenty-Five

Mama hadn't left Hixon anything in her will. She'd given it all to the sorority. But Muriel didn't follow suit. Didn't spite Hixon in death but blessed him instead. She gave him her property, every asset, even her Ford Fiasco—a pet name she'd given it before Hixon met her. At first Hixon protested to the lawyer, Mr. Jo Ed Thornton, saying he must be mistaken, but Joe Ed just smiled and said, "Hixon, she was clear as a cloudless sky. She wanted you to have it all—to give you a legacy, 'a rightful inheritance' is how she put it."

"Thank you, sir."

"There's more to it, but I am not obliged to tell you."

"What do you mean?"

"She had me place what's next in her house." Joe Ed stood, shook Hixon's hand.

Hixon thanked him, then left the office in a flurry, his mind pacing back and forth between sadness and joy. He'd struggled most of his life, never having enough, but perhaps now the fight for daily bread was over. Out of habit, he still prayed God would provide it. And forgive him his trespasses. And lead him not into temptation.

Hixon crossed the lot quickly, then got in his own car, which ran slightly better than Muriel's Fiasco. He drove across town, past the place where they found Daisy, past the graveyard, past the lake until he reached the county road. He turned right. In his rearview mirror, he watched the white lines blur behind him, then said a prayer out loud to the open skies stretched out before his windshield. "Lord, you gave me this land and house and money for a reason. Please show me what you want me to do."

Every mile that sped underneath the car niggled his stomach, while an afternoon storm spat rain on the windshield. He hadn't had the courage to see Muriel's place since she died. Would she be watching as he went through it? Would she grab his attention from heaven using God's holler of cracked lightning and then weep a storm of tears in empathy? Or had heaven silenced her forever?

While clouds boiled the sky, a wound unfolded—not from missing Muriel as much as missing his own mama, who never really cared. The wound didn't open with a concise incision, but by a ripping, tearing, gnawing bite of his heart. While his tears inched their way from eyes to chin to lap, Hixon felt all the grief of his life tear into him—making everyone seem like Mama in his mind. Sure he talked the talk, made it sound like he loved folks. But it was talk. Truth was every single person in the world frightened him to tears. Only Muriel burrowed into his fearful heart. Only Muriel saw the wounded boy he'd been. She healed him in nearly every way, pointing him to Jesus. And now her kindness rent his heart.

The rain thinning, he loped to Muriel's front door, then opened it with the key Joe Ed had given him. He smelled Muriel there, felt her presence. Could almost hear her laughter. All of it together weakened his knees. He removed his black shoes, then his socks. This was holy ground, after all. Hixon splayed himself on the carpeting like a young priest being commissioned. He sobbed—was it minutes? Hours? A single ray of sunshine angled itself through Muriel's nine-paned window, blazing his eyes. He blinked, then stood. Seemed the storm wore itself clear out, leaving behind blue sky and a shining sun.

He surveyed the house's insides—a brown couch and an orange loveseat, a central stone fireplace with burned-up logs, a dining table with a shellacked tree trunk as its base. He could see Muriel's knotty pine cabinets through the doorway beyond the dining room. Everything may have looked mismatched, but it smacked of home. Though it was neat, the dust of long disuse covered everything, begging him to scatter it away and live within Muriel's four walls. He scanned the room again, this time spotting an envelope propped on the table, his name on its front.

He opened the envelope carefully. A single sheet of paper held a handwritten note.

Dear Hixon.

He scanned the letter, remembering how he'd snuck a peek when she still took breath. Missy. He would honor Muriel by wooing Missy. But how, exactly? How does a handyman who loves Jesus chase nobly after a waitress who blames Jesus? Hixon read to the place he'd left off. Muriel's writing scrawled haphazardly now, barely legible. She continued:

By now you've gotten the lawyer's instructions that all this is yours. Most of it's a gift of grace meant to bless your socks off.

Hixon looked at his bare feet. "Oh Muriel," he said to the house, "how right you are."

There's only one hitch.

He shivered now, like when God came near. God seemed to be far away these days, in the wake of his grief, but he prayed again for his nearness. Holding the letter, Hixon felt a hush of his presence, like God had whispered these words to Muriel just for him today. He sat at Muriel's table, tracing a line with his finger through the dust. He continued reading.

I have a feeling Emory'll need a new house, something that won't hold Daisy's memory. (You know I love you, but your house in town is not acceptable. You can't woo a woman with taxidermied squirrels. Understand?)

Hixon nodded. Though he was a handyman, his home needed more work than most in Defiance. His foundation was slipping off the pier and beam. His windows didn't open and close easily. His kitchen lay in ruins, with a small hole in the floor where you could see earth and an icebox from the fifties that grumbled and moaned through the night.

And I've had Joe Ed draw up the papers to give my house equally to her, so if you don't ask her to marry you, you might find yourself in a frustrating situation! How's that for a twist?

Even from heaven, Hixon could hear Muriel laughing. But the echoes of her humor frightened him. Really ask Missy to marry him? Why did Muriel add this as a condition? Did she know something? Did God whisper the end of the love story in her ear as she lay dying? All this depended on one stubborn, angry woman. A white woman in a prejudice-stained town. A broken woman. A woman bent on saying no before he ever got up the courage to ask the question.

I know she's hard. I know it. The thing is, I used to be a lot like her, Hixon. And I changed. Maybe it's better said that Jesus changed me. I'm sure folks thought it was too late for me. But with Jesus, it's never too late. Be Jesus to her, Hixon. That'll break down the walls. Think of it as a way to redeem your mama. Your way of making things right with her. Something tells me if you win Emory, you'll win some healing. You know I love you or I wouldn't say all this. Now get to work. You have to woo a needy woman, and you've got some hope to rekindle. May it all happen like a campfire, warm and bright. May God surprise you with love. It's my dying wish for you. Be loved, Hixon. Be loved.

She signed her name Muriel, then drew a heart, a cross, and a fish after her name.

"Why do you sign your name like that?" he'd asked a week before she went to glory, when he noticed the signature on her utility check.

"The heart is mine." She looked at him with Jesus' eyes shining through her in Hixon's darkened living room. "Jesus made it new. The cross is to remind me that making my heart new cost Jesus his life. And the fish is to remind me that he has a plan for me, to fish for others, bringing their hearts to Jesus for healing and wholeness."

Could it be the same for him? He liked to think so, wanted to believe his life was all about helping others find that kind of love. But was it true? Could he wish that for Missy when it meant his heart would be crucified in the process?

Hixon stood. He crossed the floor, no longer wanting to linger in the home he'd have to sell. When he closed the door behind him, he locked it. Keeping the house safe was important.

Keeping his heart safe was too.

Twenty-Six

I got in my car, my mind bent by a couple six packs. I still don't know how many." David coughed.

"You always held your own," Emory said, looking away from his eyes. The tone of his voice sounded like Rod Serling just before something creepy jumped out at the characters of *The Twilight Zone.*

"It was a lie, you know. I just acted like I held my own. Truth was, I was smashed most of my life. That night was no different."

"When?"

"A year ago."

"Why didn't you—"

"Tell you? I just didn't." David backed his up his chair, creating a good foot between them. "So I was smashed. I drove here, or tried to, but the road kept moving and blurring before me. I shook my head, tried to clear it, but the world kept tilting sideways and endways. I told myself to brake, but my foot decided something different. It hit the accelerator in a fury. My tire caught the gravel, which apparently sent the car off kilter. Police said I flipped it going probably eighty-five miles an hour. They said my car must've tumbled over itself four times. It finally set itself down in the middle of a cow pasture. The first thing I heard when I came to was mooing. Then my own voice, swearing. I couldn't feel anything below my torso."

"That's terrible," she heard herself say. She tried to imagine a car flipping so many times, how that would paralyze someone as strong as David.

"So here I am," he said plainly. "Half a man, but every bit as whole."

"Whole?"

"They say folks get Jesus when they fight in a war. I don't know why I didn't meet him in 'Nam. Oh, I shouted his name now and again, like some sort of life insurance policy. But after the accident, it was different. God became personal."

"So you got religion?" She felt her face get hot. Great, now he was going to save her. She readied herself for the Roman Road.

"Not exactly." He wheeled farther backward toward the fireplace mantel. "Not religion. More like a friendship, or peace."

"I'd rather not talk about this." Emory picked at her cuticles, biting one and making it bleed. She looked at her watch. More than an hour to wait for Angus. An eternity, she thought.

"Listen," he said. "I don't want to shove anything down your throat."

"That's nice to know."

"Sarcasm never did become you."

She shook her head, then stood. "It's such a nice day. I can pass the rest of my time outside."

"Please don't go. Please." He wheeled closer. "Not before I tell you something. There's something I need you to know. Please sit."

She shook her head, then turned and walked out the door. A pleasant breeze ruffled her hair like a sky embrace. She smelled winter coming, but the warmth still felt like spring—when Daisy laughed and smiled and played and hoped. A lifetime ago. Another world. In a moment, her girl was gone, leaving a quiet house, but a roaring pain deep in Emory's gut. That pain grunted and growled and hollered until she silenced it with drink or pills or pot. But every morning the grief pressed in again. She gulped a deep breath of East Texas air, hoping to settle herself. The door pushed open behind her.

"I need to say something," David said, squinting into the sunlight.

"Sorry? Is that what *you* need to say? To make yourself feel better?" She felt her voice crack. "To get rid of every ounce of guilt just by saying a few words? How convenient. How very convenient."

"Would you let me finish?"

Emory crossed her arms. "Go ahead."

"I *am* sorry, but that's not what I need to say. I'd love your forgiveness. I long for Daisy's. But whether that comes or not, I rest in Jesus' forgiveness now. He's set my heart on fire."

Emory remembered the anonymous prayer. "Are you praying for me?"

"Sure."

"I figured it was you."

David looked at her, his face the picture of confusion. "Emory, let me say this: I have this gut feeling, see. When I met Jesus after the accident, I think he gave me a special ability."

She'd heard how blind people could smell better, hear better. It all made sense. Now that David couldn't walk, he could do something else better—to compensate. God didn't have to figure into the equation, but she humored him and asked, "What ability?"

"I have dreams."

She leaned against the house. "We all do, David. I've had my share."

He sighed. "On the day Daisy went missing, I had a dream about her. She was alone in a church. Someone, a man, I think, walked in behind her, put a hand over her mouth, and dragged her through the woods."

"Are you trying to spook me?" She wondered if he was making all this up, especially after she'd conveniently told what she knew.

"He took her to a clearing. I couldn't see his face—it was painted."

Emory stood up straight. "Painted?"

"It was dark, so I couldn't make it out, exactly, only that I knew his face had grease paint on it. He hollered the word *death*, and then I woke up. I prayed for Daisy. And when I heard ... "

"You ran."

"I can't run, Emory."

"There are many ways to run."

"True. But I was in Mexico when I had the dream. I heard about Daisy after it. I didn't run. I came back."

"And here you are."

He looked at her. "Here I am. I'm going in. You can join me if you'd like, or you can stay outside. Your choice."

"Convenient words," she hissed. "My choice. Like it was my choice to have a baby."

"It was your choice."

"And my choice to raise her alone?"

"You're right. You're always right. But you want the truth? I left because I couldn't be around you anymore. You and me, we were poison to each other. You should know that better than me. I left for your own good."

"My own good. An interesting use of words."

"You know how we fought. I didn't think it was right, bringing a baby into that mix. Besides, I was a drunk. I had no business—"

"You had every business! Do you know how many nights I had to rock my baby to sleep? How many nights she screamed out from a bad dream, asking for her daddy? How many times she begged me to tell her who you were? You know what I thought when she first went missing? Do you know?"

"No," he whispered.

"I figured she'd finagled your name out of me when I was drunk or high."

"You're still doing pot?"

Emory shuffled backward. A maple seed helicoptered to the ground. "What does it matter to you?"

"I have nothing to say in judgment."

"You just did by asking the question. It's not like I'm a heroin addict."

"No, I can see that. Why don't you tell me what you thought the day Daisy went missing?"

"I thought she left to find you."

Silence stood between them. A late-staying bird chirped happily in the maple tree above, then flew away into the blue November sky.

"I wish she had," David said.

"She had your eyes." Emory pulled out Daisy's fourth-grade picture, her favorite.

"My eyes aren't as good as they used to be. Can you bring it closer?"

She held it a foot from his face. "Take it away," he said, eyes moist.

She did. He backed the chair into the house. Once inside, he shut the door.

A sudden wind blew browned maple seeds free. They circled and twirled around Emory in a happy dance. She shook her head, fighting a memory. But it came back full force, grabbing her face to pay attention.

"Make 'em fly, Mama." Daisy handed Emory a handful of maple seeds—brown-winged and paper-dry. Her blonde hair shone in the August sun. Ten years ago.

Emory threw them all heavenward, watching them dance to the ground while Daisy clapped and danced and sang. "Are they alive?"

Today with the stench of death so near, she would've said, "No, they're dead. Get over it." But that moment she knelt before Daisy, held both of her small hands in hers. "They're as alive as you are, baby."

"Then make them fly again."

So she did. Again and again and again.

But all she could do today was crush them under her feet.

Twenty-Seven

Trees sped by one by one, standing tall against a fading sky. Red ditches ran along the roadway for miles and miles as Emory and Angus left Burl proper and motored toward Defiance. All Emory could do was wonder how many people lived beyond the wall of her heart, and whether she knew enough about people to let a few in.

"You all right?" Angus yelled back to her.

"Yes." Her tears moved from her face to her ears, sticky and sweet, like beer on skin. Tears and beer. She hated one and loved the other, could stiffen herself to abandon one, but could not give up the other.

Angus slowed through Defiance, taking the corners deliberately. The police made their monthly quota by pulling over anyone going more than three over or sliding through a stop sign California style. Emory knew Angus couldn't risk it, what with the bulging package of weed tucked into the back of his jacket.

He braked in front of her clapboard house. She looked up in a flurry, fully expecting Daisy to come barging down the steps, scolding her for not coming home to make supper. Emory stood. No little girl bounded down the stairs, hair flying, perfectly pronounced words scattered by the wind.

It sickened Emory to gaze upon the empty stairs, the closed door, the latched gate. But what needled her more was the sudden realization that she'd never let Daisy into the citadel of her heart, except when she was high, and Daisy told her in no uncertain terms that her affection then didn't count one smidge. "Love me when you're thinking straight," she'd said like a nursery rhyme, over and over and over until once Emory screamed, "Enough!"

Angus tapped Emory on the shoulder. "I need to go, and you have work. Let me walk you to the door."

She turned to face him—his deliciously wild eyes, his tumbled-down hair, his face that sung sincerity—and wanted to wrap her arms around him and plaster him with a kiss. The urge came sudden upon her, like a thunderstorm in summer, from blue sky to storm gray in moments.

Angus looked at her, his head cocked, his eyes smiling. "What?"

"Just this." She obeyed her crazy urge, flung her arms around his neck, bent near, felt the brush of his lips against hers, then kissed him again. He wrapped strong arms around her, their torsos so close she felt the rhythm of his heart hammering through his shirt.

During the kiss, she thought, Yes, I can do this. I can let people in. I know who to let in and who to keep out. Such logical thoughts while her heart thumped joy in her chest.

Angus pulled away. He laughed, then stopped. He cleared his throat and nodded to something beyond her. "Good day, Hixon."

Emory spun around to see Hixon, flowers in hand, eyes toward the sidewalk. Her face burned. "Hixon."

But he walked by her, never saying hello. She watched him walk toward the woods, dropping flowers one by one, marking his trail like Hansel and Gretel.

Angus watched, too, then bent near for another kiss.

Emory intercepted him with her right hand. "No, it was a mistake."

"A mistake? That's what you call the best kiss either of us has had?" He tried to pull her to him.

This time she slugged him hard in the gut and walked down her unbuckled pathway, her feet touching Hixon's handiwork. She slammed the door. Not just on Angus or Hixon, but on the whole wide world. It felt good, slamming. Really good. But it also felt like another death, like her heart stared at the sky with unblinking Daisy eyes, never to dance with love again.

The mail sat piled on the floor, skewed this way and that. Emory picked up the whole stack, then threw herself on the couch with it. An envelope caught her eye, with that same familiar typesetting and a Burl postmark. She ripped it open.

> Stations, Lord. Stations.
> Bring Emory to Daisy's stations—
> Where she walked her last days,
> Where she finally rested.
> Help her to be there, really be there so she can grieve.
> Take her back, Lord, starting with Daisy's grave.
> Wrap your arms around her there, hold her heart.
> It's breaking; or maybe better put—it's broken.
> Teach her through grief to let you in so you can heal her.
> Make it so she loves again. Amen.

Emory stared at the words. Blinked her eyes and read them again. "David," she muttered. The ebb and flow of his printed words made her feel eerie. Here she'd seen him today, and now he was sending nameless prayers, asking her to go to the place even he hadn't dared to go. Why her grave? Why the prayers? She sat back on the couch, closed her eyes. Maybe it was guilt, pure and simple. Maybe he felt so terrible about his absence that he tried to make it up to her with pious prayers, never having the guts to sign his name, 'fess up. That was it. He'd lied to her before. Why not now?

The letter's instructions, David's really, told her to go to the places of Daisy's last days. Told her to spill grief on Daisy's grave and leave it there once and for all. Right. Wouldn't that be terribly convenient for everyone? She could be a controlled woman who smiled sincerely. No one would have to pity poor Emory ever again. All because she followed in the footsteps of her ex's words. He could be the hero of the story, which made things ever more poetic as he wheeled himself around in an electric wheelchair. A hero indeed.

The sun angled its way into the living room, making the dust dance. She watched it for a long time, wondering if there were such a thing as light making someone dance. It seemed to be with Muriel. Even when she couldn't dance, her eyes did, "All because of the light of Jesus," she'd said.

But no light could make Emory dance, she knew. Even the searchlight Brother Bob Keller used to scan the sky when he tried to sell used cars wouldn't be enough to set her feet to flight. Emory sighed. This was her life. This. An ugly couch, a stash of pot, and a little girl's bedroom emptied of laughter.

She looked at the letter, tossed it aside like junk mail, and swore. Mary Jane angled in and out of her legs, purring, but she scatted the cat away. Emory Chance. Lone woman. With no one to love her. And no one to love.

She closed her eyes. A knock at the door roused her.

She opened it. No one was there. She started to push the screen door out, but it hit something. A pan. No note. No one to be seen this way or that. But chicken and dumplings stared back at her from that strange lady's dish. Ethrea Ree, was it? She picked it up, smelled the still-warm chicken, and fought to keep her head.

Her mama's chicken and dumplings was the only thing she

remembered fondly from way back when. Emory took the dish to the kitchen, set it on the table, and breathed in Mama. She grabbed a crusted fork from the sink and dove into the soupy, dumplingy, chickeny concoction. Oh, sweet Lord, it was good. But even in the eating, a bitter, metallic taste invaded her mouth.

"Emmy, that's for company, not for you."

Her stomach growled. Roared. Bit itself in fury. And the dumplings, which Mama made with such loving care, made Emmy wish her mama's hands would reach that way toward her. But that was not to be. Mama dumped the pot of chicken and dumplings into a serving container—a mottled blue and white bowl Mama loved more than the sky itself—and handed Emmy the pot. "You can lick it clean if you'd like."

She said it like she was doing Emmy a favor, like she'd was the queen bestowing a blessing on a commoner. Even then, Emmy believed it to be true. She could hardly wait for the pot to cool down. She hauled it to her own little table—a wooden bench she'd found on the side of the road. She sat on a fruit crate—another find—and ran her right index finger through the now-congealing chicken broth. It tasted like beauty. And perfection. And love. All mixed together. She mmm-ed her way through the dregs of the pot, all the while thanking Mama for the pleasure of licking it. Not one dumpling. Not one sinew of leftover chicken. Just broth, broth, broth circling lips that curled upward in bliss.

Emory ate a dumpling now, made bitter from the memory. Mama's prized possession—her skills in the kitchen—were never to be given to her. Not in the form of food or knowledge. When she asked Mama for her recipes, when she still had a mind in her head, Mama said, "I had to scrapple my way through the kitchen, figuring those recipes all by my lonesome. They're mine. Not yours. I will take them with me to heaven's kitchen. I didn't much like cooking for you, but I think things will change in the hereafter. Angels will be grateful, I'm telling you. They'll cherish my cooking. They'll appreciate my biscuits and gravy."

Emory sat on the edge of Mama's bed, tears wetting her cheeks. "Please, Mama. Just one recipe. Chicken and dumplings."

But Mama said a flat, "No."

"What about Daisy? Don't you want your granddaughter to keep eating chicken and dumplings long after you're gone?"

"No," she said again, her breath ragged. "I don't want to be remembered at all. Why do folks think they're so high and mighty that they need to be remembered, anyway?"

"So that they make a difference," Emory heard herself say, scarcely a whisper.

Mama pulled herself up and leveled pale blue eyes Emory's way. "Don't get yourself caught up in such nonsense. I didn't make any sort of difference. None at all. And you won't either. It's the way of life."

Emory now sat at the table while the chicken grew cold. She pushed it away in the same manner Mama had pushed her away, with indifference. Though her stomach growled and rumbled inside her, she took the dish and put it in the fridge, not bothering to cover it. She trudged to her bedroom, took off all her clothes, and lay on her bed, her eyes staring vacantly into the ceiling light, counting the dead flies in its tray. One. Two. Three ... Thirteen. She stopped counting. Daisy was thirteen when she choked and died. She counted until she reached the end—thirty dead flies crowding for space under the sixty-watt bulb. One dead fly for each year of her life.

How fitting.

With a sigh deeper than Defiance's water supply, Emory got up. She put on her waitress uniform, glanced at the extra stash of pot, and looked at her watch. No, not enough time to take a hit before work.

She passed Daisy's room. Her bed still stood unmade. She

couldn't abide it anymore. She grabbed Daisy's sheets and bedspread, even her pillow. In a heap she wrestled them out the back door and threw them into her burn barrel. A lighter from her uniform pocket flicked to life under deft fingers. She tilted the flame toward Daisy's sheet, waiting for it to catch fire. It smoked, and then fire curled around it, slowly devouring the sheets that once cradled Emory's daughter.

If only forgetting Daisy could be that easy.

Twenty-Nine

Hixon had swung on that tire swing whenever Mama had boyfriends over. Back and forth, twirling in circles with his head back, tongue out as if it were licking the sky. He could stand and pump his legs, then jump off into the dirt beneath him, his knees dusted brick red.

Hixon spun this time, trying to twirl his anger clear to Alabama. His mom was with a nameless man, broad shouldered, dark hair flecked gray, and a fake, syrupy smile. He hated the man instantly, particularly when he patted Hixon's head, his eyes amused. "I've always wanted to touch a Negro's head, but up till now I never had the chance. It's spongier than I expected."

Mama didn't say anything. She laughed instead. "It's not easy taming it, if you want to know the truth." She sipped lemonade on the wide verandah of their yellow and white house.

Nameless Man nodded Hixon's way, smiling again. He looked at Mama. "It's downright good of you to adopt him."

Hixon felt the man's words in his stomach first. Is that what he thought? That Mama didn't give birth to him? That he was a pathetic orphan boy who Mama took in? Always, always the men in Mama's life gave him that same pitying look, but none had ever said this. Hixon looked at his mama, waiting for her to straighten the man out.

"Don't flatter me so." She took a long drag of a Lucky Strike, drained it completely of its smoke.

Hixon noticed the lipstick pressed on the cigarette's tan filter—a kiss redder than cherries. He watched her mouth, but didn't say a word. He knew his place, even at ten.

"Well, it's not often a white woman would take in a colored orphan child is all." The man leaned back on the clapboards.

She smiled. "Did you ever see a situation and just know God had chosen you to do a particular thing?"

Hixon shrank back, dreading the rest of Mama's words. He longed for the swing, but knew he couldn't leave until Mama said so.

"Sure," the man said. "When I saw you. The good Lord told me to court you, and here I am."

"Well, that's how it was with me and Hixon. He needed a home, and I had one. Plain as that."

The man laughed. "You're a saint, you know that?"

"You may go now, Hixon." She winked at Nameless Man. "Two hours. Be back in two."

Hixon nodded, retreating to the swing he now twirled on, watching the clouds pass through the sky like they were on their way somewhere. Like they knew where they were headed. So unlike him. He thought he knew where he came from, only to hear his mama concoct lies to flatter a man. He thought he would grow up to be somebody. But under the shadow of her lies, he knew the truth. Though she pushed and heaved him into the world after a one-night-stand with a black man, she considered her duty done once his brown bellybutton was severed from her white body. Once the knot was tied, the blood wiped away, the screams quieted, Mama regarded him as a rescued orphan, she his caretaker, he her problem.

Only Frank treated him with respect and kindness. Mama's real boyfriend. But Mama spent her life upsetting Frank. And while his twirling slowed, the familiar rumble of Frank's car pulled him from cloud watching.

"Hixon," Frank hollered. He shut his car door with a flourish. "How is my sweet, sweet boy?" He smiled.

But Hixon couldn't smile back. Mama was with Nameless Man, who had parked his Cadillac in the alley. Seeing Mama with yet another man would send Frank away, Hixon knew. "Push me," he said. Begged really.

"I can push a little bit, but I have something to ask your mama. Is she in?"

"No." He looked away, couldn't lie with his eyes with Frank looking at him that way, all sincere and kind.

"Nonsense. I know she's home." He motioned for Hixon to get on the swing. He pushed him high in the air, then spun him so he'd twirl and swing. It roller-coastered his stomach. But still he said, "More, more."

Frank laughed. While Hixon swung helter-skelter, Frank made his way to the house, one step at a time. Hixon tried to jump off and hurt himself, just so Frank would tend to him, preventing him from seeing Mama with Nameless Man, but the momentum held him in his place. Even as a man he remembered how the tire smelled—a warm rubber odor he used to find comforting—as he dragged his feet along the ground.

Shouting erupted minutes later. Hixon clambered down from the swing, praying Mama would come to her senses and realize Frank was a kindhearted man, that he'd make a good father. But when the front screen door slapped the house's face and Frank appeared alone and red-cheeked, Hixon knew. It was over.

Frank walked down the porch steps, head down, eyes wet. He stopped in front of Hixon. His large hand rested on Hixon's head like he was blessing him. "I'm sorry," he said. "I thought ... " He looked away, put a hand over his rough face, covering his mouth. "I thought we'd be a family."

Hixon sat on the dirt and cried, not loud like a girl, just tears that dropped like overripe fruit to the ground, dotting the earth.

Frank bent down. “I want you to promise me something. Can you do that?”

Hixon nodded but kept his eyes on the dirt.

“Someday you’ll be old enough to marry. Do yourself a favor and marry a faithful, sweet-tempered woman. Don’t get yourself hoodwinked by a pretty face. She has to love you with everything inside her and not have a wandering eye.” Frank stood, wiped his hand under his nose. He sniffed, then shook his head. “Here.” He reached to lift Hixon from the dust.

Hixon stood.

Frank wrapped farmer arms around him, crushing him against his chest. Frank smelled like cut grass and sweat—the most glorious smell Hixon’d ever known. He wanted to stay that way forever, wrapped like a burrito in the embrace of the only father he ever knew. But as soon as Frank’s arms weakened, as soon as he pulled away and took a long, sad look into Hixon’s eyes, Hixon knew. This was good-bye.

Frank fished through his pocket, his left one. He held out a single gold ring. “I was going to ask her to marry me.” He took Hixon’s right hand, pressed the circle of metal into Hixon’s palm, and closed his fingers around it. “For your bride someday,” he said. Then he turned on worn cowboy boots and left Hixon behind. Opened the car door. Shut it quiet. Motored away. Leaving Hixon with the sting of his memory and a simple gold ring.

On his porch, Hixon held the ring in his hand, touching its smoothness, wondering what he would do with it. Missy and Angus’s kiss festered like a disease in his heart. *Why, God? Why couldn’t things be easy? Why couldn’t you bring me a sweet black girl to marry? Why this one? She doesn’t even love me. She barely notices me. And she loves another man. What are you asking me to do? What purpose?* All these questions circled around him like vultures above a coyote-eaten carcass. He sat on his porch, hands now clasped behind his head, his weight shifting the porch swing back and forth in a quiet rock.

No, God couldn't be serious. Hixon knew he got things wrong sometimes. Sure, Muriel was convinced—but that was because Hixon told her his secret and she let it take flight. The prophetic gift others had thought true of him had proven terribly fallible. God didn't whisper to him Daisy's killer. He didn't give Hixon step-by-step instructions as to how to woo Emory Chance. In fact, he made it near impossible. Hixon had once heard Hap holler from the pulpit, "When God wants to do an impossible task, he takes an impossible person and breaks him." Was he the impossible person? Or Emory? Or both? And what kind of earth-shattering breakage would open the dungeon of Emory's heart? What kind of ripping apart would Hixon be called upon to experience in order to win her?

"Lord," Hixon said to the tree beyond his porch. "I can't do it. She loves someone else. And I'm feeble and needy and my skin's the wrong color. Please send someone else."

The creak of the porch swing was his answer from the Almighty for seconds, then minutes. Until a familiar resounding opened his mind. *She is not who she will be*, the voice said. *Patience.*

Hixon smelled the smoke first, then saw it coming from behind Missy's house. He ran around the now pristine white home and stopped when he saw Missy standing in her uniform, a thin, pale hand raised in the air while smoke circled around her. She didn't cough or choke. She didn't do a thing. Just a raised fist to the heavens and a mouth as silent as death. Hixon coughed, but she didn't turn around. His bride. Or at least God thought so.

He walked over to her, put a tentative hand on her bony shoulder.

She jumped, then turned to face him. Tears angled down her cheeks. "Dead."

"What?"

"She's dead. And I'm the rendering plant. I'm burning her scent." Her voice sounded hard as granite, as determined as a weed pushing its green might through a cracked sidewalk.

"I'm sorry," he said.

"Sorry doesn't help. Nothing helps."

For a long time he said nothing. Because she spoke the truth this time. Nothing on earth could help her, he knew. Not even him. When God told him he was to ask her to marry him, he believed he could embrace her pain, squeeze it completely out of her. But pain couldn't be pressed out. And she certainly wasn't managed so simply. No, nothing could help her now, only Jesus. While the smoke swirled around her, depositing speckles of ash in her hair and his, he said yet another prayer. *God, I can't do this. She has to choose you first. How can I ask her to marry me with her heart so hard? Oh, Jesus, she doesn't even love me. It's Angus she loves.*

Missy turned his way. "He's praying for me," she said.

"Who?"

"David."

The name pounded in his heart. Daisy's father—the man she once loved. Three men vying for one closed heart. He felt the ring in his pocket, circled his thumb and pointer finger around it. *Patience*, he told himself. *She is not as she will be.*

But she had so far to go. And looking into her eyes while ashy snow flittered down around her, all he could see was his mama's wandering eyes.

Thirty

Emory saw sadness there, haunting Hixon's tree-bark brown eyes. While Daisy's bedding rendered itself into the atmosphere of Defiance, an ember of longing burned dimly in her heart. Hixon. The man who painted her house, along with Jed Pepper. The man who repaired her walkway. The man who protected her, prayed for her, watched out for her. The man who saw her kiss Angus—the one who could charm the eyeballs out of a billy goat. She looked away from Hixon while Daisy's memory smoldered and Hixon's eyes cast themselves to the earth. No. She couldn't lose herself in his eyes. No matter how kind he was, how tenderly he cared for Muriel, no matter how he seemed to touch every soul in Defiance with hope and love, she could not give her heart to him or any man. "I'm late for work," she said. She hugged herself as the sun slipped below the trees.

"I could walk you there."

"I walk alone," she said.

"Good-bye, then. I'll head home. But I can walk you to the corner. It'd make me feel better, especially with Daisy's killer still on the loose."

"Suit yourself," she said.

They hadn't walked a half a block when the familiar sound of a rattling tailpipe motored down the street behind them. Angus. He slowed until he was even with them both. "Well, looky here—the handyman and the waitress taking a stroll. It's downright romantic."

Emory faced him. "Cut it out." She felt Hixon's tension behind her.

"Just a joke." Angus laughed. "You're late, aren't you?"

Emory looked at her watch. He was right.

"Hop on and I'll give you a ride."

She looked at Hixon.

"You hop on," he said. "Since you're late."

"Be safe," she told Hixon. She maneuvered onto the bike and put her arms around Angus's waist. She saw Hixon wince. Two men. One who flattered her ego and ignited her desire. One whose kindness wooed her heart. Why couldn't they be made into one man? She waved to Hixon, mouthed good-bye, but he turned in the direction of his home, not saying a word.

Angus deposited her at Little Myrtle's and told her he'd pick her up after her shift. "Maybe we can have ourselves a little party. A crazy little gathering."

"No," she said. "I'm over all that." She said it with surprising authority, like maybe she meant it this time. Angus propped the motorcycle on its kickstand and placed both hands on her waist, pulled her to him. She looked away, but felt desire rise up in her. She snuck a look into his eyes, but they seemed distant, vacant, cold. She pulled away. "I've got work. And don't bother picking me up. I can make my way home just fine."

But it was close to midnight when she got off work, and a storm wrestled the trees. Big Earl offered a ride, but she refused. She wished she hadn't. What was left of brown leaves clinging to the trees now fell to the ground, spinning and shimmying to cold cement. Emory had no coat, so she hugged herself while the wind shrieked through Defiance. She walked fast, and then felt the sudden urge to run. In a flash, she thought she heard footsteps behind her. She looked back. Nothing. Just an empty street, cars with dead eyes staring back, and a buzzing streetlight above.

She didn't run, but her heart did. With each step she comforted herself by knowing she was closer to her home. One thousand steps. She'd counted them once. At five hundred thirty seven, the footsteps behind her became distinct. A heavy-soled shoe, like a man's dress shoe. It was too muddled to be heels. Too loud to be sneakers. She turned quickly, only to see the street empty, no steps slapping the sidewalk.

She squinted, thought she saw movement to her right. Emory swallowed, hoping to swallow her fear too. She didn't.

At step seven hundred seventy seven, the footsteps recommenced. This time she didn't turn around. Only a few hundred more steps, and she'd be home. She could call Officer Spellman if she wanted. Yes, that would be a good idea.

She turned left onto Love Street, ever-hearing footsteps. She walked faster. So did the steps. She turned around, only to see a swinging gate, creaking on rusty hinges below a flickering orange streetlamp. She slipped off her shoes so her feet hit the pavement. She'd always been the best runner on bare feet, with no shoes to interfere. She ran the last steps home, her lungs retching at the effort—thanks to years of smoking. When she stopped at the gate, Emory's heart jumped into her mouth. The front door of her home gaped open.

Thirty-One

Emory looked behind her, not remembering if she'd heard more footsteps when she ran to her house. Love Street stood deserted, quieter than Defiance before a thunderstorm. From the front door of her home, she heard the radio blaring but nothing else. For a brief moment, she debated hightailing it to Hixon's house. But remembering his wounded eyes and the obscenely late hour, she changed her mind, gulped down her heart, and swung open her picket gate. She said Angus's name out loud, hoping he was playing a joke to get back at her for pushing away his party invitation.

No one answered back.

At the door, she gasped while ammonia burned her eyes.

Someone had hurricaned the living room, overturning furniture, emptying every desk drawer, and marring the walls. Yellow and red smeared them like a child's finger-painting. And the smell of ammonia permeated the room. Emory swallowed. "Angus? You in here? This isn't funny." She stepped into the house, worry forcing its way into her stomach. "Not funny at all."

She reached the radio, which had been tuned to her least favorite station, and turned it off. As she stepped away from it, she realized whoever came into her home didn't steal the radio. Why would someone come into her home to destroy it and not take anything? "The can." She looked up on the high shelf where she kept her stash of pot.

It was still there.

"Oh, God."

Emory's eyes burned as she crossed through the living room into the kitchen. The phone was still there, thankfully, but everything else spelled chaos. The fridge, wide open and running, was emptied of what little she had in there. Someone had thrown a mayonnaise jar against the back wall. Some white globs clung there, while others had slid down into a heap on the linoleum below, spiked with shards of glass. The intruder's foot had smashed ground beef into the flooring. She grabbed the phone. Her hand shook as she dialed.

Officer Spellman told her to lock the doors and wait in the living room. He said he'd be there in a few minutes. But she couldn't sit still. She had to see what else had been done. She grabbed a knife from the kitchen, clutching it in both hands. The knife trembled before her as she entered her bedroom. It looked like the living room's twin—the nightstands toppled over, paper covering the floor, that same terrible smell—worse than the rendering plant. Her clothing lay in heaps on the floor like casualties. She pulled open the dresser where she stashed money and jewelry. Though everything else was out of her dresser, that drawer looked as if it had not been touched. The money sat there like it always did. Her jewelry too.

In the distance, she heard the scream of Officer Spellman's squad car. He'd be here soon.

She stopped in front of Daisy's room, the knife still in her shaking hands. The room looked like it had when Emory left it—nothing overturned. No drawers opened. Nothing smashed against the floor. Nothing on the walls. Except for one thing: a single shoe sitting in the middle of Daisy's sheetless bed.

Thirty-Two

Emmy walked everywhere as a child, even skipping the streets of Defiance past nightfall, not a stitch of worry in her step. She never wore shoes, even as the sidewalks blazed summer heat—she just ran faster. She was a lonely child, craving the attention of nearly everyone she met, but seldom receiving any. So she learned to tell herself stories—grand tales of princesses and knights and fairies who resided in the forests of the little town. And when she slept, she craved perfect darkness—the darker her room, the better her dreams of this other world. She believed in magic then. A seven-year-old's magic. And when she flicked the light switch southward, the magic appeared, always on the movie screen of her mind.

One night the dream had been so vivid that she sat upright in bed, not knowing which world she awoke in. Giant lizard-like trolls invaded the fairy forest. Just as Emmy wielded a troll-killing dagger, her eyes popped open, her breaths coming short. Someone stood in her room.

"Mama?" Sometimes Mama would come in at night when Emmy dreamed, since Emmy dreamed loud.

The figure didn't say anything.

Emmy felt around her bed for the dagger, believing she was still in the forest, hunting trolls. But her hand found only sheets. "Mama? That you?"

The figure moved closer. "No." A man's voice—a voice she didn't recognize.

Her heart thumped in her chest. Something in the way the man said no made her understand he was real, whether troll or man, and he meant evil.

She scooted toward her headboard. "Mama?" Her voice sounded cut off, like she was yelling underwater.

"She's not here. I am." The man moved into the shadowy light of the hallway. Emmy didn't recognize him. "Your babysitter."

When had Mama hired a babysitter? And why didn't she tell Emmy?

"It's time for a walk." He spat on the floor. He took two long strides toward her bed, grabbed her by the arm, and lifted her to her feet in a single, painful motion. "You're coming with me. Get on your shoes." He pointed to her flip-flops at the base of the bed. "Now."

"I'm in my nightgown," she squeaked.

He said nothing more. Once her flip-flops slipped on her feet, he pulled her through the dark house out into the inky night. He pulled her so fast she had to run to keep up. "My shoes. Can I take them off?"

He didn't answer. As they neared the forest on the outskirts of town, Emmy knew she had to scream. She sucked in a monster of a breath, but as she was releasing her yelp, the man's greasy hand, square and hard, pressed itself over her mouth and nose, suffocating her. He shook his head no, his breath in rasps, with hints of smoke. He dragged her up an incline into the forest. When she lost a shoe, he double-backed and pointed. She put it back on.

He shoved her onto the forest floor, the moon overhead lighting his smiling face and narrowed eyes. She didn't know then what he wanted her to do, but she found out soon enough, and the forest scene would haunt her dreams, replacing fairy tales with the dark story of that night. When he left her alone, she threw her shoes at the trees, tears blurring her vision. She ran home on bare feet, rocks and sticks cutting into her soles. And when she thrashed through the doorway of her home and locked the doors, she blazed on every single light in the house, and waited for Mama to come home in the light of the darkest night of her life.

The light switch that'd turned off for fairy dreams now stayed in the on position, chasing away the nightmares.

That memory, the terrible night she tried to keep locked behind a dungeon door, rushed into Emory's mind as she stared at the solitary shoe and the police sirens grew louder and louder. A pounding at the door shook her back to the present. She put down the knife on the hallway floor, turned and walked barefooted to the front door, and unlocked it. Officer Spellman entered, out of breath, the play of blue and red strobe-lighting his face.

"What happened?" He ran a hand through his hair. "Are you okay?"

"I am fine," she heard herself say.

"When did you come home?" He entered the living room, looking at the ruckus beneath him. He pulled on gloves, then righted an end table.

"Just a few minutes ago, right before I called you."

"Anything taken?"

"No, that's what's strange. Nothing. Not my money, my jewelry, my radio, my— " She stopped herself. Not her pot. Not exactly something to say to an officer of the law. She looked down at her feet.

"So a vandalism. Nothing more."

"Yes, I suppose. But there's something you need to see." She led him to Daisy's room and pointed to the bed. "Daisy's other shoe." She heard the tremor in her voice, felt a cry come from deep inside her, but shoved it back where it came from through sheer effort.

He ran to Daisy's bed, then stopped in front of the shoe. "There's a note here." With his gloved hands, he picked it up. Looked at the front of a thin, half-ripped sheet of paper, then the back. "I'm not sure what to make of this." He motioned for her to come.

"Read it," he said.

> Dear Mama, Please come and get me. I'm in the forest. He's trying to be nice, but he's turning. Tell Jed it's not his fault. It's not yours either. I love you. I miss you. Daisy.

Each word hit Emory in the gut, slicing through her like the knife she once carried, though the cuts these gave were jagged, raw.

"Is that your daughter's handwriting?"

Emory nodded, reading the words over again, looking for clues. She'd been in the forest too. Just like her. Though Daisy hadn't escaped with her shoes or her life. And Emory hadn't found her.

"The reason I'm asking is it just seems strange is all. Why now? And are you sure this is her shoe?"

"As sure as I am that it's her handwriting." She remembered Daisy's other shoe in the window and retrieved it. "See?"

Officer Spellman nodded. "I'm going to call in the rest of the team to sweep your house. Do you have somewhere else you can sleep?"

"I don't know."

"She can stay with me," a voice said from the doorway. Hixon's voice.

Emory faced him. "I can't."

"Please," he said. "I'll keep you safe."

"Safe," she said to herself. As if that word could be casually thrown around like it was the truth. No one was safe, she knew. Especially not her. Certainly not Daisy.

Hixon extended his hand her way, invitational like. "When I make a promise, I keep it. I'll keep you safe."

Officer Spellman raised an eyebrow, looked back and forth between Emory and Hixon. "He's right. You can't stay here tonight."

She nodded. "I need to get my stuff." She retreated to her overturned bedroom, shoved a few things into a shopping bag and followed Hixon out into the cool night. Still barefooted.

Thirty-Three

Hixon choked down tears, tried to keep them locked inside. There lay Missy in the living room, on the couch. Last night when Missy walked barefooted into his home in the middle of the night, he scampered to put sheets and a blanket on the couch, trying in vain to tuck in the corners hospital style. She climbed onto the couch without a word, still in her clothes. She turned toward the window, the sheets gathered up under her chin, a whispered thank you on her lips.

In the morning, she lay in the same position, but this time the sunlight blessed her face. She is beautiful, he thought. He wanted to come near, to stroke her hair, to pull strands away from her cheek so the light could kiss more of her face. Watching her made Hixon realize that maybe God knew what he was talking about. With Missy wordless and carefree, asleep on the couch, he could picture it perfectly. Their courtship. Their wedding. Their home together. Her laughter. Hixon catching each tear with a kiss.

In the quiet of the morning, Missy's sleep reminded him that a hard woman could have soft edges. She was just a woman, after all. A woman with a past. A woman with heartache living inside her chest. But a woman nonetheless. All at once, God's voice shot through Hixon, through his chest, reverberating in his heart. *Treat her like an orphan*, he said. *Before you think of her as your wife.*

Orphan.

The word stung him. He didn't even know Missy's past. Was she an orphan? Was God giving him insight into her life? Or was it something different? He slipped out of the living room into the kitchen, where he put a scoop of coffee into the percolator. Missy deserved more than instant coffee. He waited for the coffee to brew, then poured a generous amount into a mug and took a sip. As the sunlight angled a little higher in the sky and spotlighted the table, he remembered Gentry. The boy had come by Hixon in a scattered way, through a friend of a friend who'd taken in the orphan boy but could no longer cope with his antics. Gentry was nine years old when he came to live with Hixon. At first it'd been pure bliss, Hixon like a kindly uncle who let Gentry do whatever he wanted because he felt so bad for Gentry's orphanhood. But soon the folly of that made Hixon realize the boy didn't need freedom, he needed restriction. Rules.

And when he set rules, Gentry hollered and disobeyed over and over, trying to push Hixon away from his heart. He scrapped and fought and spat. He broke Hixon's heart until it lay open and bleeding.

In Swan Field on the edge of town, Hixon cried to God. "Everything I do, he pushes away. Every time I try to love Gentry, he runs the other way. What do I do, Lord? Help me. I am not a father. I don't know what to do."

God whispered guidance, calming Hixon's heart. Giving him strength and resolve.

He's an orphan.

He is wounded. All he knows is self-protection. All he knows how to do is push back. He cannot trust on his own. Your love must come longer and swifter than his resistance. It must be relentless, continual. No matter what, be there. Affirm your love even if he spits at you. Keep the rules intact, but just as much, keep your love constant.

When Hixon came home after God's instructions from Swan

Field, he returned to an empty house. His wallet missing. And Gentry gone for good. The grief Hixon had felt in his empty house had felt like today's grief. A helpless pain he couldn't remove if he wanted to. Jed filled that place, touching on his father nerve. Maybe that's why he hadn't spent time with Jed lately. Maybe Jed would end up like Gentry—running far away. Though he knew Jed wouldn't do such a thing, nor would Hap Pepper permit it, Hixon still felt sad when he spent time with him. He and Gentry had that same look about them.

Hixon remembered God's words to him, massaged them a bit in his heart. Missy an orphan. What was God asking of him? To love and love and love and love only to have her cut bait and run away with the remainder of his heart?

He took another sip of coffee, letting the warm liquid coat his throat. It all made sense. Missy as Gentry. Gentry as Missy. Both pushing back. Both wounded like he'd been. Both stealing his heart. He sighed, opened his tattered Bible sitting on the table. In the concordance in the back, he found the word *fatherless* and flipped through some verses, hoping for strength, guidance.

In Psalm 82, he read, "Defend the poor and fatherless: do justice to the afflicted and needy. Deliver the poor and needy: rid them out of the hand of the wicked. They know not, neither will they understand; they walk on in darkness: all the foundations of the earth are out of course."

True, true, true. And remembering Missy's house thrashed into disarray, Hixon knew he must deliver her from the hand of the wicked. Someone was after her, he knew, and it made him sick inside. God had made it all clear. He was to defend her. Be sure she experienced justice. Keep her free from Wicked's probing hands. Be a light when the darkness swirled around her. To keep her course when she veered.

Poor fatherless Missy, he mourned. His orphaned bride-to-be. Hixon's heart swelled in that moment, coffee cup in hand,

Bible opened to Psalm 82—his instruction manual for Missy in the coming weeks and months. He smiled and thanked God. What seemed impossible just a day ago now seemed possible. He stood, took his coffee cup to the sink and rinsed it. He poured another cup for Missy in his only good cup—a china teacup he'd found at Goodwill years ago, hoping someday to have a wife to give pretty things to. No cracks. Just a ringlet of roses around the rim in gold and pink and green. He placed the saucer underneath and smelled the rich coffee, scenting his pathway to the living room. It clinked as he carried it.

"I brought you some coffee." He nearly sang the words.

In the place where she'd been kissed by morning light lay only twisted sheets.

Thirty-Four

Chasing. Breathless. Trees bending branches down to capture her. Was this another trip? Had she taken Angus's little pills again? All at once Emory wished she hadn't. Taking trips on the back of little pills no longer felt safe. Or right.

But here she was in the woods, sweat driveling down her face—an odd thing as winter nearly grabbed Defiance. A noise behind her, like the rustling of leaves, made her turn. Nothing. She ran, but briars and long-twining shrubs grabbed at her ankles, bloodying them and preventing her from running away free and clear. Her heart leapt within her, pounding her temples. Footsteps behind her thumped in the mossy earth, but she wouldn't turn around. A deep sense of dread crept into her soul then. Somehow she knew that if she turned around to face the owner of the footprints, her life would be over. Whatever she saw would twist her life worse than she'd so far known. So she clawed and detangled her legs while blood ran down her hands.

Far off in the distance, she saw him.

Kind eyes, a true smile. Hixon. His arms outstretched to her. But she couldn't reach him, and he didn't run toward her in rescue.

Trapped by sticker bushes, she heard her breath come louder and louder in the fight. She looked up, hoping to gain strength from Hixon's kind face, but in that moment he disappeared.

The ache of losing him then made her cry out in the night. Despair lurked behind her, she knew, but the fight she'd had under Hixon's eyes drained from her. She splayed herself prostrate on the dry, brambled earth, thorns piercing her everywhere. Usually careful to keep her tears deep inside, she gave that up, too, letting them wet the dirt, filling the dryness with so much water that a gully formed beneath her, cooling her body, salving the sting of a thousand thorns.

She sobbed, really wept, while the parade of her life played in front of her in mockery. Her childhood. Her mama. The loneliness. The man in the woods. The loves she'd hoped would fill her empty heart, only to leave her feeling emptier after she gave herself away. The icy fear that crept into her soul when she found herself pregnant. The battle with drugs she never seemed to win. Her splayed out like this on her living room floor the day Daisy went missing. Daisy's empty eyes staring at a sterile ceiling.

Something inside her told her to turn around. It was not a gentle voice, but the angry voice in her head. The voice that told her she was nothing. The voice that strangled her with her own worthlessness. The voice that enticed her to take just one more hit. The voice that mocked her. This voice told her to turn. And like a slave under the control of an evil master, she obeyed.

Where someone should've stood were two shoes. Daisy's shoes. Nothing more.

Emory tried to holler, but nothing came out of her mouth. She felt death grip her throat then, strangling her breath. She fought. Oh how she fought—like a drowning girl grasping at air. But the breath wouldn't come. Maybe death would be better, she thought. She gave up the struggle, hearing the voice in her head: *You're not worthy of this life. May as well give it up.*

In that moment, that great giving up to the hereafter, she smelled something. What was it? It smelled like home and company and grace—if grace had a smell. Coffee. Yes, coffee.

More than anything in her life, in that moment, she needed and wanted coffee. She struggled for breath, gobbling in a mouthful. Her eyes opened. And suddenly she wasn't in the thorn-infested woods, Daisy's shoes chasing her. She was in Hixon's house, sheets twisted around her torso like brambles in the woods.

She saw light coming from the kitchen doorway and knew Hixon had made that coffee. He would be here soon. *Stay*, a voice told her.

But she disobeyed. Barefooted, she ran back to a coffeeless, ramshackle home, knowing all the way that she didn't deserve one ounce of coffee from the hand of a kind man.

She didn't look behind her this time.

Thirty-Five

Alone in the house, Emory pulled down the can of marijuana, rolled a joint, and lit it. But the smell soured her stomach. Her only friend, this white stick, had failed her this time. Maybe there was nothing on this earth that could make her whole. Joints beckoned her to bliss and escape. The little pills sent her on adventures—but they never quite lived up to the imaginary adventures she'd conjured up as a child or read in the pages of a book. Empty promises, the pills were. And left her feeling even more hollow after the fact.

She squelched the joint by plunging it into a glass of water, then dropped it into the can and took the whole thing to the toilet. Poised like that above the bowl, Emory felt the can's weight, as well as its pull to her. She tipped it toward the bowl, stopping just short of letting the dried leaves flutter to the toilet like green snow. No, not yet. Not with her house in disarray, with Daisy's note to haunt her. She pulled the can back to herself, pulled the plastic lid tight and walked it safely back to its place behind *War and Peace*.

Someone knocked on the door. She jumped, then told herself to calm down, for heaven's sake.

After making sure the can was hidden, she opened the door to see Ouisie and Jed standing there, cleaning supplies in hand.

"We've come to help," Ouisie said.

Emory looked at Jed, hated him again. He breathed. He ran. He stood. He thought. He talked. He moved. All things her Daisy wasn't doing. She nodded his way, then looked at Ouisie. "I don't need help."

Ouisie pushed past her. "Yes, you do. Don't be ridiculous."

Jed stood on the threshold, not leaving, not entering, as if he knew the awkwardness of the situation his mother apparently didn't understand. It made Emory mad and appreciative all at once. At least he knew his place. Though he was alive to have a place at all. Emory's mind put a thumbtack in the note Daisy wrote, while Jed stood there and Ouisie started cleaning. She should tell him what it said, now that it was in the hands of police. She should. But she didn't want to. Instead, she muttered a half-baked, "Come in," and turned her back on the boy who dared to live.

"Who did this?" Ouisie righted Emory's coffee table.

"How should I know?" Emory eyed the coffee can's hiding place behind *War and Peace*, wondering if Ouisie would spy it. What would she think if she found it?

Ouisie sat on the couch, her yellow cleaning gloves gesturing at the end of animated hands. "Daisy's killer, must've been. Did you lock your doors?"

"I don't remember."

"You don't remember?"

"Last I checked, you weren't my mother." Emory heard Jed laugh. She tried to push down a smile, but it came anyway.

Ouisie hmphed. "I can't help it. Once a mother, always a mother."

The words hung in the stale air like lazy mosquitoes on a summer day. Mother. Ouisie was a mother. Is a mother. But Emory only was. Never to be again.

Jed stood before Emory, like he knew how to rescue folks from his mama—his timing perfect. "I noticed your trim was peeling," he said. "I brought some brushes and paint. Mind if I go outside and fix it?"

"Suit yourself."

Jed stepped outside.

But that left Emory alone with Ouisie the mother. Ouisie the woman who didn't need to know secrets. Ouisie who should mind her own business. Ouisie who stood up and started messing with stuff.

"I can take care of myself." Emory paced while Ouisie pulled out window cleaner from her bag of cleaning supplies and started cleaning the ketchup-smeared windows.

"Like you are now?" Ouisie hummed something indistinct while her gloved hand circled the glass windowpanes.

Emory sighed. She might as well join the cleaning brigade. Maybe they'd even get the smell out of the house. Vinegar, was it? They worked side by side, quietly and quickly, in a semblance of friendship Emory actually enjoyed. Ouisie was her longest friend in the world, though they both held things back. She'd shared the man in the forest story with Ouisie alone, hinted at it to Daisy, but swore them both to secrecy. Those kind of secrets made for closeness she never felt with any other living soul on this earth. So she cleaned alongside Ouisie, hoping she wouldn't stumble across dope or pills or any other secrets while they tried to erase all signs of the vandal's destruction.

On hands and knees, Ouisie scrubbed the kitchen floor with a brush and a pail of suds, Cinderella style. She looked up at Emory. "He needs you," she said plainly.

"Who needs me?" Emory expected Ouisie to share the gospel with her, much like her husband Hap would do. How God needed her in his army, how precious she was to him.

"Jed."

Not God. "Oh," Emory said. "I don't particularly need him."

Ouisie stopped her scrubbing and looked up, her hair a stringy mess. "It's not all about you, Emory. The world, you know? You're not the only one who's been hurt by Daisy's passing. I know it sounds heartless. I know I shouldn't even bring it up, since I can't begin to understand losing a child. But I love my son, and he needs something from you. I've told it to you before. And I'll keep saying it until the words mean something."

Emory sat at her dinette. Looking down on Ouisie, she remembered looking down on Daisy, her matted hair, her cold hard stare, her lifeless body. "Maybe if your son hadn't left my Daisy alone, we wouldn't be having this conversation." Even as she said it she felt a pang in her heart. She'd left Daisy too. Only earlier. And more often than Jed ever had. She couldn't forgive Jed. Because if she did, she'd have to pardon herself. She couldn't do that. Wouldn't. Mothers were supposed to know better. Were supposed to protect. Listen. Empathize. Be there. All things she wasn't.

Ouisie sat back on her haunches, then plopped onto the floor, crossing her legs like a schoolgirl listening to story time in the library. "That's just how he feels," she said. "It's an anvil around his neck, bending his head forward. It's chained to him. He has the key that would unchain him but refuses to use it. And as I've been praying, I believe you have a key too. You can set him free from the weight. Only you won't. Why, Emory?"

"I can't. That's all," she whispered.

"Won't is more like it." Ouisie stood and wiped her hands on her pants.

"Your husband, he writes sermons about me." Emory grabbed a sponge from the sink and started cleaning the fridge's front. "Tells all the kindly folks of Defiance about my wayward ways. How I deserved Daisy's death. How I lack scruples. Don't think it doesn't get back to me. Since we're being honest here and asking pointed questions, do you mind if I ask if you ever defend me? Do you ever stand up in the church and say something to better folks' opinions of me? Or do you let them swallow up his words?"

Ouisie sighed. She picked up a picture frame that'd been pulverized by the vandal, and started picking out the glass shards from its frame. "You know I can't do that."

Emory scrubbed dried mustard from the fridge handle. "So we both have things we can't do."

"You're right. So right. I'm sorry. It's just that as a mama—"

"Please stop talking like that." Emory felt tears in her eyes, this time letting them spill. "Every time I hear the word mama, do you know what it does to me?"

"I'm sorry."

"It plunges me into the deepest pit, and I can't claw my way out of it. And the terrible thing about it all is I'm not thinking about Daisy. I'm thinking about me and my own mama—how she did me wrong. How she never quite loved me. How she didn't believe me. How she kept herself far, far away from my heart." A wail threatened to erupt from inside her. She pushed it down. "But what's worse than that, Ouisie, is that when I look in the mirror, I see her in my eyes, haunting me. I see me doing what she did. And now that Daisy's gone, I can't take it back." She slid down the fridge onto the floor, holding her face in her hands, desperately courting control but not finding it. Fists pressed the tears back into her face, but they flowed anyway.

Ouisie sat next to her, stroking her hair, whispering "there, there,"—things mamas should do. Things she didn't and now could never do.

"I'm sorry, Emory. You're so strong. So capable. So unlike me. I figured you were getting along fine somehow. I don't know why I thought that, other than I see myself as the weakest woman on this earth and think no one can measure up to me in that department."

Emory huffed in air and removed her fists from her eyes. She let out an exhausted breath—it felt like the longest breath she'd held her entire life. Having someone bear a little of the war inside her head jostled her heart, woke it up a little. "Thanks," she said.

"I'm going to redouble my prayers for you, okay?"

Emory nodded.

"And as far as Jed goes, part of that's my fault for not having enough faith. Perhaps it's that God has the key to his freedom, not *you* necessarily. Somehow it's easier for me to put it all on you rather than trusting God to set Jed free in his timing. Does that make sense?"

Some of it did. Some of it didn't. Emory nodded anyway. God was that great mystery in the sky—sometimes angry, as in Hap's rendition of him, sometimes sweeter than honey, as in Hixon's view. Ouisie's seemed to be a combination of the two. Angry and sweet. But Emory mixed them all together and added fickle. What kind of God would take an only child from a mama who could no longer apologize? Who could never improve as a mama, her neglect always and forever lingering in the past, stinking it up? But maybe, just maybe he was also the God who sent a friend today to clean up what some criminal destroyed, a friend who listened like no one else. Maybe.

As they scraped, polished, and scrubbed together, Emory found herself smiling in the midst of the chaos of her home. A flicker of hope ignited something inside her. In the living room, she spied the side of her Mary Jane can while Ouisie beat rugs outside. She pushed it farther behind *War and Peace*, vowing this time to destroy it. Once Ouisie left. Maybe she didn't need the can of dried leaves after all.

Thirty-Six

Whoever did this took careful precaution not to be found." Officer Spellman paced Emory's living room that evening, his eyes full of concern. "I really think you're in danger."

Emory swallowed. Echoes of her time in the woods so many years ago leapt into her mind, the fear hazing through her thoughts, grabbing her by the throat. She remembered how she kept the lights on, afraid to sleep, afraid to tell her mother, afraid of every creak of the house. All because of one man. And here she was again, reliving her childhood nightmare. "I'll be fine," she said.

"I can't promise it."

Emory felt tears again, but this time kept them inside. No need to let the officer see her worry. "That's okay. My guess is that whoever did this meant to scare me—nothing more. He probably doesn't like all your poking around and used me to give you a warning. The best thing I can do is go on with my normal routine, unaffected."

"I don't want you going anywhere alone, you hear me?"

Emory laughed. "Look around you. Do you see anyone else living in my house? I live alone now."

"I'll continue my patrols here. And can you please not walk to work? Use your car for once."

"I don't work tonight, but it's something to consider when I do."

Officer Spellman shook his head, rubbed his chin with one strong hand. "Consider isn't the right word. It's something to *do*."

She saluted him. "Yes, sir."

At first his face was somber, but then it relaxed into a wide, infectious grin. He covered his mouth with his hand, trying to hide the smile, then looked away. "I'm serious," he said. Emory felt compelled to kiss this man who wanted to protect her. But then she'd add another man as a notch in her belt. One was too many. But David, Angus, Hixon, *and* Officer Spellman? Four, an overwhelming majority. Seemed she had more protectors than she'd ever had in her life, but she didn't feel any safer.

When he left her behind, she sat in her home, all clean now, thanks to Ouisie Pepper. Daisy's smell usually lingered in the nighttime, but she couldn't smell her anymore. She chastised herself for burning Daisy's linens, for forever erasing a part of her daughter. Is this what it felt like to face grief? A gradual, excruciating letting go of pieces of her child she'd never experience again? Death and death some more, she thought. That's what it felt like. Daisy gone missing. Daisy found. Daisy buried. Daisy everywhere in the house as a reminder. The reminders slipping away one by one. Until there was no evidence Emory had ever borne a child.

When Emory found out she was pregnant, the last thing she wanted was to have a baby dependent on her. David wanted it. She knew she'd had no training for motherhood, no business raising a child when she'd probably just end up hollering at it. She made an appointment in a beige office in Tyler to take care of the problem. She told herself it wasn't a baby, right? She wrote her full name on the receptionist's fill-in-the-blank paper. She tried to smile at the other distressed women in the waiting room, though her stomach tilted toward unease.

She touched her belly, wondered a bit. No, she wouldn't think about growth. Couldn't. She leafed through last spring's *Family Circle*. Her eyes fell on a two-page spread of mothers and babies, laughing, playing, wearing matching Butterick patterns, sewn by loving grandmothers as gifts to their daughters and granddaughters. Streamers floated through the fake-set air. Emory could almost hear the giggles.

She slapped the magazine shut. Curious red eyes glanced her way. She looked down, unable to control her own tears now. It was as if every woman in the waiting room understood the other. Understood that they were making a choice not to have matching clothes with babies without faces. Why was she crying? It wasn't like her mother would sew clothes. It wasn't like she wouldn't sneer Emory's way, laughing at Emory's predicament, no doubt with a "So now you'll understand my terrible life" wafting behind her like smoke from the unfiltered cigarettes she breathed through. Mama wouldn't take kindly to grandmotherhood, she knew.

Emory placed a hand on her stomach again, swelled enough to make top of her bell-bottom jeans feel like a girdle. Tears stung her eyes again, but she did not wipe them away. She remembered her days living with just Mama in the back of someone else's grand property, settled into the heart of Old Defiance before it burned to the ground. An acre lot in town, surrounded by a wrought iron fence. An imposing mansion preened near the street, three stories into the air. Columns, a porch, and gingerbread molding crowned the home of Edgar and Elsa Cunningham. They'd taken pity on Mama way back when and given her the carriage house out back to live in when she found out she was pregnant. Until Mama's drinking got so bad they had to kick her out.

Emmy's first memory lived there, now a part of scorched earth, with nothing to show for it. She was three years old or maybe four. Elsa found Mama stretched out on the little porch swing in front of the carriage house, sound asleep. Emmy watched as Elsa smelled Mama's breath, then made a face. She reached her pale, gentle hand Emmy's way. Emmy took it, all the while looking back at Mama, who slept the afternoon away. Elsa let Emmy take a bubble bath. She brushed her hair gently, never tugging like Mama. She let Emmy put on powder from a large round box on the back of the toilet. It smelled like roses.

Elsa returned with two gifts. A beautiful yellow dress with lace at the collar and daisies on the hem, and a doll wearing the same dress, only miniature. "I'd meant it for Christmas, but the good Lord told me today's better than any other day to celebrate him. So here you go."

Emmy clutched the doll she spontaneously named Daisy to her chest, even before she put on the beautiful dress. She sang Daisy songs, stroked her hair, told her everything was going to be okay. For one sweet afternoon, Emmy played—really played—without worrying whether she'd make Mama mad. She took off Daisy's dress, then put it back on. She propped Daisy under the great big tree out front, spreading a blanket for a tea party Elsa delivered. She told Daisy her secrets. And somehow Daisy whispered back, "You're a great mama."

Mama must've heard because that was precisely the moment she discovered Emmy under the tree. She swore at Elsa, who stood at a distance, Mama's words slurred and syrupy. "I nearly lost my head worrying about my baby. Thought someone kidnapped her. But no, it was you. My friend. Spoiling her." She grabbed Emmy by the arm and dragged her through the well-groomed yard. Emmy heard Elsa's crying and hollering behind her, but the ache in her shoulder kept her trying to keep up with Mama's dragging. Even so, she clutched Daisy like she was gold, never letting go.

She told Daisy her secrets. Took her swimming. Shared her hopes. And Daisy always listened. Emmy needed to pour her life into this doll. Needed to nurture her, keep her safe and happy. Looking back, Emory knew she was playacting her own longing. Being the mama her mama never was. In hopes that maybe Mama would watch her and catch on somehow. That she would see the loving care Emmy poured into Daisy and do likewise. But life never ended up the way Emmy hoped it would. Daisy's presence and Emmy's fawning over her only made Mama drink more, swear more, throw things more. Sometimes even Daisy. Every ounce of mothering Emmy poured out on Daisy became Mama's fuel to be nasty.

Daisy stayed with Emory her whole life—the only constant in a sea of swirling chaos. Daisy's beautiful golden locks now tortured themselves into dreadlocks, her eyes now faded, the blush of her cheeks worn off with too much hugging. But Emory still loved that doll. Still loved her to pieces. Even alone in a stark room with wet-eyed ladies, she wished she'd brought Daisy with her for comfort and company.

She told herself it was Daisy that made her run from the office when Emory Chance was called. Said she needed to get something first. Someone, really. Because that stupid, beautiful doll saved the life of the only thing Emory Chance did right. Daisy the doll saved Daisy the girl. And now the living, breathing Daisy was gone. Forever.

Emory went to the living room closet. She rumbled through boxes, tore through grocery bags, pushed aside winter coats she'd soon need, until she found the doll. She retrieved Daisy doll, her dress in tatters, her eyes unblinking. She looked smaller, more ragamuffin than Emory remembered. She carried Daisy to the paisley couch. She bent her legs out in front of her, sat her beside Emory like they were girlfriends having a chat. She smoothed the ratted hair, petted it really. "Thank you," Emory said to the night. A movement outside, accompanied by a twig-snapping sound made Emory suck in a breath. She grabbed Daisy, pulled her to herself and hugged her to near death—her heart pounding a fearful rhythm into Daisy's plastic chest.

Thirty-Seven

More rustling. More noise. Emory snuck to the living room curtains, Daisy still in her arms. With her nose, she pushed away the tiniest section of drape and looked outside. Nothing. Just trees, now leafless, bending slightly in a winter-like wind. Maybe that was it. Clacking limbs in the wind. Emory let out a breath. Almost.

A pounding at the door made her drop Daisy. She didn't know what to do then. Pick up the doll that clattered to the floor in a plastic heap? Answer the door? Call Officer Spellman? The pounding rattled the door again.

Her hands shook now. She felt sweat trickle down the back of her neck, though it wasn't hot outside. She hesitated, the knock no longer there, but echoing in her mind. In one brave lunge, she swallowed her fear and opened the door. Wind howled in the empty space there. No one. She stood on her porch, holding herself against the cold. Her gate angled open, the night silent. Part of her wanted to run out into the night and confront this jerk, whoever he was. To chase him for once, to ransack his place, to put the fear of God in him. She stepped into her yard, not knowing whether she'd run to catch the phantom that pursued her or if she'd hightail it back to her house. Instead she stood there under the tree where Jed apparently lost one shoe to the killer. She slid against the rough trunk, pulled her knees to her chest, and rocked back and forth, cradled only by herself.

"Oh, God," she said to the sky. Just "Oh, God."

The cold got the best of her, pulling her back inside. She closed the door and fastened Hixon's locks. Daisy lay face down on the hardwood floor. Emory picked her up, took her to the pristine-clean kitchen sink and turned on warm water. First she ran her hands under the water's warmth, wooing the chill from her stiffened fingers. Then she put the stopper inside the sink and squeezed dishwashing detergent inside. "Your bubble bath, ma'am," she told Daisy.

With careful sponging, she cleaned Daisy's worn face and washed her matted hair. She dried her with a clean kitchen towel, wrapping it around Daisy's head turban style. Finished, Emory took the now-clean doll into Daisy's room and flustered through Daisy's bottom clothes drawer, where she kept her old doll clothes. Emory chose a dark green corduroy skirt and a pink and green and pale yellow plaid top. She snapped the blouse in place. She found a pair of faded white underpants and two socks, mismatched, but both yellow. Emory pulled on black patent leather sandals over Daisy's yellow socks. She found a comb in the bathroom and gently combed Daisy's hair straight. Daisy didn't holler, didn't protest. She took each stroke, pasted smile unchanging.

"There you go. Now don't you feel better?" Emory took Daisy into her room and perched her on the dresser. "You can watch over me here, right?"

Daisy didn't nod.

Emory fell into bed well after midnight. She watched the ceiling for a long time, straining to hear knocks. None came other than the creaking of her old rented house. She smelled dishwashing detergent on her hands, enjoyed the fresh scent. If only her life could be as clean. If only a bar of soap existed strong enough to clean away all her regrets, her fears, her stupid mistakes. But not even lye or carbolic acid could clear away the muck she'd made of her life. She trembled under her bedspread. In one fluid motion, she rose, crossed the room, and grabbed her Daisy doll. She held her close, all the while wishing that when she woke in the morning, fairy tale magic would have transformed plastic into her baby girl—alive and laughing.

Thirty-Eight

The word had come to Hixon at 1:25 a.m., real quiet-like, like a dove's whisper or a squirrel's ascent up a smooth-barked tree. "Protect her," God said.

Hixon shook his head, clearing away the deep sleep. "Lord, is that you?"

"Protect her," God said again.

Hixon knew enough about the Almighty to understand that when he said a thing twice, he meant it with an exclamation mark. Like all those verily, verilies Jesus said. Hixon put on a pair of pants with a heavy sigh. Anything he did seemed to push Missy away. Even so, he knew enough not to mess with God's clear commands, especially not in the middle of the night. So he walked to her home, whistling his fear away into the night. Winter felt near, and he thanked the good Lord he'd had enough sense to bring a jacket and a blanket along. It wouldn't freeze, that was for certain, but he felt the chill in his leg bones as he hustled his way to Missy's.

Ablaze as always, Missy's home shone on Love Street like a shiny penny in the sunlight. He stopped at her opened gate, wondering why Missy left it hanging like that. He looked up at the house, noticing his handiwork. He and Jed painted it last summer under the sun's hottest gauntlet, taking it from derelict status to sensible splendor. The walkway before him was his doing alone. It took some work, but once it heaved up from the red earth, the path finally walked a straight line to her porch steps, level as could be. Maybe he should've included Jed in the project. Perhaps.

He walked on seamless stones, creaked up the stairs, then stood at the door. At this hour, knocking would frighten Missy. So instead, Hixon did what protectors do. He stretched out on her welcome mat, his body a front-door obstacle. He pulled his ratty blanket over himself, made his two hands into a bony pillow, and shut his eyes.

Thirty-Nine

She woke up with Daisy nestled under her right arm, knowing David's mysterious words about the grave were meant for today. Today she'd venture there, to Daisy's resting place. Whether God would show up in bodily form and squeeze out the pain remained to be seen, but she felt a strange sort of anticipation as she thought about it. Hixon believed that way, she knew. He seemed to eke out his life knowing God was playing peekaboo around every bend in the road. That he would show up, bringing surprises to each day. Emory saw God more like a jack-in-the-box. Life wound around and around and around in intensity, each day coiling in on itself until God popped out in the midst of whatever terrible thing she faced and startled her to tears. Problem was you never really knew when he'd spring up. Or whether he'd stay put. Days like that, it was easier to believe he didn't exist at all.

She propped Daisy on her sheets, all at once realizing it had been months since she made her bed, really. So she set Daisy aside on her dresser and stripped the bed, throwing the dirty linens into the wicker hamper in the corner of her bedroom. She stretched blue and white striped sheets over her bed, making hospital corners with the flat sheet. She de-enveloped her pillows, stuffing them into fresh pillowcases from the linen closet. It felt good to do something so normal, so domestic. It occurred to Emory that people strung out on drugs didn't bother with housekeeping, and that perhaps today was the first day of her life when she truly believed she could live without them. She looked over at the Daisy doll, staring at her with expressionless eyes, that painted smile confirming the truth, perhaps.

Though the day looked gray and cool, she pulled on a pair of sweatpants and a T-shirt, wanting to feel the cool on her skin and breathe in a new day. She thought of taking Daisy with her to the porch but decided against it. No use in giving folks something to talk about. Defiance already thought her peculiar.

She unlocked the front door, then tried to push the screen door, but it wouldn't budge. She half-expected to see another Ethrea Ree dish blocking her way, but it wasn't food—it was Hixon, lying across the threshold. "What on earth?"

Hixon jumped to his feet, a blanket half covering his torso like a toga. "Missy," he said.

"What are you doing here?"

He looked in her eyes right then. The grayest of days made the brown in his eyes all the browner, like earth becoming earthier. "Protecting you."

"Protecting me? Why?"

He rubbed his bristled chin with one hand. "The Lord told me to. Last night. So I came."

"So I see. Any reason why you didn't let me in on the Lord's command, Hixon?" Emory thought of her Daisy doll, wondered if Hixon saw her through the living room window. Had he been spying on her? Peeping in?

"He didn't say to knock. Besides, it was way past your bedtime."

She tapped her fingers on her sweatpants. "And how do you know my bedtime?"

Hixon stepped back. "I don't. I just figured."

"You figured."

The cold air between them said nothing. Not a car sped by.

No workers jaunted to the rendering plant. It seemed like the two of them were the only souls alive and awake in Defiance. It made Emory uncomfortable.

"Coffee," she said.

"Coffee?"

"Do you like it?"

"Yes, I do. I tried to bring you some—"

"Just come in and quit your talking. I'll make you some coffee before you're on your way to protect the rest of Defiance."

He followed her into the living room. "But my job's to protect *you*."

"Don't bother," she hollered behind her on the way to the kitchen.

She clanked dishes while coffee brewed, all the while trying to figure out what to do with a man who slept across her doorway. Part of her smiled inside. Her own father never protected her. Maybe he would've, had he stayed around long enough. But even his absence she blamed on Mama. Mama drove Papa away, Emory knew. But Emory didn't have a choice in the matter, being too young to run away and too scared to cross her mama. Papa had done what he needed to do. She pictured him on an island, surfing the afternoon away, always thinking about Emory but too afraid to find her.

But Hixon was different than Papa. He stayed. Emory pushed him away, scratched at him, but he braved his way back to her every time. Maddening man. She brought them both coffee, setting his in coffee-colored hands.

"I assumed you wanted it black. You don't seem the sugar and cream type. Am I right?"

"Yes," he said. "You must be a good waitress."

"I am." Emory thought of Daisy's grave and David's message. She wondered if she should go alone, wondered, too, if she should tell Hixon about the knock at the door late last night. Or maybe it had been him.

"When did you come sleep on my porch? What time?"

"Must've been around two. Why?"

She swallowed bitter coffee. How could Hixon not make a face when he tasted it? "No reason. Just curious."

"When do you work again?" Hixon asked.

"Tonight. But this morning I need to run an errand."

"I could go with you."

"I'm not sure. It's personal." She cradled the cup in her cold hands, letting the coffee's warmth soak into them.

"I don't have work today, so I'm free. It's up to you."

Loneliness, something she'd made friends with growing up, gnawed at her today. A cleaned up doll couldn't fill the frightened parts inside her, nor could it say anything of comfort when she sat horrified on Daisy's final resting place. Emory swallowed. Weighed the kindness of Hixon versus her own need for independence. "Would you come with me to Daisy's grave?" She wasn't sure it was the right decision, but Hixon's smile seemed to make her words take power.

"It would be my privilege. When do you want to go?"

"Now. I need to go before I chicken out."

Hixon nodded, then stood. He reached his hand her way, but she didn't take it. No sense in getting his hopes up. She pushed herself up from the couch. "I'll get my keys," she said.

Forty

Mama's grave remained undecorated. Only Emory would know where it was, the smallest marker the only stone she and Daisy could afford. Emory didn't cry when she heard the news that her mama's heart had stopped, that the lung cancer had taken over in vengeance. Daisy eyed her when the phone call came. "I see. Yes. Thanks for letting me know."

"Is it Grandma?" Daisy asked, wide-eyed.

"She's gone to heaven," Emory told her, surprised at the lack of emotion she felt. She'd envisioned a deep grief unfurling like a war flag in an angry wind, but the air around her felt still, stagnant. And grief didn't erupt. Didn't even trickle.

"I'm sorry, Mama," ten-year-old Daisy said. She wrapped spindly arms around Emory's waist, squeezing hard, trails of tears wetting her cheeks.

Emory unpeeled Daisy's arms. "No use in crying. Preachers will tell you she is in a better place."

"Do you believe in heaven?"

"I don't know. I hope so."

"But if you don't believe in heaven, does it mean you won't go there? Grandma said heaven was for well-wishers."

"Maybe she was a well-wisher in secret." Emory brushed away Daisy's tears. "That's too much for a young girl to think about. Just believe Grandma's not suffering anymore."

They sat on the paisley couch covered by the quilt Daisy loved and didn't say a word for a few minutes while the weight of Mama's passing settled into Emory's mind. Grief didn't live there, just relief. All at once, she felt guilty about her relief. What kind of inhumane woman felt relief when her mother died? How could that be? Maybe it was that Emory was predetermined to head down the same angry path Mama trudged. And Emory had little fight but to give in. So she couldn't really blame Mama, if that were the case, now could she? If she were going to turn out the same way, anyhow?

Three stones down from Ethrea Ree's deceased husband sat Mama's unflowered grave. Daisy clutched a bouquet of dandelions and placed them on top of Mama's etched name. Daisy cried — a low, deep wail only an old woman seemed capable of. Emory placed a tentative hand on Daisy's head, all the while knowing she should say, "There, there," or "Everything's going to be okay," but she kept her lips shut as tight as the grave. No sense in indulging Daisy's affection for Mama. No sense at all. Emory'd spent her life pouring out affection for a mama who never bothered to return the favor. She'd given her heart over and over again, only to be shushed or pushed or scowled at or stiff-armed. Relentless, Emory was — always needing more and more love, grabbing after it, but never, ever receiving it. And now, with the grave beneath her feet, she could give up the illusion that a mama on this earth would love her.

Death had its way, both with Mama's absentee affection and Emory's pursuit. Daisy stiffened her back after the last tear trailed down her pink cheek, like she had readied herself for the world. Emory felt the same stiffness in her back — a determination to live life on her own terms, needing no one, grieving no mama. When they walked away, Emory vowed never to return to Mama's graveside. Even when Daisy's body was lowered into a gaping Defiance mouth, she didn't bother to walk one hundred paces to her left to see how the old woman fared. And today, with Hixon as her witness, she didn't intend to make the trek either. Mama was dead. That was that.

She drove her car, staving off the early December chill with a blast from the heater. The sky remained the same gray it'd been yesterday, making her wonder if every day from here to forever would have the same complexion. She'd heard about places where this was so—Seattle, Portland, London—and for a brief moment wished herself in one of those cities. What would life feel like if the weather always mimicked your mood? Next to her, Hixon cleared his throat. "Got a cold?" she asked him.

"I'm guessing my throat doesn't agree with outdoor sleeping." He smiled her way.

She caught his smile in an instant, but then looked at the road as she pulled out of her driveway onto Love Street. Before she made it to the next intersection, a loud rumbling motor roared behind her. Angus in her rearview mirror. He pulled her over Officer Spellman style, except that he brought his bike to her window. He motioned for her to open it. While she cranked the window, her stomach soured. She could feel Hixon stiffen next to her.

"Well, well. On a pleasure ride, I see?"

"Not exactly," Emory heard herself say.

"'Morning, Hixon." Angus saluted.

"Good morning," Hixon returned, his voice clenched.

"I have a present for you, Em."

"Interesting," she said. "Why don't you leave it on my doorstep. I'm in a hurry."

"A hurry. Ain't that a pretty picture? Emory Chance and Hixon Jones cruising Defiance. Won't the heads turn!"

"Leave us be, will you?"

"Us? Now you're an 'us'?" He smiled, and for a second Emory lost herself in his easy grin, remembering suddenly all the reasons she pined after him in the first place. While the motorcycle idled and exhaust perfumed the air, Emory's mind raced.

Hixon leaned over. She could smell him—a mixture of sleep and sweetness all wrapped together. "Thanks kindly for bringing her a gift. But we need to get going, if you don't mind."

"There's that pesky word, *we*." Angus spoke with that same smile, but something dark lurked beneath his words.

Hixon settled back in the seat, quiet as a ghost tired of haunting.

"Just let it be, Angus. Hixon's my friend. He's helping me do something I can't do by myself. That's all. Don't get all weird and emotional on me."

"Interesting choice of words. Weird and emotional." He drummed his fingers on the window casing. "Some folks would use those words to describe him, you know."

Emory revved the engine. "I need to go."

"See you around." He winked.

She watched Angus pull away to her left, circling back to her home. He'd be putting his present on her porch, she guessed. Or would he take the opportunity to vandalize her home while she was gone? The thought had bothered her the moment she walked into her ketchup-stained home. On a binge, Angus was capable of anything, she knew. At least she would have Hixon riding home with her. To protect her.

She let the car idle awhile in the cemetery's parking lot—a ghost town of a lot, thankfully. The last thing she wanted was a crowd while she paid Daisy her respects. She turned off the car, letting the cool silence wash over her. Hixon seemed to know she needed quiet. He nodded her way, then got out of the car, leaving her alone with one thousand angry thoughts. Why would David demand she go here? And why wouldn't he do this himself? If he'd gotten religion like he said he did, why didn't he change his absentee-father status before Daisy left the earth? She knew her daughter would've given everything to see her father just once. But David sat—oh did he sit—on his religious laurels, not bothering to care that he'd fathered a child. And now, in a strange twist, he demanded she do the thing he'd probably never do—say a proper good-bye. 'Course, if he'd never said a proper hello, maybe it made sense. You can't say good-bye to someone you never bothered to meet.

Emory leaned her head on the steering wheel. She could do this. She could. And maybe standing at the grave would finish a chapter, or maybe the book of her life. Maybe she could say good-bye and mean it, and then some wasting disease would rid the earth of her. One could only hope.

She opened the door, remembering David's words about embraces from God and grief. Her heart fluttered an anxious rhythm inside her ribcage. It beat loud to the steps she felt herself take toward the lone black man standing on the hillside where Daisy slept. When she neared the spot, Hixon turned to her and said, "I'm sorry."

"Sorry?"

"It's gone."

"What's gone?" Was this some sort of religious talk Hixon said to help her grieve?

"Daisy's headstone."

"What?" She ran the last few yards to Daisy's grave. Hixon was right. Daisy's gray, shiny stone—the one a stranger paid for—was gone. "Maybe they never put it on." She remembered the funeral home telling her when the stone would be placed above Daisy's resting place, but she hadn't been back since to check on it.

"I've been here before," Hixon said. "The stone was here. Now it's not."

Emory sank to the brown grass. A red square of earth proved Hixon's words right. Who would take Daisy's stone?

"We'd best tell the police, don't you think?"

"I guess so," she said.

Hixon sat next to her, but he didn't touch her. They sat like friends on a cold hill, neither speaking for a long time. Emory broke the silence. "Why would anyone do this? They didn't take anything else, did they?"

Hixon looked at her. "No, the grave's intact. Probably just pranksters from the high school. A silly dare."

"It doesn't make sense."

"You're right. Which is why we need to let the police know."

Emory sighed. Hixon took off his jacket and wrapped it around her shoulders, careful not to touch her.

"I was supposed to come here, do something, I guess," she said to the grave. She meant to end her words with "expect something, God maybe," but she chose to keep those expectations inside.

Hixon stood. "You still can. I'll wait in the car."

"No, stay." She reached her hand his way, held his work-worn hand, and then let go. "I need you to stay."

Hixon nodded, tears in his eyes. "Whatever you want, Missy."

She knelt at Daisy's patch of earth, empty-handed, just as she'd been at Mama's grave. Only this time she didn't feel relief. She didn't stiffen her back and resolve to withdraw from the world. She whispered instead, letting her words become the flowers that decorated Daisy's final resting place. "I'm sorry, baby. Sorry I didn't try harder to find you. Sorry I didn't— " A rush of tears washed down her face. She felt Hixon's hand on her shoulder, felt the square of warmth. She half-expected a shimmering light to break through the dreary clouds and spotlight Daisy's grave. God's only answer seemed to be hazy drizzle, mixing with Emory's tears, saturating her to the skin. Wasn't that just like him? Take her at her most vulnerable point, in front of Hixon no less, and send a message of rain.

What was it David had written? That God would embrace her here? But pursuing God felt a lot like pursuing Mama in that moment. She'd reached a tentative hand his way only to be spat on from the heavens. She forgot Hixon's warm hand. Forgot her apology. Forgot the reason she even needed to be there. Once God's hand withdrew into the clouds, sending rain instead of sunshine, despair instead of hope, she pasted Mama's face on his, knowing him to be just as cruel. And she fancied Hixon and David as God's emissaries, neither to be trusted. She shrugged Hixon's hand away and stood. "I need to get home."

"That's fine. But let's swing by the police station first."

Forty-One

They rode in silence to the station. She waited for Hixon to get out of the car, knowing he'd trot behind it to get her door. When he did, she peeled away from the curb, not looking to see his reaction. She needed to get home. Needed to see what gift Angus brought. What had she been thinking—that the God who never bothered to protect Daisy would suddenly show up at her grave, giving Emory hope and joy and peace? Ridiculous. While the windshield wipers batted away drips from the sky in a hasty rhythm, Emory let her mind yell at herself.

No one's to be trusted. Not even Hixon. You're a fool to think he can be.

Idiot! Why apologize for Daisy when it's God's fault in the first place. You let him off the hook!

But let me remind you that you were a terrible mother. Never there. Doing drugs.

Don't you think the world would be better off without you? What exactly do you contribute? You sit in your house and smoke pot. You deliver food to customers. That's it. Nothing more. Useless, that's what you are.

Emory's tears blurred her vision. She shook her head, trying to rid herself of the voices, but they shouted louder, demanding release.

She pulled into the driveway and parked the car out back.

She ran around to the front of the house, hoping for a gift from Angus. As promised—Angus always seemed to keep these kinds of promises—a single lunch bag sat propped on the doorway. She opened it, peered inside. No pills stared back at her. Just a slip of paper.

Em, I'm taking a road trip today. I'll be back later. If you need anything, well, you'll have to cope on your own until tonight when I'm better supplied. Sorry. Angus.

Emory balled up the note and the bag. She unlocked the door, then threw it open. Not even Angus would help her. But as she stood in the living room, the world spun around her. The walls felt oppressive, pushing in on her, about to vice her head. She remembered the pills that she never flushed. She pictured herself fishing them out, putting them in the medicine cabinet. Relief pushed the incoming walls away from her. Gave her a jaunt of peace. She ran to the bathroom, opened the cabinet, and greedily fingered the plastic bag. She grabbed one pill, turned it over between index finger and thumb, smiled down at it. David's letter had insisted she go to stations, starting with Daisy's now-unmarked grave. She'd obliged him this one time. But now it was time to go to her own station—a station of bliss and escape. She placed the pill on a willing tongue, bent near to the faucet, drank from it like a thirsty dog, and let the pill slide down her throat.

She went into her bedroom, stripped down to nothing, then pulled on her nightgown. She stretched the covers over her, smoothed them, and waited for the fairy-tale trip to begin. And, oh, how it began.

Forty-Two

She flew. Really flew. High above Defiance, Texas—the little houses like Monopoly houses on straight, straight streets. Only they weren't green. Most were white. She soared still higher until Defiance looked like an ant pile, and she a gigantic hawk circling above. If only life would be so carefree; if only she could fly above it, unaffected by the fighting and crawling and spiting beneath. She swooped in a wide-winged dive so that her face grazed the earth. Suddenly she was standing on Daisy's grave, the headstone still missing. A small voice came from behind.

"Mama, why didn't you come looking for me?"

Emory turned around, her body no longer a bird's, but her own. She saw Daisy then, but she wasn't thirteen. She was three, clutching the Daisy doll and her frayed yellow blanket. A thumb plugged her mouth.

"I did, baby," Emory said.

Daisy unplugged her lips. "Well, you didn't do a very good job of it, did you?" The voice was thirteen-year-old Daisy's, but the body stayed three.

Emory sank to the earth, laid herself flat on the grass face first. Daisy stood in front like a headstone, not saying a word. Emory felt each blade of grass like a sewing needle, poking into every pore of her body. Tiny streams of blood flowed rivulets out of her. She welcomed it all. Let her strength leave. Let her blood drain onto Defiance before three-year-old Daisy. Let her pay for not being the mama she was supposed to be.

The thought occurred to her that God was terribly weak, or maybe completely stupid. If he knew all about her, all about her lapses, her weakness for drugs and men, then why didn't he take her out? Maybe he did know all that, but he was too weak to strike her dead. Maybe, just maybe, God needed help. So Emory did her part by staying very still while her heart pumped every ounce of blood onto Daisy's grave. They could both share a bed, then. Side by side, she could hold her baby and never let go—a perfect, fitting solution.

But then Daisy wailed—so loud Emory thought a scorpion had stung her. She looked up. A shadow crept around her daughter, engulfed her, so that Emory could only see a haze of Daisy. She screamed a three-year-old's scream—terror shrieking from a small mouth. Emory stood, woozy, and tried to wrap her arms around her shrouded little girl, but her arms swept through Daisy like she was humid air with no form. The shadow rose from the earth like steam after summer's gully-washing rain. Daisy misted upward toward the skies of Defiance until she appeared like a gray rain cloud, her scream sounding more and more like the call of a dove so very far away.

Emory's hands reached heavenward like a TV preacher's. She jumped, hoping to launch into her eagle ways, but her body didn't fly. Instead it sank. Daisy's grave became a muddy mess, sucking her down until the mud slurped around her chin. Emory relaxed. This was the end, she knew. Something tight—was it the mud?—choked her breath. As mud sopped into her eager mouth, she smiled. No more life. No more pain. No more regrets. All would be well. Finally.

While mud filled her mouth and she tasted its grit and her nose sucked in slickened dirt, she heard another voice, hollering from another county. Who was it? Was it Daisy?

"Daisy," she tried to say. She couldn't, of course, because of a muddy mouth, so she thought it, somehow knowing Daisy could hear her in the hereafter. "Daisy, I'm coming. It won't be long now. Just you wait real patiently, you hear?"

But it wasn't Daisy's voice. Emory felt her eyes rollick back in her head, like the tendons holding them in place had been cut, her eyes like marbles on an incline. The voice was a man's. A familiar one. Who was it?

Her eyes saw nothing now, at least not the muddy world. Rolled back the way they were, they saw her optic nerve, her brain, the blood pumping it pink. She thought it funny that she would be watching her brain die. How many people could say that?

That voice again. This time closer.

No more breath came. The mud took it all away. Emory smiled, content to let the ground pull her deeper in, closer, closer, closer to Daisy's world—a place where maybe she could try to make things right.

"Missy!"

Who was Missy? She felt her mouth open, her nose breathe, her neck un-tighten. "Nooo," she said. "The mud. Where's the mud?"

Someone shook her. "Missy, it's me. Hixon."

Her eyes flew open. "What're you doing here?" She remembered being with Hixon at Daisy's grave, but hadn't that been years ago?

"Please, it's not worth it."

"What?"

Hixon pulled her to himself, rocked her back and forth like a good mama would. "Don't leave me," he said.

"Leave you?" she croaked. Her tongue and tonsils felt so dry. Dry as Ajax.

"It's a good thing I came by."

"Where am I?"

"At home, in your bed."

"In my bed?" She looked around, then noticed herself. A nightgown. The bathroom door splayed open. She remembered the little pill. She groaned. "Oh, no."

"You had your sheets wrapped around your neck, Missy. If I hadn't come—"

Emory felt her anger. It felt like a rigid spine and a hard, cold stare. "I'd be happy. Finally. I was going to see Daisy. To make things right. To rest in the earth with her. And you stopped me."

"Thank God," Hixon whispered.

Emory pulled away from his embrace, suddenly realizing she'd been cradled there. "God is no one to be thanked." She fell back onto her bed into a twist of sweaty sheets. "He is weak and stupid."

Hixon stood. "That's not true."

Emory's head spun in such a way that Hixon's face looked like several—a kaleidoscope Hixon. She laughed.

"What did you take?"

"I took up too much space on this earth. That's what I took."

"Don't talk nonsense." He bent toward the bed, uncurled the sheets, and pulled them over Emory.

"Why? Don't you like my nightie? Am I too brazen for you? Too unholy?"

Hixon shook his head. "You're talking nonsense." He walked to the window, his face brightened by the late-afternoon light. "Jesus, you've gotta help me here."

"He can't help you. He's weak." Her words sounded sloppy. Her tongue felt like a cow's tongue in her small mouth.

Hixon turned toward her, his eyes a mixture of anger and pity. "I know this isn't you, Missy. It's something you took. You didn't flush those pills, did you?"

"Pills, pills, pills. What does it matter to you? You're a black man in a white woman's house. I could call Officer Hank Spellman, you know. Get you arrested."

Hixon held up his hands. "I'm not here to hurt you. I just saved your life."

Emory sat up. The room tilt-a-whirled around her. "That's a matter of perspective."

"I'm not leaving until you're done with this trip, Missy."

"Trip, trip. I'm on a trip. Hixon's a dip. A dippy drip." She could see his eyes move from pity to hurt to anger. She smiled and waited for him to let into her, Mama style.

Instead, he kneeled at the foot of her bed, his hands clasped behind his head, his face buried in her blankets. "Jesus," he prayed. "Jesus. Jesus. Jesus." Over and over again, he said Jesus' name like a crazy, mumbling man.

The whole scene made Emory burn inside. "Just quit it, you hear me? This whole town, they talk about Jesus. All y'all do. It's like he's the answer to every problem. Now wouldn't that be convenient? Well, tell me this, Mr. Jesus Talker. If Jesus is the answer to every problem, why didn't he rescue my Daisy?" She took a deep breath and shrieked, "Why?"

Hixon looked up, the name of Jesus still on his lips. "I don't know," he said. "I wish I did. But I do know he can help you today."

"Help. I think I'm pretty much beyond that, don't you?"

"The truth? Sometimes I do. But Jesus keeps telling me to keep praying. So I pray. Because the absolute, God's honest truth is something I've learned personally. No soul on this God-made earth is beyond redemption, Emory. No one. His arm is long. His reach stretches into the most wretched places."

Emory felt her head, pressed her hands into her temples. A roaring freight train lived inside there, pounding, driving, tracking, wailing.

"I need to know where those pills are."

"They're mine," she said. And she meant it. She didn't have anything left in this world—other than escapes. Even as the little pill wore off, she craved just one more. And then maybe another one. Every single day. Who needed work? Who needed food? Who needed a roof over her head? All she really needed was a little pill to escape the daily-ness of her pain.

"I will find them. And I'll get rid of them. Then I'll make sure Angus stays away."

"Why would you do that? Why would you take them from me?"

"Because I— "

"Never mind." She sank back into the bed, longing for sleep, as if suddenly sleep became a gorgeous man who beckoned her, wooed her to himself. She closed her eyes. "My pills," she said. "Mine."

Forty-Three

Missy fell into a fitful sleep. Hixon knew that some of what she said was true. If he were caught in the bedroom with her in the state she was in, he'd be in a pickle. So he had to move quickly. After talking to Officer Spellman about the missing gravestone, he knew the policeman would investigate, concluding his time by stopping by Missy's.

Hixon took off his shoes so he wouldn't wake her, then padded to the bathroom. A plastic baggie—the one Missy promised she'd flushed—stood open in the sink, pills inside. He dumped them into the toilet, shut the door to the bathroom as quietly as he could, and flushed them. He opened her cabinet, looking for more pills, but found nothing.

He paced to the living room, scanning the bookshelves. A coffee can peeked out from behind a large book. He grabbed the can, then sat on the couch. The lid came off easily. Inside rested at least three cups of marijuana and a stash of rolling papers. He shook his head. Why, he asked himself. Why? Why would God call him to marry a woman like this? Who hid dope and took little pills that made her strangle herself? It didn't seem right. She sure didn't fit the Christian woman ideal he wanted to marry. He'd read about the Proverbs 31 woman, sewing clothes, feeding servants, all before dawn. Well, Missy, she was about the farthest you could get from that industrious, godly woman.

Her anti-hero, he thought. Hixon shook his head, tried to remember God's encouragement to him.

She won't be as she is now.

Treat her like an orphan.

A car pulled up to Missy's. Hixon looked at the can as footsteps neared the porch. Panicked, he re-lidded the can, put it back on the shelf, only farther back, and ran barefooted out the back door.

Forty-Four

"Ms. Chance!"

She heard her name calling from her sleep. Another man's voice.

Emory opened her eyes, the world blurring around her like a fast-moving camera pan. She shook her head. "Hello?"

"Can I come in?"

"Officer Spellman?"

"It's me. Mind if I come in?"

"No, wait just a second." She jumped out of bed.

Her head, oh, her head. Throbbing, pounding, she felt like her brain was being sifted. Or tortured. Or beaten with a club. She pressed both hands to her temples, shut her eyes against the light. The room smelled stale, like Daisy's after she'd been playing outside all day and she'd left her sweaty clothes in a pile on the floor. Her tongue was thick on the roof of her mouth. She tasted metal. And bile. Woozy, she remembered the door and who stood there. Officer Spellman. She could not be in a nightgown when he came in now, could she? No. She lifted it over her head as she plodded to the dresser, but her feet tripped over something. Shoes. Hixon's shoes. He had been here, right? Had he? Yes. Yes. Yes, he had.

In a flurry, she opened the bathroom door, hoping to see her little friends peering at her from a happy plastic bag so she could hide them. Instead the bag had been wadded into a heap and thrown in the trash next to the toilet. Hixon had flushed them. Had stolen her friends.

She stretched on a T-shirt and a pair of jeans. In the mirror above her dresser, she roughed up her hair. Then she sat on the bed, put her face in her hands, and let genuine tears flow. After all, she'd miss those pills. "Come in," she hollered to Officer Spellman.

She entered the living room a disheveled mess just as Officer Spellman came in the door. The look on his face was beautiful to her just then. Terrified. Concerned. Those thick eyebrows knitted together with lust for her and a stitch of officerly kindness.

"Are you all right?" He paced the room toward her.

"Taking advantage of a friend," she mumbled.

"What was that?"

"His shoes," she said. "Too scared when he heard you. Left without his shoes." She sat down hard on her rocking chair. She knew she didn't have to work hard to have vacant, scared, traumatized eyes. Her whole life had been such a thing. She quickly looked behind her to see if her can was still there. It winked at her from behind *War and Peace*. At least he hadn't found that. She drummed her fingers on her leg, waiting for the officer to speed off after Hixon so she could take one long drag to settle her mind.

"What's that? What's that about shoes?" He sat on the couch, opposite her. "I'm here for the gravestone. The marker's been taken, just as Hixon said. I'm telling you, Miss Chance, this is fishy—and frightening."

"Hixon," she said. "Took advantage."

"What?"

"His shoes are here." She made sure her crazy-tired eyes met his. Made her hand tremble as she said it.

"Hixon's?"

"He tried to—" She broke down in tears, mourning Hixon's

treachery, stealing those pills, sending them to kingdom come. How dare he?

"You're saying Hixon came in here and tried to—"

"Go look in my bedroom. He left something behind."

She put her head in her hands and cried some more. She heard footsteps, felt them in the balls of her bare feet on the wood floor. Officer Spellman swore, then pounded back to the living room. She looked up.

"These are his?"

"Yes, sir." Emory sniffed.

He bent low before her, locking his eyes to hers. She looked away.

"This is a serious charge. Did he try? Or did he go through with it?"

"He *tried* to strangle me." She pointed to the ring around her neck, where the sheets had nearly snuffed her life out. "So I kicked him where it counts. And he ran barefooted out of the house." Inside herself, she smiled. Emory couldn't live life with a do-gooder following her around everywhere, poking his brown nose into her business. She wouldn't. Though a small thought wiggled its way into her heart, that Hixon was an honorable man, and truly the only one who ever truly loved her, she wrestled free from it like a snake shedding its skin. Good riddance, she thought. Now she could do whatever she wanted. When she wanted. How she wanted.

"I need to talk to him. You lock the door behind me. Is there anyone you know who could come over and take care of you? To keep you safe?"

She almost said Hixon—her automatic response—but choked his name back inside. "I'll call Ouisie Pepper," she said.

Officer Spellman rose, Hixon's shoes dangling from his hands like a hangman's noose. Maybe because they were. The smile she smiled way deep inside surfaced, but only as the door shut firmly behind Officer Spellman. Then came the regret.

Forty-Five

Where else would he go but home? His house, normally a catty-cornered mess that welcomed him with open arms, looked alarmingly haunted in today's light. Like it wouldn't co-coon him inside but suffocate him with inward-moving walls. Still, he mounted rickety steps and opened his front door. He could still smell Missy in his front room. Her scent of fresh, clean soap and a hint of springtime honeysuckle still clung to the sheets she slept on. He sat on the couch, touching the sheets, thinking.

How could one man change one woman? Was it even possible? He couldn't change Gentry. He hadn't even tried to change Jed. Why would God task him with such a thing? There were entire civilizations that rebelled against God Almighty, and even he couldn't turn them back to himself. That pesky free-will problem rose its ugly-beautiful head before him. Missy had an ample dose of free will, he knew. And she intended to use it to the nth degree. Remembering the pills, the way they swirled down the toilet, gave him no hope. Because more pills would find their way into her home.

Helpless, oh so helpless. His mind teased the word, tossed it around, worried about it all. How does a man woo a woman who walked such a path? He felt so terribly small. So helpless.

She won't be as she is now.

Treat her like an orphan.

Hixon sighed, letting all his helplessness flow out of him in the breath. As he breathed in, he prayed that God would fill his lungs with hope. And power. And strength. "Dear Jesus," he said to his living room. "I'm helpless. I can't change her. I can't even change myself half the time. You have to intervene here. If you really are calling me to marry Missy, you'll have to work in her heart. I can't do it. I can't make her not crave drugs. I can't change the way she pushes everyone away. I can't. I can't. I can't." Tears ignited a deep, deep sorrow—even deeper than when his mama died or Gentry left or Muriel passed to the heavens. Because it felt like the final betrayal. With Mama, he'd risked his heart, but then got streetwise and moved far from her poisoned ways. He'd tried loving Gentry, but Gentry left before Hixon's heart was fully engaged. And Muriel, well, her leaving felt sweet in some ways, and he knew he'd see her again. Though he'd risked his heart with her, she didn't run the other way with it. She carried it sweetly to heaven's gates—as a deposit of what would come in the hereafter.

But Missy, oh, with Missy he'd risked parts of his heart he hadn't known were alive. Secret parts. Wishing parts. Hoping parts. For years, he had deadened his desire for marriage, believing God was calling him to be a missionary to Defiance—like the apostle Paul—unmarried and unhindered. For a long time, he contented himself to rest there, to be God's servant to this crazy town. Every little flicker of light on the blackness that could be Defiance filled his heart with joy. When he befriended Jed last year and got to see him grow in Jesus, it was enough. Helping Muriel when she was a new widow blessed him beyond words. But meeting Missy and hearing the Almighty's mandate changed everything. He had to come to that place in his life with Jesus where he 'fessed up that all along he never really wanted to be single, that he'd had a monsterlike desire to have a companion for life, one to hold, one to love, one to be one with. And cracking open that door just a little bit opened his heart wide.

And now it felt as if Missy slammed his heart in a cruel doorjamb. He smarted in a way he hadn't known, with a sorrow deeper than grief. That trickle of hope that soon became a flood now had nowhere to go.

He shook his head of the tears. Told himself to pull it together. Asked God again to give him the strength he needed to love this maddening woman. To love her even in her unloveliness. Even when she pushed away. Even when her mind frayed from too much dope. Even through that. Oh, God, even through that. After all, she would not be as she is today, he told himself. She's a frightened orphan like Gentry. She needed constant, abiding, God-breathed love in a steady, flowing stream.

Hixon stood, paced the room, smelled her scent.

Yes, by God's grace, and only by his grace, would he love her. His trying by himself suddenly felt hilariously silly. After all, God wooed Hixon to himself, hadn't he? And Hixon had been as far away from God's holiness as a runaway from her abusive family. So, so far away. If God could bridge that chasm, surely he could woo Missy home. Truly.

For the first time in weeks, though his heart felt raw, Hixon's mind settled into peace. He didn't have to do this courting thing alone. God Almighty, the Lover of his soul, would be there to help him. Of that he was sure.

A knock sounded hollow on the front door.

He opened it. Officer Spellman stood in the doorway, holding Hixon's shoes.

Forty-Six

Ouisie came just as Emory picked up the phone to tell her not to come.

"I'm here," she called out as she squeaked open the screen door. "Are you okay?"

"I don't know," Emory said. And she meant it. What kind of human being would accuse someone like Hixon of treachery? But then again, why not? He'd been a pest, anyway. Back and forth her jumbled mind talked in her head, swinging from terrible guilt to a self-satisfied smile. All in one head.

"Hello." Ouisie waved a hand in front of Emory's eyes.

"Sorry," Emory said, still rocking on the rocking chair. "It's been a horrible day."

"So you tell me. You seem awful calm after Daisy's gravestone's gone missing. And what's this business about Hixon?"

"He tried to choke me."

Ouisie sat on the couch. She looked directly at Emory, but Emory looked out the window. "Hixon? Are you sure?"

She didn't say anything, just pointed to the bruising around her neck.

Ouisie came close. Looked at the bruises. Shook her head. "Let me just ask you one question." She retreated to the couch, sighing as she did. "When was the last time you were high?"

Emory said nothing. How could Ouisie ask such a thing? She

thought Ouisie was her friend, but here she was acting just like Hixon, poking her nose into Emory's private business. Emory's head screamed all sorts of things to her, residual thoughts from that little pill that started all this nonsense. She wanted another one right now—to stand up and excuse herself and let one slither down her throat with a can of beer to ease its journey. She could see the beer can dance in her mind, the pill, too, all in a welcoming jig, beckoning to her. But Hixon had made all that impossible today. He and his flushing ways.

"What did you ask?" Emory smiled sweetly.

"It's no mystery and you know it."

From deep inside a memory firecrackered into Emory's mind—a blessed diversion. He stood in her doorway years ago, a father of two small children, a glint of hunger in his eyes. His wife hadn't put out for months—depressed after her second was born. And he needed Emory. Really needed her. And, oh, how he wanted her then. Under the cover of doing a handyman job in town, he grabbed her furiously in muscled arms, carried her to the bedroom and hungrily took her, over and over again. She'd felt delicious at the thought, warmed inside from his need of her. Seven months this tryst—as he called it—happened in a passionate joy. Until his conscience eroded him, sapped his strength, took away his passion for her. He'd even whispered "I love you" in her ear, that he would leave his wife and kids and start a life with her. Did she like California? Then, yes, it was settled. But it wasn't settled. Because the conscience, the thing he called God-breathed grief, pushed him away from her. Forever.

"Excuse me a second," she said. She went to her bedroom, crashed through her closet until she found it. She carried the birdhouse back to the living room and placed it on the coffee table. "Hap made that for me."

Ouisie eyed the birdhouse but said nothing. Clearly, she was not understanding.

Emory cleared her throat, looked at her only friend in the world, and leveled her eyes. "Your husband has a mole on his upper left thigh," she said. And let the room's silence say the rest.

Forty-Seven

Hixon looked at his innocent hands, turning them over. His palms faced the ceiling above like he was saying "I don't know" with them. Empty hands. Accused hands. Helpless hands. His hands could not unlock the room that held him. He saw sympathy in Officer Spellman's eyes, but he had a job to do, and he had enough evidence to keep Hixon in this room for the time being. An accusation. Hixon's shoes. No alibi but Missy.

Missy. Her name brought bile up the back of his throat, stinging his tonsils. She was the worst kind of orphan, worse than Gentry. Not only did she lash out at herself mercilessly, but she reached sharp fingernails his way and gouged his soul. Even when he was found not guilty—though he couldn't necessarily rely on his own innocence—he would be left with her accusation ringing in his head. That accusation, in the soil of Defiance's gossip circles, would become tried and true fact. No matter where he went, folks would whisper and point about the black man who dared to force his way with a white woman. Even if Officer Spellman unlocked the door, he would never be free on Defiance's streets. Never again. Her word had seen to that.

He looked at his hands and thought about the wounds of Jesus that pierced just below his holy palms. Hixon's own piercing happened there years ago when hope seeped out of him like water from a broken water balloon. He'd taken a razor, criss-crossing his veins until the blood flowed red onto white sheets, and Hixon felt life pour out of him. But by some strange miracle, the blood congealed, clotting on the skin and stopping the flow of death. Hixon lived. He bore the scars to prove it.

But Jesus bore scars others gave him. He looked down on the mass of humanity below him while he agonized on the cross, blood pouring from wrists—blood that didn't congeal. He said those frightening, beautiful words, "Father, forgive them; for they know not what they do." All at once, in the dank gray of the nearly empty room, he understood Jesus afresh. Missy had pierced Hixon with untruth. She had intended for him to suffer and didn't seem to have conscience enough to reconsider her words. Coldhearted, she was. And empty of love. Just like those Pharisees who sent Jesus to his death. Like the Romans who obliged their jealous rage. Like him, Hixon, who did enough sinning in a lifetime to shame Jesus onto the cross one hundred fold.

He suffered for someone else's sin. He could feel the weight of it on his shoulders, the tension spreading angry fingers upward into his cranium. And she wasn't the joking, likeable Peter, either. In a way, she was Judas, feigning interest one minute, giving a hint of humanity and vulnerability in a flash-second, but kissing him with death the next. His quiet life in Defiance came roaring to a halt, thanks to her betrayal. And he didn't even get a kiss to show for it.

He could get out of this room in one minute, if he chose to. All he'd have to do is holler for Officer Spellman and tell him the truth—to indicate where the stash of pot was, to explain it all. The marijuana would collaborate his story beautifully. He could shift blame to the real criminal.

Hixon cradled his head in his hands. Could he send the blame Missy's way? Everything jumbled in his head like bingo balls waiting to be sucked down a vacuum tube. Thoughts pinged and ponged crazy-like. Bits of sermons he'd preached. Snippets of Scripture he'd read and read again. Pieces he'd studied in books. And a little hint of Muriel's words.

Speak the truth in love. *So I should tell the truth.*

Love covers all sins. *So I should keep my mouth shut.*

Jesus was silent before his accusers. *So I shouldn't try to defend myself.*

But Jesus spoke the truth to his disciples, often saying hard things. And he was love with skin on. *So I should love Missy enough to expose her to the truth of her actions.*

Why not rather be wronged? Why not? Is that like turning the other cheek or giving a cloak to one who asks? Is it like walking the second mile?

Don't throw your pearls before swine. *So I should take care of myself, get out of here, and then never, ever darken the doorway of Missy's home again.*

If someone rejects you, wipe the dust from your feet. *So, yes, I should do that. Give up this silly notion that I'm supposed to marry her.*

Do unto others as you would have them do unto you.

Hixon stopped there. He sighed, breathing in stale air, then releasing it in hopelessness. He couldn't do that to Missy. He certainly wouldn't want his friends to expose all his secrets. Defiance was a feeding ground for rumors—the juicier the morsel the better. If he exposed her coffee can of green leaves, the whole town would smile smugly, confirmed in everything they'd already known about Emory Chance. But he knew better. He knew there was something of value hidden way deep inside. She was simply a person who had been bludgeoned by life. Maybe that's why he understood.

She won't be as she is now.

Treat her as an orphan.

Though Hixon considered himself a visionary from time to time, he still had a hard time wrapping his heart or mind around

Missy's being any different than she was today—spiteful, angry, distant, cold. But God said those words to him plain as truth. And God had a wily way of keeping his word. He had with Hixon.

And what about orphans? Didn't they steal sometimes to get food? Because they'd been thrown out into a cruel world with only themselves to scrap their way through life? Missy was like that, he knew. She clawed out a living, using her wherewithal. Her grit. Would the law punish an orphan for stealing in the same way it'd treat a hoodlum? Hixon shook his head. He'd heard about tough love, how it was the only way to help a drug abuser. Is this what God was asking? To be tough? Or gentle? To enact judgment? Or respond with mercy?

All he knew was that as he sat in the narrow room with a buzzing fluorescent light above, he hadn't made up his mind.

Forty-Eight

Ouisie stood, her eyes aflame.

Emory thought throwing the truth out there would crush her friend, send her shrieking grief into the afternoon air. But she hadn't expected this. Not rage.

"How *dare* you?" Ouisie paced the floor. Seven steps to one end of the living room, seven steps back. "How dare *you*?" She shook her head. "My friend."

"It was a long time ago," Emory said. Her voice sounded stifled, like she didn't have enough air to ignite it properly. All that effort she'd made to push Ouisie far, far away was coming to nothing. Because Ouisie didn't leave. She paced.

"A long time ago," Ouisie repeated. "How long, Emory? Why don't you tell me the story? I'm all ears." She sat on the couch, then crossed her arms over her heart.

Emory sank into the rocking chair and started rocking, hoping the motion would help her get the words out. It didn't. She kept as silent as Daisy in the grave.

"What's wrong? Don't have the guts to spill it now? Did you think I'd run out of the house hollering and crying?" She cleared her throat. "I may not be the strongest woman, Emory. But I'm stronger than you might think. Years of marriage to that man have given me a tough hide. I can take a lot. Like details. I can take all the details you're willing to spill. It would help me make sense of things, besides."

Emory rocked. And thought. And remembered the touch of Hap on her skin. She shook her head. The whole affair seemed suddenly dirty and shameful. Where before it had been a delicious secret—and the fact that she'd been able to keep that secret gave her a distinct feeling of power over every woman she'd met—it now felt like a tragedy. She, Emory Chance, could have an affair with Hap Pepper and keep it dead silent—even from his wife—for all those years. In a town that thrived on spicy news, she'd kept the spice capped. And for what? So she could sprinkle it on her friend like a weapon? She felt sick inside. If a mirror were put up to her face at this moment, she'd have to turn away, afraid of what she'd see in her eyes.

"I'm waiting."

"I'm sorry," Emory whispered.

"Oh, that's helpful. Gee, thanks so much. You're sorry. That clears up everything. Let's go have dinner and celebrate our friendship. Let bygones be bygones and all that."

Emory's stomach curdled inside her. "It was just after you'd given birth to Sissy."

"When he repaired the cabinets," Ouisie said, a blank look on her face.

"Yes, then."

Ouisie looked out the window. One tear settled into the corner of the eye Emory could see. It spilled down Ouisie's white cheek, then dripped onto her blouse. She didn't brush it away. "Do you have any idea what my life was like then?"

"You were tired. I knew that. And you didn't pay attention to Hap's needs."

"Oh, yeah. His needs. That's a good one. While you were having sex with my husband, did you ever stop to think that I had needs too? Needs that were *never* met?"

Emory shook her head. She didn't want to hear this. And yet part of her felt cleansed in the effort—cleansed and shamed all at the same time.

"I was a mess after Sissy was born. I had Jed to take care of and an infant, and a husband who demanded the house be the same clean as before. But I couldn't seem to get out of bed. Couldn't seem to function."

"That's when you started drinking," Emory said.

"I'd already started by then. It helped me get through. To cope. To wade through my sadness, just a sneak of wine at night, or a couple extra tablespoons of cough syrup to calm me to sleep. And then"—Ouisie's defiant eyes turned weepy—"then I felt I'd lost Hap. He'd kick me in the bed at night when I tried to hold him. Told me to leave him alone. That he was tired." She swallowed. "Of course I knew something was wrong. Usually nothing deterred Hap from nighttime relations. And all the while he was getting them here. Tell me. Did you do it on this couch?" She slapped the cushions.

Emory coughed, then choked on her spit. But Ouisie didn't get up to help. She coughed some more, finally righting herself. "I don't think that's necessary, do you?"

"Oh, I think it's entirely necessary. So did you?"

"Yes," Emory said. "There, but mostly in my bedroom."

"Care to tell me how he was?" Ouisie's ache appeared to turn back to cold rage.

"I don't think this helps." Emory concentrated on the rhythm of the rocking chair.

"It's helping me—if you're after forgiveness. But then again, you don't seem to be the least bit sorry. Your mouth might've said the words, but I don't see regret anywhere on your face."

"I *am* sorry."

"Really."

"I don't know how to tell you I'm sorry. Not really."

"You can start by telling me everything. And I mean everything. How long. How it started. What you did. Did he love you? That sort of thing."

Emory swallowed her shame, opened her mouth, and vomited the whole sorry story into the room. She held nothing back.

Forty-Nine

The parade of men in and out of her mother's life had soured her. Made Emory make a vow: *I will never entangle myself in the affairs of men!* It sounded lofty on her tongue, in her mind—the way the words sounded British. The exclamation point of the sentence came at sixteen, just as she was planning life on her own. Jimbo Perkins had been Mama's catch of the month, and despite telling herself not to get attached, Jimbo wooed her to his side. Took her to get ice cream. Asked her about her dreams. Encouraged her to make something of her life.

It wasn't like Jimbo and Mama were married or anything. But one day, Jimbo sat across from Emory biting into a Dilly Bar at the local DQ, his face drawn into agony. "I followed her, Em. And you know what I saw?"

Emory let her dipped cone remain as it was. From underneath the hard shell of chocolate, vanilla ice cream melted, running little streams down the cone and onto her hands. She knew this story. Heard it played out a hundred times. Seen it a few too. "She was with someone else," she said.

"You're right." He took another bite.

She wondered how he could eat at a time like this, but then she remembered the way his belly played over his belt. When Jimbo was hurt, he ate. And apparently he'd been hurt a lot, being a sweet, trusting man and all. "I'm sorry," she said.

He stood. "Women who do that to a man—affairing and the like—are only after ripping apart the world. Promise me, Em. Promise me." He put one large hand on her shuddering shoulder. "Promise me you won't end up like your mama."

Tears busted through her eyes. She put her sticky hand on top of his, looked into Jimbo Perkins' eyes, knowing it would be their last time together, and made him a promise. Said she'd never be Mama. Not in one million years.

But it hadn't taken even a decade for her to fool around with someone else's man—to dip her toe, then leg, then body into the pool of Mama's ways. Emory stared at the mirror now, a full look in her bathroom mirror. She saw the face Ouisie Pepper glared at, then wept before, then slammed the door on. Mama's face. Mama's eyes. Mama's ways.

Could a person come undone? She pictured herself a giant ball of yarn, knotted around itself, tightly coiled. In one quick moment, Ouisie Pepper, with that broken heart and pain-strewn life, took a pair of scissors and cut the knot, then kicked the ball, leaving Emory to spin wildly, pieces of herself unraveling before her eyes. And she could do nothing to stop it. Rolling, rolling, rolling, the ball moving this way then that in a chaotic dance. The room spun.

Boiling emotions came so close to Emory's throat, she nearly cried out in pain. She sat on the closed toilet, shoved her head between her knees and breathed. One. Two. Three. Four. Five. In with the good air. Out with the bad air. In. Out. In. Out. Her vision haloed for a moment; the world of the bathroom shrunk to a small circle at her knees. Don't panic. In. Out. In. Out.

She pulled at her ponytail until it hurt, hoping a bit of pain would bring her back to the present. Was she losing her mind?

Emory stood, splashed water on her face. Mama stared back again. She'd always thought her face ugly, a terrible thing for a daughter to think, she knew. But it was true. She seemed hideous to Emory, gargoyle-like. And now Emory looked exactly like Mama. Rounding face, eye wrinkles, lost-looking gaze, a hint of a frown in her smile even when she deliberately tried to be happy. A pessimist's face.

Fifty

Hixon sat. Had he spent his whole life waiting for something to unfold? Something good? Though he never made anything of himself other than to help people and build things on the side, he'd always found joy in it all. Now, with that threatened, he wondered if all that do-gooding had been worth it. Love folks then let them walk all over you. The longer he sat at the table in the middle of the buzzing room, the more he took this kind of inventory. Still, Missy's face haunted him. He tried to imagine her expression as she lied to Officer Spellman, but he couldn't. This perplexed him because he felt he should be able to discern her betrayal—hadn't he seen it all along in her eyes?

Hixon shook his head. He cleared his throat. The noise echoed off pale green walls. Footsteps clacked down the tiled hallway behind him. The door opened. He turned. There, in front of Officer Spellman, stood Missy, her hair in a ponytail, her eyes like a hungry Doberman. Well, he could picture her now, as if he'd been using binoculars, seeing the world in a blurred mess only to readjust and see it clear as day. Those eyes spoke betrayal. Nothing more.

Fifty-One

Emory felt the authority of Officer Spellman behind her, felt the seriousness of his role. Felt her betrayal in her throat. She swallowed.

"Sit, Ms. Chance." Officer Spellman motioned to the chair opposite Hixon.

They'd be less than three feet apart, she saw. Which meant she'd have to look into those eyes and not shrink back. She sat but stared at her hands.

Officer Spellman paced back and forth. "Here's the thing," he said. "I'm not sure what happened between the two of you, but I've got this sneaking suspicion all is not as it appears. I'm going to let the two of you talk. I haven't filed charges because I'm thinking it's unnecessary. But since your accusations, Emory, are of a harmful nature, I will stay in the room with you. To protect you."

Hearing the word *protect* made Emory feel even worse. That was Hixon's job, the job he wore like the officer's badge, and here she was being protected *from* Hixon. She remembered looking in the mirror, seeing Mama's eyes, living Mama's life. With Mama, it was always everyone else's fault. Always. And she felt herself wanting to slip into that way of thinking. Problem was Mama's blaming others was like a pit of quicksand. Once you put your toe in it, you were up to your neck in blaming.

Hixon shifted in his chair. He said, "Missy."

She looked at him. Saw the contours of his face, wondering for the first time how old he was. Those eyes had seen a lot, she could tell. The lines around his eyes and mouth revealed years of laughter, even though he'd slit his wrists. Was that how life was? Up and down like that? Heartache and laughter? Even so, he seemed so far away from heartache. That is, until she forced it upon him.

She stood. "He didn't do anything." She wouldn't look at him, instead leveling her eyes Officer Spellman's way. "You want the truth?" She was ready now. After spilling her terrible secret to Ouisie and feeling the agony and beauty of confession, she was ready to come clean, whatever it took.

"The truth is what I'm always after." Officer Spellman nodded Hixon's way.

"The truth was Hixon came to help me. But I was— "

Hixon stood. "I shouldn't have disturbed her. I wanted to tell her that you now knew about the missing gravestone and that you'd be by. She was asleep. Which is why I took off my shoes. I didn't want to wake her. When you came by, it startled me, and I ran."

She jerked her head his way. Saw anger and love mixed together on his face. Why was he doing this? He could've cleared himself with one word: *drugs*. But he hadn't. He should have. She would have. She already had.

"Ms. Chance." Officer Spellman stood in front of her. "What you alleged is very, very serious. Such an accusation could incarcerate Hixon the rest of his life. Are you telling me that you lied to me?"

"Yes." She fiddled with her hands. A phrase she'd heard once in church years and years ago fluttered into her mind. *Hands that shed innocent blood*. Only it was her words that crucified Hixon today. Ouisie too. Studying her hands, she suddenly wanted to rid the world of herself, to cut up her wrists again, to let death swallow her up once and for all.

"Hixon could press charges, you know."

"I know," she said. "He should."

"That won't be necessary." Hixon stood, pushing the chair away from the table. Its metal legs screeched along the floor. "I have a feeling what she really needs is some good old-fashioned rest, and more time to heal from Daisy's death. Folks do crazy things when they're grieving. They lash out at anyone because they don't know what to do with their pain. I understand that. So if you don't mind, Officer Spellman, I'd love to be on with my day."

"Absolutely."

Hixon stood next to the officer, not looking Emory's way. She was invisible now, she knew. She'd crossed the last line in Hixon's ability to forgive and be kind, and now she was a shadow, a mist. She deserved it, but the way he talked to Officer Spellman made her stomach turn over in grief. She'd lost two friends today. Two friends she hadn't cherished enough but now wished she had.

"Listen, I told her I'd protect her. Someone's out there, wanting to harm her, I'm convinced. But as you can imagine, with her saying those things about me, I'm not the person to be protecting her anymore. I'm giving you that mantle. You promise me, Officer Spellman, that you will protect her."

"Of course. I've been patrolling her street since the break in. And I'll keep it up. You can count on me."

Hixon looked at Emory. "I trust your word. I believe you'll keep her safe." He turned to Officer Spellman. "I need to go. Thanks for bringing her in. For everything."

They shook hands. Hixon left, leaving her alone with Officer Spellman. He sighed, shook his head back and forth, and led her out of the precinct. "I'll let you know if I find out anything else about what's been happening. In the meantime," he said to the cold sunny day, "rest. And learn the importance of telling the truth."

"Okay."

"I'll take you home."

"No, I'll walk."

She figured he'd argue, but he didn't. Officer Spellman simply turned toward the station, leaving her alone on the sidewalk, regret her only friend.

Fifty-Two

Onto the floor, her mail slot had spat one solitary letter. With the same E m o r y C h a n c e typed. Great. Another holy reminder of her failure from David, probably her last friend on earth. She tore the envelope, ripping free the inevitable prayer-letter.

Take her to the other grave, Lord.
She needs to weep there.
At the place where life ended, may it begin for her.
Because nothing's too big that you can't forgive it.
No one's too far that your arm can't reach.
Meet her there. In the place of death.
And resurrect Emory. Dear Lord, make it so.
Amen.

She took the letter to the rocking chair—the exact place she spilled her affair to Ouisie and lied to Officer Spellman. Her betrayal chair. She looked around. It was as if David were reading her mail, or understood her days betrayed. How could that be? He who was paralyzed, how could he know how much she needed resurrection today? He who would never walk again on this earth? Maybe David was right. He couldn't use his legs, but he now had the special ability to walk into the future, seeing what would happen.

What did she have left in the world? No more friends, other

than a detached, letter-writing David. A job that she would probably lose if she didn't do her shift tonight. Angus, who probably would never come around again unless she begged him for pills. She had no one to come home to. No connections with anyone other than Officer Spellman's nightly patrols. That was it.

She did have whoever it was that wanted to frighten her. She had the tattooed man, her thrashed house the evidence of his ability to destroy and scare. That she had. Maybe he spent his days watching her from behind trees. Maybe he could read her thoughts. Maybe everything that happened was a part of his plan. Kill her daughter, then stalk and kill her. She looked at her wrists while she rocked. Though it seemed like relief to slit them now, the thought completely immobilized her. Pulling a sharp knife across veins—she'd done it once—and freaked out when the blood drained from her. It had been the worst kind of trip. The room darkened, she remembered. This very room. And she felt fingernails scratching at her ankles, claws pulling her down, down, down to a place of wailing. Gargoyle eyes peered around her, pierced her fear, letting it spill out like the blood that flowed from her wrists.

"Mama," came the only voice that didn't torment. "Mama."

Still the talons scraped her flesh, making the blood seep further, haloing her head in darkness. The worst trip she'd ever taken.

"Mama, what have you done?"

Daisy's voice. Daisy's sweet voice. The only good thing she'd done in this world. She forced open her eyes. When she saw her daughter's terrified face, the demons clawing her into the pit suddenly vanished in the light of Daisy.

Even at seven, Daisy seemed older, more mature than Emory. She calmed her mama down and called the ambulance that whisked her away to Tyler, to stitches, to doctors with concerned expressions and talk of suicide watch.

Seeing Daisy's face had been enough to make her want to live then.

But now no one's face appeared. Only the memory of her own in the bathroom mirror. More and more that image felt like the clawing ones beckoning her to wailing and gnashing of teeth.

So she ran. Flat out ran. Away from the mirror, the rocking chair, Daisy's room, the memories of her trips in that house, the knife against flesh, the emptiness. Barefooted and cold, she ran toward David's destiny, to the place he assigned for her, in hopes that the tattooed man would be watching, would follow, would rid the world of her once and for all.

Winded and hair-mussed, Emory neared a ditch next to the road that, if you crossed it, would grow an incline through the forest, steeply, steeply until it broke out flat into an open field surrounded by trees. She stopped. Measured for a moment whether it was time. She looked behind her, seeing only the sun stare quietly at her. No one was following her. Yet.

She jumped the ditch, grabbing long stalks of dead grass for support as she climbed toward the trees. Everything inside her screamed stop, but she didn't listen to those voices. A great compelling, like Huckleberry's call to the Mississippi, forced her forward. She huffed through a stand of pines. Cold, lowering sun filtered through lazy branches, the same sun that angled through the kitchen window in the mornings. Dust danced above the forest floor too.

She broke into the light. Squinting, she turned toward the place Daisy'd been found. A nondescript mound of dirt loomed before her, just a few paces away. Police tape fluttered from sticks poked into the earth. The tape flew unattached, free in the wind, but it made no sound as it moved. The whole earth fell silent. No birds. No grass rustling. Just a great empty stillness that settled into Emory's heart like a rock.

She walked toward the mound, then stopped. She took

small steps until she stood above the dirt pile. Shovels had once marred the pile, she could see. But beyond the small mountain of dirt was a hole in the ground, a gaping, gnawing mouth that had eaten Daisy. She stepped into the hole, then sat, her hands smoothing the dirt walls around her. She looked up at the wide sky, bluer than blue, and wondered if Daisy had prayed to that sky, to the God who lived there but never rescued souls on earth.

The walls of the hole pressed in on her. She couldn't see Daisy's eyes there, but she felt her, strained to smell her. "Daisy," she said. "Daisy." And nothing more. Emory sat in the hole long enough for the shadows to shift above her, enough to think of a thousand things to say and yet keep silent. The earth turned, she knew. But in this moment, it answered her grief with silence. Blessed, terrible silence.

She stood, her head poking out of the hole, seeing the trees the way Daisy saw them when someone choked her breath away. She felt her own neck constrict, felt heavy suffocation in her chest. She slurped in air like a greedy swimmer surfacing from a long dive underwater. Yes, she could breathe. She could. Even when Daisy couldn't.

She crawled out of the hole and stood. It would be a beautiful metaphor, she knew, if crawling out of that hole meant a change for her. But she felt no different. And, if anything, the weight on her chest only grew heavier, pushing down on a heart already crushed by life and her own lies.

She dusted herself off and skidded down the incline toward the road. She walked home, wondering why God hadn't resurrected her like David said, then wishing the tattooed man had followed her, choked her, and sent her flying into Daisy's hole. Nothing ended as she hoped. She could feel the weight of folks peering at her from dirty windows, making their speculations, passing their judgments about the crazy barefooted lady. That was Defiance, she knew. She'd love to say she didn't care, but she did. She spent life worrying about the opinions of others, even Daisy's. And now her opinion didn't exist.

Because Daisy was gone.

And Emory had no way to better Daisy's last thought of her. She didn't deserve to.

Fifty-Three

Hixon saw Missy walk out of town a few times, observed the way she kept her head high, her blonde hair trailing behind her like bending wheat under the wind's weight. But today was the last day he wanted to see her. So he prayed he wouldn't. He expected her to stay put, anyway, after the day she had. But as he accelerated on his way out of town, he saw her again, on that same road, with that ponytail.

There walked Missy—a pinprick of a woman in the distance. He could tell it was her by the way she walked. Confident, but haunted. Willowy but strong. Perfect in every way, but flawed down to her marrow.

As he neared her, everything stopped.

Or at least it seemed to. His heart. His will. His hope. Everything but his foot pressed to the accelerator.

He drove nearer, watching her wind-whipped ponytail. He searched her face for recognition, but her eyes kept to the road, as if she needed to concentrate on the Missy shadow before her to keep going on with life. He nearly rolled down his window to holler her way, but his hand wouldn't move either, thankfully. He'd had enough of her for a lifetime. Only the steady pressure of foot to gas kept her rolling nearer, nearer, nearer.

Now pulled even with her, he saw her lips, neither smiling nor frowning, her face as white as a paper napkin, so different from his milk chocolate skin it startled and frightened him all at once.

In a terrible moment, Hixon could see the two of them walking hand in hand in Defiance, see it like a sharp photograph. But just as clearly, he could see the wagging heads of people not accustomed to such a thing, black and white joined hand to hand. He could hear their words: "Chocolate and vanilla, they don't mix, boy. Best keep to your own." He could see the tears Missy'd cry at the thought of it all. Defiance wasn't an easy place to live as a single mom. He knew she bore those words when Daisy was alive. Only pity had kept the gossips quiet as rabbits of late, but Hixon decorating her arm would unleash their flapping tongues mercilessly, he knew.

And besides his crazy fantasies, he knew they were just that. Terrible dreams that would never come true. Funny thing, though. It wasn't black and white that kept them apart. It was her heart—her lying, distant heart.

As those thoughts knotted through him, he watched her fade away in his rearview mirror until she was less than a dot on the road. She was farther away than she'd ever been, he knew. And no matter what he did, Hixon couldn't drive the distance between two hearts. Not today. Probably not ever.

Fifty-Four

Emory came home empty-hearted. Like a zombie readied for a life of lifelessness, she instinctively donned her uniform, splashed water on her face, and made her way to the car. She unlocked it, got in, turned on the ignition, and drove to Little Myrtle's. She parked by the dumpster, readying herself for the smell when she opened the door. Smelled it did. She hung her sweater on her hook, put on her apron, winked at Big Earl, and went to work clearing dish-strewn tables, smiling, and taking orders. This was her life. Her empty, empty life. It wouldn't be resurrected. And it wouldn't be snuffed out by the tattooed man either. Neither of those things. Life would be waiting tables, sleeping, paying Clyde Van Tassell finally, and trying to fill hollow days.

Someone snapped fingers behind her. She turned. There sat Angus in booth seven, that sly smile on his face as if nothing happened between them.

"Howdy, purty girl."

"Howdy, yourself. You sound like a cowboy."

"I am. Just got back from servicing a dude ranch in Burl with Curly. Business is good on the ranches these days."

She poised her pen above her order pad. "Is that so?"

"It's so. I swung by an old haunt and got me some good stuff too. What do you say we go out and have ourselves a little fling?"

"I don't think so."

"Ah, come on, Em. Just a date. Like real people. I'll take you—"

"So you'd like coffee and a piece of pie." She glanced behind her at Big Earl, who was tsking her with his eyes.

"Knock it off, Em. This is me you're talking to. You kissed me, remember?"

"Or do you want a sandwich? A nice grilled cheese and fries? Or maybe a french dip. Please don't order chicken-fried steak."

He leaned closer. She could smell him—a mixture of axle grease and Old Spice. "I'll wait for you. Bring me some peach pie, will you? I may as well enjoy something while I wait."

"One piece of peach coming right up," she said, a little too loud.

He remained there while she swirled salt in the bottoms of the coffee pots, cleaned the counters with diluted bleach until they gleamed, then dragged a gray mop over greasy black-and-white floors. He stood, paid his bill at the register, then nodded her way. "I'll meet you back at your place," he said.

Big Earl placed a hand on Emory's shoulder as Angus left. "I'm not much for meddling."

"Since when?" Emory said.

"Just listen, okay? He's bad news. The last thing you need in this world is bad news, Emory. You've been given a gift."

Emory laughed. "A gift? Care to let me in on it? Last I checked there weren't any gifts waiting around for me." Though as she said it, she remembered the cross-stitch—the words about fires in forests.

"Just this: the gift of death."

"I'd hate to come to your house come Christmas time."

Big Earl motioned her to the booth Angus once occupied. "Sit."

She sat in the vinyl booth. Best to oblige her boss, who had taken to telling her often that other girls, pretty ones, too, had asked after her job.

"When Myrtle died, I thought my life had ended." He pulled a strong hand over his gray-stubbled jaw.

"You loved her." Even saying that out loud made her ache. When would anyone say that about her? Did Hixon? Not likely anymore.

"Yes, with everything inside me. So when she died, I died too. I had no one to love anymore. And not having anyone to love shriveled me up inside." He fiddled with his hands. They were vein-roped and half-trembling.

"But you seem fine."

"I am now." He looked out the window into the winter night. "I am now. But it took me some time."

"How long?"

"A few years. But here's the funny thing. Her death actually changed my life for the better, once I let it. That's why I told you that you've been given a gift."

"I don't see any way out of my life the way it is, Big Earl."

"I know you don't. But open your eyes, Emory. Keep 'em wide open. You just never know when things will change. The grief will lessen. And as it does, you'll find yourself laughing again. Getting stronger. Becoming a different you. A happier you. A you who can withstand more trials than most people."

"That's sweet of you to say, but I'm not the kind of person that good stuff comes out of, if you know what I mean. I birth trouble."

"I see that. Which is why I'm being your daddy for a second and telling you to stay away from Angus." He grabbed her attention, stole her gaze. "And what he sells you."

So it wasn't a secret after all, her drug abuse. Great. Did the whole town know? "I need to go." Emory scooted out of the booth.

"It's not too late." Big Earl crouched in the booth, then stood slowly, his arthritis and his girth no doubt keeping him from springing up as she had.

"But if folks here know, then it is."

"Prove them wrong, Emory Chance. You hear me? For Daisy's sake. For yours."

Angus sat on her porch, a smug look set into his face. She blew out her breath as she pulled behind the house. Instead of coming through the back door, she walked around to the front, hugging the chill to herself. She'd forgotten her sweater.

"You fixin' to let me in, darling?" Angus stood.

She walked up the steps, legs leaden, heavier than her heart even. "No. Not tonight. I'm worn out."

"I've got something for that, you know."

She crossed the length of the porch and stood three feet from him.

He smelled like gum. He smacked it and smiled.

"Cut it out. I'm going to quit, Angus."

"So you say." He reached her way, grabbed her hand in a flash, and pulled them both onto the porch swing.

"Do you ever think there's more to life than money and drugs?" Her words sounded hopeful to her, like she was a child wondering how a star was made or whether fairies lived in trees.

Angus laughed. "You getting all philosophical on me, Em?"

"No. Not exactly."

Angus settled his right hand on her left thigh. "Sure there's more. Lots more."

She took his hand and placed it on his own thigh for safe-keeping. "Let's not."

"Well, this is something new. Did that Hixon fellow pour some religion and piety into you after all?"

Hearing Hixon's name drawl from Angus's lips made her sick to her stomach. "Quit joking about him."

"It's so fun, though."

She shifted in the swing, inching away from Angus just a little. "Are you happy?"

"I'm sitting next to a pretty girl here. Heck yeah, I'm happy."

"Stop it, okay? I'm being serious."

He put his arm around her. "You look cold."

She plucked his hand from her shoulder and gave it back to him. "I'm fine. Just answer my question, will you? Are you happy?"

"I'm not sure what happy means, Em. Sometimes I think I am."

"When, Angus? Tell me what life is doing all around you when you're happy." She watched a low cloud move in a slight winter wind, revealing the half face of a blue moon. They rocked beneath it in a moment of quiet.

"It's not really life that does the doing, Em. It's when my heart is settled inside me, all quiet like. Then I'm happy."

She chewed on the words in the silence of the cool night, willing herself not to tremble so he wouldn't try his arm trick again. But his words made sense. It was the inside of a person that made them settled. Not circumstances. She saw that in Ouisie—married to a perfectly awful man, but still able to love and give and go forward. Somehow. And Hixon too. He hung his head when he left her today, but she knew he'd make it through. Somehow. And Muriel had cancer stealing her heartbeats, but she smiled in the middle of it all. Somehow. "I guess you're right in that. It's something inside. But what happens when the insides are all messed up?"

"Are you asking for honesty?"

"Yes. If you're willing to spill it." She trembled again, but he didn't settle his arm around her. She let out a breath. It curled misty gray in the air, evaporating into the evening.

"I take something to help me along."

"Yeah," she sighed. "Me too."

"Listen," he said. "I'm not much for this kind of conversation, you know. It's getting late, and I need to get going. It's been fun, though." He stood, his angular body dark against the moon-lightened sky. Its blue cast a halo-shadow around his long-haired head from behind, creating Jesus out of Angus. Now wouldn't that be interesting?

"That's fine. I understand. I'm tired. It's been a long day." She watched him turn, walked down those creaking stairs, and place one shoe after another onto Hixon's foot path. He opened and shut the picket gate, mounted his motorcycle like he'd been born for such a thing, and revved away into chilly Defiance.

She didn't wave good-bye.

But then again, neither did he.

Fifty-Six

It seemed a good day to finally pay Jed a visit. Hixon knew his heart had been so entwined with Missy that he'd neglected Jed Pepper the past few months. Sure, he'd talked to him at church now and again and encouraged him when he could. His prayers were often seasoned with Jed's name. But he hadn't really been there for the boy who protected his family from his father's preacher-rage, and the guilt from his neglect compelled Hixon to make the journey to the other side of Defiance.

As he walked in the chilled morning air, he prayed, his words reaching as high as the clouds and bouncing back to earth. Did God hear him? There were days, weeks, and months when he'd swear on his Bible that God always seemed truly near. The season of God's visitation, he'd called it. But then he walked through a desert with Jesus, not hearing, not seeing, not experiencing. At first he thought it was a test, to see whether he would follow God if his mouth didn't speak, but soon that kind of faith wore as thin as the coat he wore today. Somehow, though, King David and all his sad-toned psalms pulled him through the journey—not that David's words were magical, but that David seemed to walk in Hixon's shoes. Knowing someone else understood made all the difference.

He passed Missy's house, remembering God's first words to him when he came out on the other side of his spiritual desert:

"You will marry her." Hixon shook his head at the memory. He'd responded well, then. In the excitement of offering his entire life to God, he'd almost been reckless in his obedience, straining to hear, jumping to follow any heavenly directive. "Yes, Lord," Hixon told God.

And then the parched heartache began.

But this was not a desert like the first. The first was lonely, without God's constant voice, but this time was different. He heard from God, but Missy kept pushing him away, severing pieces of his heart with every sharp word. Her words made God's seem small, dried up, not enough. Hixon picked up his pace, turning right on Forrest Lane, trying to concentrate on his journey to Jed's.

But Missy's house stayed in his mind long after he turned the corner.

"What am I supposed to do?" He said it to the wind that picked up a scattering of dried brown leaves. He hoped, perhaps, that the breeze would fly his words to Jesus in an instant. Leaves blustered while his feet plodded steadily along, his breath white in the winter day. Truth was he was blustered too. When it came to Missy, he was a dried out leaf, scattering, skittering here and there, unanchored to limb, to trunk, to roots. She was the tree, he knew. And her fingers let him loose to crunch under boots, to fly on the wind, to decompose in the dirt.

God must've been in the wind, hearing Hixon's plea in an instant as Hixon prayed. Sweet as a tree-ripened peach in summer came God's voice.

If you do anything, you'll get the glory for turning her around. Release her and let the wind of my Spirit change her. Then I'll get the glory.

Simple words, those. And true. So terribly true. Hixon felt release and anguish roil inside him. Release because he'd felt the last few weeks that he'd come to the end of his own abilities with Missy. He didn't know what else to do to bring her to Jesus.

Anguish because he knew he could do nothing but sit back and watch God take her to the deepest pit—the kind of pit God brought him into. Hixon understood those pits—the darkest, dankest, scariest place to be, where all you can do is look up and hope someone stronger could pull you out. Or turn your back and muster the strength to scrape your fingernails along the bottom, digging that pit deeper and deeper until the light above becomes a pinprick.

"Dear God, let her reach up. I give her up to you. Release her to your ways. Your mysterious ways. I can't change her. You know I've tried. But if I did change her, I'd wear it all like a badge of honor, forgetting to give you the glory. Take her, Lord. She's yours anyway. You're the only one who can change a life, and she's the only one who can reach for you. I can't do her reaching for her."

The words settled into the morning. Naked trees absorbed them. Hixon turned left onto Jed's road, exhaling slowly, praying for strength. Hoping Jed would forgive him for all that absence. And relieved that God, once again, took a heavy weight off his already-bent shoulders. His whole life was a gaggle of relationships like this. Some that needed mending. Some that needed releasing. Some that needed tending. He walked up the porch steps, putting on his tending hat.

Standing at the doorway, he hesitated. Yelling and banging erupted from inside. Shrieking, too, coming from Ouisie. The words hollered weren't distinct, but they sure sounded desperate and angry. He poised his hand at the door, wondering if this had been a good idea. Then again, it being Saturday and all, he knew Jed and Sissy would be in the midst of all that screaming, so he swallowed and knocked as loud as he could. Silence answered back.

A sweating Hap came to the door—an odd thing for a December morning. He looked like he'd just played a tennis match. "Yes," he said, his voice as cold as Hixon's breath.

"I wondered if I might talk with Jed."

"Now's not a good time, Hixon."

"Please, I need to talk with him."

Jed pushed around Hap, his eyes so much like Gentry's, it took Hixon's breath. "I'll be back," he told Hap. "Sissy too." Sissy slipped behind her father, a waif of a child, her eyes bigger than her coat buttons. She wore a tattered old coat, fit for a teenager, only she wasn't one. Far from it.

Hap shook his head. Anger rattled in there, Hixon knew. He said a silent prayer for Ouisie's safety, then placed his arms around the two children, leading them down the steps. He didn't say good-bye to Hap. Didn't need to either, since the door slapped shut right then.

"What's going on?" Hixon led them away from the house.

"I'd rather not say." Jed kicked a rock across the gravel driveway.

"You and Sissy up for a brisk walk to town?" Hixon pictured the interior of his wallet. Not much cash there since he waited for Muriel's estate to be settled, but enough for a little something. "What do you say we head to Little Myrtle's for a treat?"

Neither answered. But they walked through Defiance anyway. Hixon knew sometimes kids needed quiet to get their heads on straight. 'Specially after a battle of yelling inside their house. They turned right on Forrest and walked quietly, just their shoes on pavement making any noise. Together, they turned left on Love Street—still quiet. They passed Missy's house. Hixon breathed a quick prayer.

"She's the problem. Her." Jed pointed at Missy's house.

"What's that?" Hixon stopped. Looked back at Missy's house.

"Your girlfriend, Miss Emory."

"She's not my—"

"Her name keeps flying from Mama's lips."

Hixon felt sick inside. He didn't want to know.

While clapboard homes and brick ranch-style houses inched by, Jed continued. "Seems she and my father—the preacher—had themselves a little fling."

Hixon felt a cold rock settle into his gut.

"Don't talk about it," Sissy whimpered. "Mama asked us to keep our mouths shut or all of Defiance would be talking."

"Shush yourself, Sissy. Hixon isn't Defiance. He's Hixon. Even though he hasn't been around much."

Another boulder settled inside him, filling Hixon with cold fear, draining the last bit of hope from him. He neared Little Myrtle's, thankful Missy didn't work days, and stood briefly beneath the neon sign. He looked over at Jed. "First things first. I'm sorry." When the sorry dropped from his mouth, he exhaled. "I've let my life spin out of control a bit, and I've neglected you. There's really nothing to say except that I'm wrong about all that. I've let you down."

"You can say that again." Jed's voice was edged with sarcasm.

"I deserve that, okay?"

"I forgive you." Sissy's sweet voice filled Hixon's heart.

"Thanks, Sissy. But I want you and Jed both to know that I'm taking responsibility here. I should've kept close." Hixon found himself shaking. "Before we go in, let's agree not to talk bad about Miss—Emory."

Jed laughed. "Oh, yeah. That'll do us all some good. Sweep more stuff under the rug. Do you know what your girlfriend did?" He looked at Hixon. "That woman you are pining after had an affair with Hap when I was a kid and Sissy was a baby. I would say that's our business. Especially since Mama's been crying and sobbing and weeping and wailing all yesterday and today."

"You shouldn't have to shoulder all that. Shouldn't have to know." Hixon saw the anger in Jed's eyes, saw Hap's fight living there.

"Well, it doesn't matter much now, does it? We know."

Sissy started crying. "Mama and Daddy—are they going to divorce?"

Hixon turned, looked at Sissy's innocent face, only to find a world-worn adult's anguish there—as if Sissy aged two decades in the last few months. "No one knows that right now. But God is big enough— "

"He's not big enough, Hixon. That's just talk and you know it." Jed pounded a fist into his open hand.

Hixon led them into Little Myrtle's, opening the door for them both. Hixon felt the weight of Jed and Sissy's grief, yes, but he also felt it for himself. Missy wasn't just a drug-addicted recluse pushing people away. She wasn't simply a liar. Or a neglectful mother. She was an adulterer, the other woman. How could God ask such a thing of him? To love someone like that? A betrayer? He thought of his earlier conversation with the Almighty. *Sure, Lord, you can have her. Go ahead. Be my guest.*

Hixon sighed, but the action didn't soften the heaviness in his chest. Nothing would. "Okay. Okay. My guess is that you both don't want to go home just now, am I right?"

Jed nodded.

Sissy sniffed yes.

"So let's sit down and have ourselves some pie and ice cream and hot chocolate. I'll be quiet, I promise. We'll sit in one of the booths in the back, and you can tell me whatever you want to tell me. I'll just listen. Will that suit you?"

"I like pie," Sissy said.

So that settled it.

They ate pie—Hixon peach, Jed cherry, and Sissy lemon meringue. Hixon didn't know if he had enough money for his own coffee so he drank water while Sissy's upper lip frothed with whipped cream and Jed sucked Dr. Pepper through a long straw. He looked like a kid again, much younger, slurping his soda.

Though Hixon's heart was ripping itself in two, he readjusted his tending hat, hoping Jesus would show up in the midst of their motley group of three and give them all hope and guidance and love and so much more. In giving away, he'd known before, Hixon felt healing. He silently prayed it would be so today. Give away and receive from God.

"I'm going to be praying for you all," he told Jed and Sissy.

"Thanks." Sissy took another sip of hot chocolate. "What will you pray?"

"That—I don't know. For God's will. That's a good standby when you don't know what to pray."

Sissy looked at Jed. "Wouldn't it be God's will that Mama and Daddy stayed married?"

Jed slurped the last of his Dr. Pepper, sucking the cup dry. "No." Jed's confusion was evident in his piercing eyes. "Or yes. Doesn't God hate divorce, Hixon?"

"That's what the Bible says. But it's not a simple situation." Hixon took another sip of water.

"It never has been," Jed said. "Hap's been a little better since he was sent away to rest. But all this trauma has awakened him again, if you know what I mean."

"Yes, I do. I do."

Hixon let the last bit of peach and crust slide down his throat. Big Earl always did make the best pies. Even when Myrtle was alive, everyone knew it was her husband's crust that blessed each pie. Big Earl sauntered over to the corner booth. He slid the ticket Hixon's way. "You need anything else? Refills?"

Hixon hoped no one would want one. How could he pay for that?

"Sure," Sissy said.

"Yeah." Jed held his empty glass to Big Earl.

Hixon prayed God would multiply the loaves and fishes in his wallet.

Big Earl left, a smile on his face and an indistinct song whistling from his lips.

"So what am I going to do if Hap gets—you know." Jed touched the leftover glass sweat on the table, fingerpainted with it.

Hixon didn't have advice. Nothing came to mind. What did a teenage son do when a father rampaged? Fight back? Turn the other cheek? It reminded him of Missy just then. For so long he tried to fight her will with true words, hoping she'd bow the knee. Sometimes he let her smack him upside the head with her own version of truth. A hard call, to be sure. "All I can say is that God will give you what you need in each situation. And I don't really know what that'll look like."

"That doesn't really help me."

Big Earl returned with the drinks. "On the house," he said.

Hixon sighed relief.

"Hixon?" Sissy looked at him with those blue, blue eyes.

"Yeah?"

"I'm wondering. Before you go home, can you pray for us? Like here? Is it all right to pray in a restaurant?"

"Of course it is. I happen to know Big Earl won't mind a bit." Hixon extended his hands to Sissy and Jed. Sissy took his hand. Jed didn't. He bowed his head. "Jesus," he prayed, "you know everything. Absolutely everything. I know nothing. Absolutely nothing. Help me. Help us. We're so small. We don't know what to do. Give us words to say when words are needed. Give us actions to do when actions will speak louder than words. And, Jesus, if it be your will, would you heal the Pepper family? Make 'em whole? Because they're coming apart at the seams. Help them. Be with them. Help Mr. Pepper to give everything to you. Help Mrs. Pepper to pour out her grief to you. And help these kids understand your strength. Please, Jesus. Please." He paused. Swallowed. "And, even though it seems wrong to pray, would you reach down and save Emory Chance? Lord knows, she needs you." It was his letting go prayer, the period at the end of his conversation with God earlier today.

Hixon lifted his head, squeezed Sissy's hand. Jed didn't say a thing—his eyes seemed far, far away. But Sissy's eyes glistened with a drop of hope. Just a little one. And that was enough. For today.

Fifty-Seven

Daisy skipped free under a springtime sky. Wherever her feet touched the green grass, flowers sprung up in an instant, blossoming beneath the happy sun. She laughed, her blonde hair flowing behind her like streamers on a low-flying kite. She stopped, suddenly noticing Emory there on the edge of the field.

"C'mon, Mama. You have to run. Like me. Can't you see how happy I am?"

Emory tried to speak, but no words came. She wanted to tell Daisy so many things—how she missed her, how empty her life had become, how terrible everything was—but she sensed Daisy wouldn't be able to hear such things when she ran like a race pony on that field of multiplying flowers.

"What, Mama? What did you say?"

She tried to speak again. She said four hundred sentences, a few essays, maybe even a novella, but only one sentence came out and floated on the honeysuckle breeze to Daisy's ears. "I love you," she said. And that seemed to be enough. Those three words captured all the volumes she'd tried to say anyway.

"I know," Daisy said, giggling. "I've always known."

Emory tried to step into the circle of the field—the stretch of pasture she now recognized as Swan Field—but her feet stayed muddied to the earth.

Daisy ran farther and farther away, toward a dark forest

Emory didn't recognize. Though Daisy crossed the field in minutes, and Emory could barely make out her form now, she could see an overreaching tree on the other side of the field, its giant limbs moving as if caught headlong in a tornado's path. She saw the largest of its branch arms break just as Daisy ran beneath. Emory tried to scream, to warn Daisy about the danger above, but her voice came out empty. The sickening crack shot Emory's eyes wide awake.

She felt her pulse. Swallowed, or tried. Was she alive? Really? The deadness in her heart indicated no. But the walloping rhythm said yes. She was alive. And, oh, how she wanted to take a little trip. Back to Swan Field where Daisy ran and danced and spread flowers beneath her feet.

She shook her head, her hair flying in the effort. She left her bedroom to stand in front of *War and Peace*, happy to see her can hiding there, but wishing for much, much more. Big Earl was right in every way. His insinuation about her after-work activities, spot on. Still, Emory removed the lid, rolled a joint, and lit it. Inhaling, she sat back on the couch, her eyes closed. Yes. This was what it meant to be alive. To be settled on the inside. The idea of being peaceful way down deep could only come from help outside herself. Like Angus, she needed the curl of sweet-smelling smoke to calm her fears, to match the façade of being okay on the outside with the turmoil she hid. With smoke warming her lungs, it all connected. She felt perfectly at peace—as happy as she could be with Daisy gone to heaven and her left to holler silent screams from the field's edge.

Mary Jane circled around her ankles, purring, serpentining, finally jumping and sitting on her lap—green eyes closed slightly as Emory stroked her. They sat that way a few minutes, Emory inhaling, petting, and settling her soul, while Mary Jane obliged her by purring in return.

But something poked at her as she sat on the couch. A thought. A niggling that something wasn't the way it should be.

The room didn't look right. She scanned the living room, her eyes resting on the walls, the window, the fireplace. There, on the mantel, sat Daisy's picture like it'd always been there. Perfectly positioned below the cross-stitch. The peace the pot gave now dissipated like smoke from a winter chimney. Emory stood, sending Mary Jane helter-skelter to the floor, paced to the fireplace, and ran her hand along the mantel. Her heart catapulted in her chest. Daisy, frozen in fourth grade, smiled back at her. The cross-stitch hollered its fiery message.

She knew she should tell Officer Spellman about this, but shook her head instead. He wouldn't believe her now. He would think she'd stolen the picture, only to have it magically return so she could tell a fantastic story and get attention. No, she would not be the girl who cried wolf.

She looked at the front door, seeing nothing unusual. The door's deadbolt and extra locks were just as she left them. She went to the back door. Same thing. All locked from the inside and impossible to get through from the outside without breaking the doorjamb. Hixon had done his job admirably. But this realization only heightened her dread. How did the picture get back inside? She checked every window—most of which were still as they had always been—painted shut. Around the hall corner, she heard a low-toned whistle.

It was that moaning howl she'd heard as a girl when storms brewed outside her shack of a house. The wind groaned through cracks in their clapboard, through doorways with gaps, and sometimes through windows if they weren't shut all the way. That same sound came from Daisy's room.

She tiptoed to where the whistling echoed. Daisy's wide double-hung window stood slightly open, just an inch. Whoever returned the items came this way, then tried to shut the window completely. Why hadn't Emory made sure she locked it? And who would return something they'd stolen? Why bother? Unless this person was sending a message. Shaking engulfed Emory now—the kind of trembling that didn't come from cold on the outside, but fear on the inside.

She wanted more than anything to run into the kitchen, pick up the phone and call Hixon or Ouisie. But she couldn't do that, she knew. Not after how she'd been, what she'd done, the words she'd said. She could try to drive to see David, but she didn't trust herself driving to Burl all alone. No, the only place she could go was the last place she'd seen a friendly, kind face. To Little Myrtle's. To see Big Earl.

Her hands shook at the wheel, so she gripped it tighter. The closer she got to the café, the more she hoped no one would be there—just Big Earl with his big ears to listen just to her. With no one in the parking lot except Big Earl's rig, she sighed, thankful. She ran into the restaurant, spied Big Earl, and ran straight for him. He wrapped thick arms around her. When she pulled away, she noticed Hixon, Jed, and Sissy at the counter, Hixon paying a bill. "Oh no," she said.

Big Earl looked at her, then Hixon, not a word on his mouth.

Suddenly she felt herself float above, as if she were detached, observing the whole scene. But more than seeing herself on one side of Big Earl, Hixon on the other, she smelled herself. Marijuana permeated her, nauseating her stomach. *Pathetic*, the familiar voice in her head hissed. *You come in for help and all you do is stir up trouble and let the world know you're a pot head. When will you learn once and for all that you're a worthless piece of humanity? When will you finally get it into your thick skull that no one cares a hoot about you, and nothing you do will better anyone's poor opinion of you? You may as well get out of Dodge right now. Leave these kind people alone. Go find Angus and beg him for something to help you forget. Or better yet, too much of something so you'll sleep and sleep and sleep and wake up next to Daisy in that flower field. Yes, that would be the right choice. The only choice for the likes of you. Worthless, pitiable wreck. That's you.*

She nodded, and as she did, Emory slowly materialized back in her real life, Big Earl still shut-mouthed in front of her, Hixon with a pained look beyond him.

"I didn't mean to barge in and bother you," she said.

"You are never a bother. If you ask me, I think Jesus brought you here. Wouldn't you say so, Hixon?"

But Hixon said nothing. Jed and Sissy didn't either. Emory made the mistake of looking in the kids' eyes. They knew. Jed and Sissy were a perfect snapshot of the words pulverizing her head. She was a home wrecker on top of everything else, and here was the living, breathing proof: two anguish-eyed kids not saying a word.

Here she stood, smelling like pot, clothes a mess, an angry voice in her head, standing before the only person left who seemed to care. But Big Earl's love, that fire-hot kindness, smoldered to nothing next to Hixon and the kids, like their issues against her blew out what warmth Big Earl could muster.

Emory trembled.

"I'll see you tonight. I've gotta run."

She pushed through the glass door, not turning back to look at Big Earl who was trying to say something. No, she needed to get out of there before the grief of who she'd become crushed her flat out. It was what she deserved, she knew, but Emory didn't have enough inside her to weather one more grief. Not now. Maybe never. She sprinted to her car, turned on the engine, and screeched out of the parking lot. Her destination? Swan Field where Daisy seemed to live and breathe and dance and sing. But first, Angus. Yes, Angus' place. She needed a little something to give her peace.

Fifty-Eight

Hixon watched Emory turn and leave.

"Emory!" Big Earl hollered after her, but she dashed away. The door swung shut, leaving Big Earl alone with the three of them.

"That girl. Oh, dear Lord. That girl will be the death of me." Big Earl leaned against the counter, thick hands clasped in front of his belly, his normal happy-go-lucky tone severed, replaced by melancholy.

Hixon wanted to say "Yes, I understand. Me too," but the words couldn't form on his lips. Not with Jed and Sissy with him. So he looked at Big Earl and handed him all the money in his wallet—five dollars.

"There are some folks in this world you just know will make a difference. And there are some you give up on. Emory, well, she's a mixture of the two, wouldn't you say?" Big Earl gave Hixon back a one-dollar bill.

Hixon handed it back. "You counted wrong."

"Pie just happened to be a three-for-the-price-of-one special today," he said.

Hixon held the bill, shook his head. "That's a mighty nice special you're running."

"Every so often I have one. But never mind that. Do you understand what I'm talking about—Emory being a mixture of making a difference and giving up?"

Hixon felt the weight of Jed and Sissy's sadness behind him. He couldn't answer honestly right now, so he said, "I suppose so."

"You suppose so? Look at yourself in the mirror today, will you? Hasn't God turned a train wreck into a full-steam-ahead locomotive in your life? Can't you taste the transformation?"

Sissy sat on a red-seated barstool. "Hixon's the most amazing person I know. I would say Big Earl's right."

"Come on, Sissy. It's time we headed home." Jed's voice sounded scraped clean of emotion, like a winter windshield freed of ice.

"I need to get these kids home," Hixon said.

"No you don't. We're not your responsibility. Never were." Jed grabbed Sissy's hand and walked her toward the door.

"Your father will be mad if I don't walk you home. Let me walk you. Especially considering."

"Considering what? That Daisy's gone and the killer's still prowling around? Is that it? Well, last I checked, he hasn't nabbed more kids. And I really don't want to be spending any more time with you than I need to." Jed's face reddened. "Besides, it's not like you've been beating down my door to see me."

Big Earl's eyes got bigger still. He cleared his throat. "Listen now. There's no need for all this angry talk at Little Myrtle's, now is there? If you want my opinion, and take it for what it's worth, you should let Hixon walk you home, all right? Just for safety's sake. And your mama's. She wouldn't take kindly to your roaming Defiance these days all alone."

"Come on, Hixon," Sissy said. She extended her hand his way. He took it. "Let's go home."

Hixon winked a thank you Big Earl's direction and headed out the door, Jed in front, Sissy beside. It would be a long walk to their home, he knew.

Hap wasn't there when they walked up the porch steps. The car was gone. Ouisie rocked on the porch, a woolen afghan around her shoulders. Her eyes were red, her shoulders slumped.

"Hi, Mama, we're back." Sissy ran to Ouisie and scrambled onto her lap, spindly arms and legs this way and that.

"My baby." Ouisie stroked Sissy's hair, then looked at Hixon. "Thanks for bringing 'em back safe and sound. Would you like some coffee?"

"No thanks, ma'am. I need to get some things done today."

Jed broke his silence. "You mean chasing after Miss Emory, don't you?"

Ouisie gasped. Hixon felt Jed's words like a punch.

Jed opened the front door. Ouisie's eyes followed him. He slammed the door; she winced. For a moment, Hixon wondered if Gentry left his house the same way. Was it a defiant slamming of the door or a whimpering away?

Hixon didn't know what to say to fill the silence. Ouisie sat there, petting Sissy's hair, her eyes downcast to the porch's peeling-paint floor. What could he say? He couldn't apologize for Missy; that was for sure. What she did was terribly wrong. Awful. He couldn't explain himself about Jed's comment without making a mess of things. He certainly couldn't say, "Well, um, Ouisie, it's like this. God tasked me with marrying the woman who slept with your husband. So I'm going to chase after her because I think she's off to do something destructive. And for the life of me, I can't let her do that. Though there are days I wonder if I could let Missy destroy Missy. Except that she has my heart, and if she spirals into oblivion, I'll likely follow." No, he could not say that.

"Hixon?" Sissy's voice sounded smaller in her mother's arms.

"What is it, Sissy?"

"Do you love Miss Emory?"

Hixon pulled a rough hand over his mouth. He backed down the stairs, opened his arms, then looked at the sky. He took in a deep breath. "It's like this," he said. "God calls us all to love the people he created. He made Miss Emory, so I need to love her. He made your daddy. I need to love him. He made you. I need to love you. But loving you is the easiest thing I can do on this earth. You know why?"

"Why?"

"Because you're sweeter than sweet tea; that's why." He nodded Ouisie's way, then bowed slightly to Sissy. "I'll be by again. I mean what I said. I'm really sorry I haven't been around much."

"I know," Sissy said.

"Ouisie, I'm praying for you. You know that, right?"

She nodded, still petting Sissy's head.

Hixon hurried home. He smiled at God's surprising provision in Big Earl's giving him back some of his money. That would buy gas, which would let him search for Missy by car instead of on foot. He threw a prayer heavenward. "Thank you, Lord, for giving me just enough. And dear Lord Jesus, help me to make it up to Jed somehow. Show me a way."

Once home, he jumped in the car, put a dollar's worth of gas in the tank, and headed to Angus's home, out on County Road 549. When he saw Angus with Missy the first time, he made it his business to know everything about this man, including where he lived. He accelerated after he reached the turnoff, hoping he'd get to Angus and Missy before she made terrible choices. It occurred to him while the hilly roads rose and fell beneath his tires, that he felt almost fatherly toward Missy right now. Certainly not romantic. His affection had changed from deep-seated passion to even deeper-still love. It welled out from inside him—that same kind of love the prodigal son's father must've had when he paced back and forth on his property line, searching for his son's return. Oh, dear, sweet Jesus, how Hixon longed for Missy to turn around.

But for her it wasn't really a return. It wasn't like she'd ever even lived at the Father's home in the first place. The word God had given Hixon was *orphan.* Orphans didn't leave home because they didn't really have a home to begin with.

No, for Missy it would be the first turn of her life. To walk away from the only world she's ever known to come back to a Father she's never liked much or understood. It meant her reconciling the God who didn't take care of Daisy properly.

He gripped the steering wheel tighter as he thought about the impossibility of it all. How does someone so lost become found? How does an orphan truly find a home? And how could he, a man whose heart was hopelessly meshed in hers, believe such a thing?

He slowed the car. Off the road to the right was a small field rising from the road. A dirt road snaked around the hills' berth to a single-wide on the crest. He turned in while gravel crunched under his tires. He couldn't see Missy's car, but then again, it could be hidden behind the trailer.

When he pulled in behind, he lost his breath. Missy's car wasn't there. Only a motorcycle parked against the side of the mobile home. Hixon killed the engine, opened the door, and walked to the back door. He raised a hand to knock, but the door opened. Before him stood Angus, a bong to his lips, his other hand on the doorknob.

"Well, looky here. What do we have? A star-crossed lover, perhaps?" Angus inhaled, then blew smoke in Hixon's face.

Hixon coughed, then backed away.

"I'd invite you in, but, well, you know how it is. Business is booming. No use in letting you see more than should be seen. For all I know, you're buddy-buddy with the police and will snitch on me."

Hixon thought it ironic that Angus said all this holding a bong. He crossed his arms across his chest. "Has Miss—Emory been here?"

Angus smiled. Then inhaled again. He let out his breath, smoke circling toward the sky. "Oh, it's *her* you're smitten with. You know? I've known that all along about you. I hate to be the one to break this to you, but she and I, well we're an item, if you know what I mean. I'd spell it L-O-V-E."

"If she's in love with you, then why isn't she here?"

Angus sat on the stoop below his door. "I'd ask you the same question. If she loves you, then why are you here looking for her?"

Hixon shook his head. He leaned against his car. "Look, if you love her like you say you do, you'll help me. I think she's in trouble."

"You her father or something?"

"In a way, yes."

"Kinky."

"Knock it off, will you? Please answer my question. Has she been here?"

"Yes, of course she has. She *needed* me." Angus pointed to his chest, as puffed up as a chest could be. "She left a few minutes before you traipsed up my private driveway." He inhaled from the bong again, then smiled. "And, you can count on this, Mr. Holy Pants: she will be back. She always comes back to me."

Hixon shook his head, felt the muscles in his jaw tighten. Oh how he wanted to unleash a string of choice words about now, but his firm jaw kept them inside. He was Mr. Holy Pants, after all. "Thank you for your time." The Lord, who'd taken to being silent lately, piped into Hixon's ear: *Tell Angus I love him.* What? Standing on gravel, Hixon battled the rocks in his mouth, the granite reserve in his heart. He would not tell Angus such a piece of grace. But the voice persisted while Angus blew a smoky breath to the Defiance winds. *Tell him. There's a blessing in it. I promise.*

"What're you waiting for? You can go." Angus bowed with a flourish of his left arm, the smoking bong in the other.

Hixon heard God's whispered rebuke like a roaring train in his head. Angus was one of God's creations, after all. He swallowed. And he dared to look Angus in the eyes, only to find Gentry there. A scared boy and nothing more. "Angus?"

"Yes."

"Jesus loves you." Hixon held his gaze.

A hint of panicky joy lived in Angus's stare. Angus averted his eyes, muttered a curse, and went back into the house.

Hixon thanked the Lord. In that moment of sharing Jesus' love, his hatred of Angus bled into pity. He sped down the driveway, turning left on the county road, and headed to Swan Field, the place he felt in his gut Missy would be.

He found her there, standing in the middle of the field, circling like a child trying to get dizzy, her arms spread wide. She wore no coat, no shoes—just a flimsy shirt and a pair of jeans. At forty degrees outside, Hixon figured she must've been cold. Missy sang something—a wail, really—circling around and around. Hixon stood on the field's outskirts watching his apparent bride-to-be sing sadness under an open sky. Was she going crazy? Would Hixon have to add that to the list too? Adulterer? Drug addict? Child neglecter? Crazy person?

Missy stopped her spinning and sat abruptly on the earth. She didn't utter a sound, her singing now as distant as wind in another county. She lay down on the broken brown grass and looked at the sky. Whether she had taken something from Angus and was on some sort of drug trip was hard to say. She seemed so still there, so at peace.

So many things Hixon wanted to whisper in her ear right now. But his stubborn feet kept him anchored where he stood, a mute man with a longing the size of the Texas sky for a girl who stirred his blood. He took a deep breath. His lungs gulped in the cool air. He felt the weight of the coat around his shoulders, knowing it was God's simple prompting. He took off his coat, told his feet to unstick themselves and walk, for heaven's sake, and made his way toward the silent, flattened woman.

He stood above Missy in the direct line of the sun so that his shadow fell across her face. She didn't startle, didn't even stir.

But she did look into his eyes like she knew his soul lived beyond his eyes. It danced him inside.

"You here to lecture me?" Her voice sounded almost like Daisy's. So clear. So sweet.

Hixon said nothing. Shook his head. Smiled. Then he bent to the earth and spread his coat over Missy like a mother would smooth a quilt over a napping child. He tucked her into the earth, let her be there, let her stare at the sky. As he stood, it occurred to him he hadn't really loved Missy that way. For who she was in the moment. But right now, he did. With everything inside him. He covered her with a part of himself in hopes that someday, she'd return the favor.

Fifty-Nine

Emory blinked at the dull winter sun. She felt each prick of dried grass in her back and arms. Earlier, she had felt as cold as death. But here, with her poorly clothed body splayed on the open field, she felt nothing. Numb acceptance of what would be coursed through her like blood carrying lukewarm tea to each of her fingers. The wind crisped through crackled grass. She heard it. She understood it meant that she should shudder and wish for her sweater, but none of that registered.

Even the sky mimicked her mood. A dull gray blue sky, working in vain to keep the sun in its place. No birds circled above. None sang. They'd flown south for the winter by now, singing sweet songs in the tropics, about as far away from Defiance, Texas, as a bird could get to.

Maybe heaven would be like those postcards of Tahiti up on Big Earl's bulletin board in the kitchen. Perfectly warm. White-sanded beaches that felt like powdered sugar on her toes. Unending bliss. Fruit off the tree, dripping with sweet juice. The smell of coconut oil on her skin. She shut her eyes, blacking out the day. No, heaven was a strange, fairytale dream. And though she begged fate to send her there, nestled in the arms of her daughter, she wasn't so sure she'd make the right destination. More likely death would be like shutting her eyes. One world ending, another one not beginning. Just darkness and sleep.

She opened her eyes, hoping the daylight would brighten the fear inside. It didn't.

Angus had come through again—just like he always had. In the pocket of her jeans, she fingered twelve blessed pills. Soon she would drive home and pop them all into her eager, needy mouth, then sleep away her life until Daisy welcomed her home on the other side—hopefully. But something drew her back to Swan Field, her strange place of refuge. She felt she needed to be here first, before she swallowed up her life and washed it down with a cup of Defiance water.

Earlier, when she first stood in the midst of the field, she spun. Coming from a home where sticks and mud pies were toys, she'd taken to amusing herself by spinning. Mama called her a whirling dervish then. She'd sit herself on the tire swing adjacent to the house under the giant pecan tree and twirl until her eyes blurred. She kicked up dust under her feet to stop the swing, coughing when the dust settled into her mouth and lungs. When that got boring, she'd run barefooted across the neglected peach orchard behind her home, over a dried-up creek bed into a deserted pasture and spin the day away, sometimes risking throwing up her breakfast just for the thrill of it.

In the field she spun, bookending the memory. Only she wasn't a little girl anymore. She was a woman who'd lost her passion to live. A woman with a daughter who loved to spin, too, only to spin one last time on the earth. So she twirled, arms held wide. And she sang the song David said reminded him of her: "Wildfire." She thought of Daisy being Wildfire the lost horse, how Emory ran calling her name, only to realize Wildfire had run away to the desert. In the midst of singing and spinning, Emory stopped. She couldn't grieve again. Soon it would be time to be done with grief. Why spend her last day on earth mourning what might've been? She sat on the earth, then stretched out on the bed of crisp grass that poked her back now. She gazed toward the sun, not worrying if her eyesight would leave her. What did it matter? She'd be dead by morning.

A shadow crept before her, darkening the sun. Hixon stood there, but he didn't say anything. Didn't even move. She looked into his eyes, discovering what looked like an overwhelming ache behind them. In the tiniest corner of her heart, she revived. Part of her wanted to stand up and ask Hixon what made him look at her that way—she who didn't deserve such a kind, pained look, she who probably created it in the first place.

But here he stood. Anyway. Even after all she'd done.

She found her voice. "You here to lecture me?" She hated the tone in her voice. Sarcasm mixed with despair—not a good recipe for conversation, she knew.

Hixon didn't speak. Instead he bent low. He took the coat he'd been holding in one hand and smoothed it over her. He looked in her eyes one last time. And then he walked away.

Beneath his coat, she shivered for the first time.

Sixty

Was this the last supper?

Emory saw her half-opened screen door when she drove into the driveway. Now standing above a still-warm 9x12 Pyrex dish, tinfoil tightly folded over the edges, Emory wondered what Ethrea Ree sent her this time. It was uncanny the way the woman seemed to know when Emory needed home cooking.

She cradled the warm glass container under her left arm and opened the front door with her right. Once in the kitchen, she removed the foil. The scent of chicken spaghetti wafted up from the dish. And, oh, how good it smelled.

After grabbing a fork from the silverware drawer, Emory wolfed down several bites. The noodles were perfectly done, swimming in a cheesy sauce with a hint of jalapenos and bell peppers. The chicken felt tender in her mouth, not stringy and dry. The sauce was smooth, not clumpy or overly floured. Quarter of the way through the dish, she realized two things. One, she shouldn't have eaten so much, as a full stomach would slow down the effects of all those pills. Two, if she chickened out, she still had to work tonight—in a little over an hour.

She thought about Hixon's jacket, how it felt draped over her torso, how it'd been like a hug from a friend, even though he'd been careful not to touch her. She tried to picture him just as he was, standing over her grave, that same sad face. Only this time his coat couldn't cover her coldness. It would touch a gravestone or raw earth, never her body, her limbs, her heart. Would Hixon cry if she died tonight?

She pulled out the plastic bag of pills. Inside the bag was a small piece of paper. She unfolded it. Angus's scrawled words shouted at her.

Dear Em,

The world seems to have notions about me, many of which are true. But one thing I'm not is a fool. Or an accessory to suicide. Sorry, but these aren't the pills you wanted. They're full of one thing: sugar. I'm sorry. Angus.

She expected her hand to close around the note, crumple it, and throw it across the kitchen. But it didn't obey her initial rage. Instead she read the note again, surprised at the relief that flooded through her in that moment. Not tonight. She wouldn't die tonight.

Emory dove into another quarter of the chicken spaghetti, surprised at how hungry she was. A noise startled her from the living room. She walked on quiet toes to see what happened. Her heart rested when she saw it'd been the mail dropping through the mail slot. She thumbed through the letters, threw away the envelope from Mr. Van Tassell, then spied the familiar Burl postmark. Another letter from David.

Dearest, sweetest Jesus,
Your Emory is in the fight for her life.

Emory blinked as the words hollered at her. She sat on the couch, pressing the page flat so she could finish reading.

She needs to know you love her, Jesus.
But she can't seem to feel it.
Bring her back to Crooked Creek Church—the place where it all started.

And find her there.
And love her there.
Dear, dear Jesus, hear my prayer. Will you?
Rescue her. From herself.

Rescue her from herself. That sounded awfully true. She'd been her own enemy. Because if she could remove her mama from the equation of her life, she'd still come up empty handed. Emory plus Emory equaled failure. Choices and more choices equaled despair. Stupidity plus inaction plus neglect plus drug abuse equaled Daisy's death.

But for the life of her she couldn't see how going to the abandoned church would be any different. How would that be a place of healing, when the graveyard hadn't been? She felt like she was on a scavenger hunt to find healing, only she must've gotten all the clues wrong and ended up in the wrong places. Healing would be doled out to the person pursuing the clues correctly, but not to Emory. She held the note in her hand, wishing it to be magic—not the witch's poisoned apple but the handsome prince's kiss. Would it be that everything would settle itself if she did this one last pilgrimage? Or would her life crumble completely?

Before she'd venture to the ruins of Crooked Creek Church apparently to meet Jesus, she needed to do two immediate things: take a hit from her stash and put on her uniform for work. Drugs, then diner. If only life could be so predictable.

She reached for the can, felt the coolness between her hands. Someone knocked on the door. She put the can back, then opened the door to Ouisie, whose eyes were no longer red-rimmed. Instead, she smiled.

"Ouisie? What are you doing here? I thought—"

Ouisie walked around her into the living room and settled herself on the couch. "You thought you and I were through," she said.

"Well, yes, I—" Emory sat on her rocking chair.

"In a town this small, I can't afford to lose a friend. Now, a husband? Maybe."

"But I—"

"You slept with my husband. So many times too. I'm impressed, actually."

Emory couldn't detect sarcasm in Ouisie's voice, just unnerving humor. "Listen, Ouisie. I'm not a part of your little group of Christians who knows how to—what do you call it?—repent."

"So you say." The smile didn't leave Ouisie's face.

Emory took a deep breath, all the while longing for a drag off a hand-rolled joint. But that would have to wait. She looked at her watch, only a few more minutes before she had to leave for work. "What I'm saying is—for what it's worth—I'm sorry."

"Anyone who slept with Hap would feel the same way. Lord knows I do sometimes. But I made a promise to love that man until I breathed my last, so there it is."

"There it is," Emory repeated. "How—"

"I don't know how is all I can really say. He seems upset, maybe even repentant. In a strange way, I have you to thank for that."

"I'm really only good at messing things up." Emory meant every word, felt each one in the depths of her heart. If there was a God, he made her to screw up.

"I've felt that way too." Ouisie looked out the window. "Sometimes Hap makes me think those very thoughts. Here's the thing I want you noodle on. I've got Hap, but still I have a choice to believe some of his words or discard them. Most of my marriage I've absorbed every single word, not throwing out a one. Lately, Jesus has been teaching me—"

"Do we have to bring Jesus into this?"

"Yes, we do. Just let me finish. As I was saying, Jesus has been teaching me to filter out some of Hap's words in light of Jesus' words about me. I realize, probably for the first time in my life, that I am precious to God, his little daughter he delights in. So when Hap says I'm good for nothing but sex and cleaning the house, I have two choices. I can either internalize his words as gospel truth, or I can remember that to God I'm precious. That I'm made to do beautiful things—much more than sex and housework. I call it my heavenly filter."

"I'm glad you've figured that out. Hap's not exactly good at being kind." Emory remembered some of the terrible things he said to her, even in the midst of a passionate affair.

"No, he's not. And just because he's my husband doesn't mean I have to take everything he says as the be all and end all of the truth about me." Ouisie leaned forward on the couch, resting her chin in her hands. "But here is what I felt Jesus wanted me to tell you today. You don't have Hap. Not anymore. But his voice lives inside your head anyway."

Emory felt tears touch her eyes. "But the voice, it's mine."

"It may sound like your voice, but it's not telling you the truth, Emory. You think it is—which is the problem. And it's going to drive you to your death if you can't put a stop to it."

Emory swallowed, then wiped her eyes. "You don't know what I've done."

"I know."

Emory shook her head. "How could you know?"

Ouisie held her gaze. She stood up, walked to Emory, then knelt before her. "You feel guilty for neglecting Daisy. And you think that your neglect led to her death. You are addicted to drugs. I don't know which ones or how often, but you are, and that makes you feel like a loser. You've slept with my husband, then hid the whole sorry affair from me for years. You push people away. You lie your way through life. And you're about to be kicked out of your house."

"Stop. Please stop."

Ouisie grabbed Emory's hand. "And every day you battle

voices in your head that tell you you're worthless. You entertain thoughts of killing yourself."

Emory sat back in the chair, still holding Ouisie's hand. "You're spooking me."

"I'm right, aren't I?"

She nodded. Having herself splayed out bare like that felt like a scab being ripped off a brutally skinned elbow. But the air attending to the wound felt healing somehow, even though the rawness stung.

"Believe me, the last thing I wanted to do today was to come over here and try to encourage you."

"What you said isn't exactly encouraging, Ouisie."

"No, but it's the truth, and Jesus said the truth will set you free."

"It pretty much just makes me feel terrible and sad." And a little better, she almost added.

Ouisie let go of Emory's hand and sat on the floor beneath her. "I know, honey. I know. I can lead you to the water, but I can't make you drink."

"What does that mean?"

"Only that I can tell you Jesus will take all this, will show you that he forgives you, if you'd only let him."

"Gee, thanks for the sermonizing, Billy Graham." She stood.

Ouisie scrambled to her feet. "You want to know the truth? You've grown so accustomed to the angry voices in your head that it scares you to death to let 'em go. They're like friends. Sure, they don't say the best things to you, but they're familiar. And familiarity is much safer than letting them go and trying to believe."

"I need to get ready for work."

Ouisie backed to the door, placing one hand on the doorknob. "I won't stand in your way. I came here out of obedience to share those things with you. I'll be praying, you hear me?"

Emory nodded. What could she say to that?

"One more thing before I leave." Ouisie opened the door. She breathed in the outside air, then leveled a look Emory's way. "For what it's worth, I forgive you. At least, today I do." She shut the door and left, leaving Emory with the memory of words she'd never really heard before.

Forgiveness. When she pulled on her apron behind Big Earl's kitchen, she hoped putting on forgiveness was just as easy.

Sixty-One

Hixon spent the next morning in his home, thinking over the events of yesterday. He built a fire in his sooty fireplace, relishing the smell. As flames popped and cracked the dried pine logs, Hixon nursed a cup of muddy hot chocolate. His heart felt muddied too. He'd covered Missy with a part of himself, but she didn't respond. Maybe that was the end of God's requirement. Maybe the Lord was teaching him to be kind to the unloving. Truth was he felt dog-tired of all this kindness. Wondered if he could keep doing it over and over and over again, only to see mere flickers of Missy's soul.

Today was the day he'd give her up once and for all. Stop all that hankering and pursuing. Let her walk her own path. Isn't that what the Lord wanted? For him to step aside? He'd certainly done his part. And God said if Hixon tried to help Missy, God wouldn't get the glory.

Hot chocolate drained, he readied himself for church. A fatigue he'd known years ago crept into his body, like every limb was filled with concrete. No one would miss him at church, he knew. Certainly not Jed. And having to see Ouisie fake-smile her way through another sermon didn't hold much appeal. Listening to a proud Hap cram the Bible into folks wasn't his idea of fun either. Still, he pulled on his one pair of nice pants, then ironed a white shirt until all the wrinkles pressed out. It was the Lord's house after all. And today more than any day, Hixon needed to sing songs to the Almighty with other voices alongside—with Missy far away so she wouldn't distract him. He hoped he could sing away his heaviness.

After church, Jed turned around and shook hands with Hixon, his eyes still distant, Hap's angry look living there. "You mind if we talk?" he asked.

"Not at all. I can drive you home if your parents say it's okay."

"I already told them."

"Let's go then."

Hixon had to let his car idle a bit before he'd drive it across town, so they sat in the church parking lot a few minutes while the heater sputtered to life.

"Things are different," Jed said.

"What do you mean, different?"

"At home. This morning Hap started helping around the house. And he apologized to Mama, made her eyes wet. Told Sissy and me he was sorry too."

"Sounds like he softened after the fight."

"Here's the problem. I know it won't last. So I'm waiting for Hap's next explosion. This little change can't be real."

Hixon put the car in drive and pulled out of the church parking lot. "Only the Lord knows if a man will stay changed. That's not up to you to figure out."

"I feel guilty."

"Why?"

"Well, for treating you the way I did, for one."

"Listen, don't worry a thing about that. It was my fault. All mine. You didn't do anything wrong." Hixon watched the road. The heated air of the car contrasted itself with the cool windshield, leaving a foggy haze. He'd use his windshield wipers to fix the problem, only one was broken, the other half gone.

He could hear Gentry breathing in Jed's lungs. The steady in and out agonized him. "I had a boy, once."

"What?"

"Gentry. An orphan boy who needed a home. You remind me of him." It'd been the first time Gentry's name had floated into the ear of another person, and letting Gentry go that way melted away a tightness in Hixon's neck he hadn't realized was there.

"You had a boy? Were you married?"

"No, like I said, he was an orphan, so I took him in. Only, he ran away, and I've never seen him since."

"I'm sorry," Jed said.

"He's about your age by now."

"I hope he's okay."

"I pray that too."

A hazy Defiance ambled by, while Gentry rode between them, the secret let out.

Jed sighed. "Do you ever feel guilty, Hixon?"

Hixon laughed. "Of course."

"It's just that, I feel guilty for not being happy about Hap's attempt at kindness. Isn't this what I wanted? For him to change and be the father he was supposed to be in the first place? Here I should be throwing a party, and all I can do is worry."

"A man changing is a mysterious thing, Jed. In some ways, I'd say you're right to worry. But if this small change ends up being genuine, you'll have to make peace with that. You're used to a home that's angry and violent. You know how to live in that home. But a peaceful one? You don't know about a home like that. So it's strange to you, and a bit scary."

Jed looked out the still-foggy window. "How do you see in this car?"

"I know Defiance like the back of my hand. So I make my way even when things are foggy and I can't see much in front of me. Comes from years of being in a place."

"I don't want to stay in Defiance forever."

Hixon pulled up to Jed's house, came to a stop, and killed the engine.

Jed didn't leave. "Did you hear me?"

"Yeah, I heard you. You don't want to stay here. It's understandable."

"Sometimes I think about leaving—early."

Hixon looked at Jed and noticed his strong jaw. He took note of the stubble forming on his chin. Jed was a man now, or at least coming into his own. Soon Hap wouldn't be able to keep him home. "What about Sissy?"

Jed tensed his jaw. Said nothing.

"Maybe you ought to pray about this a bit."

Jed faced him. "Like you told me you did in that burnt tree? Fake praying? I swear I don't know who is telling me the truth anymore."

Hixon shrank from Jed's words. "I was sorry the moment I lied to you about that." To his shame, he remembered telling folks he had a special prayer tree where he confided in Jesus, only to be found out. He'd never climbed that tree.

"Yeah, just like Hap is sorry for cheating on Mama. Seems awfully convenient to me. Just do what you want, then apologize. It's like Hap's years of hollering and threatening and hitting meant nothing. One burst of an apology and I'm supposed to rejoice. I don't get it."

"Allowing the Holy Spirit to change a person, well, it takes days and weeks. Maybe months and years." Hearing his words, he remembered Missy.

Jed shook his head. "Hap prayed, Hixon. He did. I'd see him when I snuck into church while he was hollering away his sermons. He'd stop mid-sentence and throw a prayer to Jesus. You tell me: how is it that a praying man hurts his family?"

"I don't understand it myself other than to say we're all a huge mess. All I can do is 'fess up to what I've done. And for my part of jading you about prayer ... about lying about praying in that burned-out tree like I was a prophet, all I can say is I'm deeply sorry."

"I know you are. And I've forgiven you. My head's just messed up is all."

"Listen, Jed. Don't go running from your problems—or the people God's placed in your life. They have a strange way of chasing you. Just hold on, you hear me? I'll be around more now, I promise."

Jed opened the door. A strange whiff of warmer air blew into the car—hardly a winter breeze. "I gotta go," he said. "But thanks, Hixon. Really."

As he pulled away, Hixon thought of Missy right then, how alone she must've felt, how empty her eyes were. But he didn't have the unction inside to follow after her this time—even if she wasn't as she should be. Driving on warming streets, nearing Missy's white home, he couldn't bring himself to stop again. Couldn't risk his heart this time. Or next time. Revving past her house, he disobeyed his own words to Jed. Running from his problems. Waiting for them to chase him.

Sixty-Two

Sunday morning brought anguish Emory's way, it being the worst day of the week after Daisy disappeared. Daisy'd always spent the morning doing everything she could to get Emory to church. Even though an avowed evening person who hated waking up with the birds, on Saturday night, Daisy set her wind-up alarm clock to 7:00 a.m. on the dot. It rankled Emory from drug-infused dreams. She remembered pulling the covers over her head and groaning. But Daisy wasn't finished. She'd clank through the kitchen, making too-weak coffee and scrambled eggs. Nearly every Sunday morning, she came singing into Emory's room: "Sunshine on my shoulders makes me happy." Then she placed an old wooden tray, covered with a checkered cloth napkin, on Emory's bed. A still-singing Daisy sat next to Emory, who hid under the covers.

"I made you breakfast, Mama."

Emory grunted.

"Come on, Mama. It's good. The eggs will get cold. It's time you got ready for church, anyway."

Most Sunday mornings, Emory growled or barked at Daisy, causing her to skedaddle from the bedroom. But Emory would always pull herself from bed, sneak around the corner in time to see Daisy through the front living room window. Daisy sat quietly on the front porch, a worn Bible on her lap, her golden hair shimmering under the morning sun as she waited for Jed's family to pick her up. Without her mama.

Emory wished she could rework the memory. That every time Daisy came in from the kitchen with a tray, Emory would sit up, smile, eat eggs, and drink weak coffee. That she would pull on some clothes and take Daisy to church. Or that she'd wake up and give Daisy a much-deserved breakfast in bed.

Today there was no coffee. No tray. No singing Daisy. Just a cold, empty house screaming Emory's neglect, fueling her regret. All on Sunday.

"It's time I get to work," she told Mary Jane. "Then church." The cat skedaddled as Daisy did at Emory's voice—right out her door. Emory dressed in her uniform for the Sunday afternoon shift—her penance for leaving Candy high and dry so many times. She pulled her hair back into a ponytail—all this without looking in a mirror.

She passed Daisy's picture and the cross-stitch on her way to the kitchen. She pulled Daisy off, looked in her eyes. "I'm sorry, baby," she said. But only Mary Jane heard the catch in her voice. Being completely alone held a heap of heartache. Emory placed Daisy back on the mantel and pulled down the cross-stitch, still puzzling over the words. " 'I will punish you according to the fruit of your doings, saith the Lord: and I will kindle a fire in the forest thereof, and it shall devour all things round about it.' Jeremiah 21:14."

But Ouisie hadn't done that—hadn't punished her for the affair—a punishment Emory well deserved. And Hixon had covered her with his coat, no judgment in his eyes, only hurt. Big Earl took her back to work last night, acting as if she'd never let him down. Praising her for her efficiency and good rapport with the customers. That's what she didn't deserve. She didn't deserve folks' kindness.

She dumped the remaining instant coffee crystals into a mug and waited for the water to boil. When she tasted the coffee, tears entered, then left her eyes. Just as weak as Daisy's had been—exactly so.

Sixty-Three

The haunting of Hixon's own words made him do it—the inevitability of them. The promise of what would be, what should be. The reminder of Missy's orphanhood. The sometimes-life in her eyes. How quickly Gentry left, and Jed's threatening to do the same. He'd been lollygagging enough, as Muriel would say. And if he didn't muster the nerve now, when would he? Thinking of Missy formed a crude recipe in his mind, one that could be changed and altered by God's grace alone. So he held the last ingredient in his hand. And prayed.

But his hands still shook as he drove to Missy's house. When she wasn't there, he nearly drove home, but he heard Muriel's voice scolding him. "If she's going to be your wife, she's worth pursuing. Any treasure is." He slowed in front of his house, turned on his blinker to turn left into his driveway, then drove straight on Elm while the blinker clicked on and off to the rhythm of his heart. He headed straight for Little Myrtle's, parked in the lot, and tried to swallow his twitches. He saw Missy through the floor-to-ceiling windows, watched her as she filled saltshakers to the brim. Remembered how Jesus had been salt, how a disciple was supposed to be salt too.

Like a good disciple, he obeyed Jesus and got out of the car.

Sixty-Four

Funny how they came in at the same time, each sitting at a different dinette across the aisle from each other. Hixon with his earnest face and Angus with his smirking one. She brought each a slice of peach pie. One seemed twitchy. The other, high.

Both made her nervous.

But it was Hixon who beckoned her to sit. She caught Big Earl's eye. The day had been slow. He nodded for her to sit. "You can take off your apron, Emory," he hollered across the counter. So she sat across from Hixon, while Angus sneered from the booth next to them.

Angus left his booth and stood in front of their table. "Ah, look at this. Daters in a diner. How sweet."

"It is sweet," Hixon said, his voice steady.

"Like two lovebirds courting."

Hixon looked at his hands.

Emory stood, then looked right at Angus, willing herself not to be wooed by his charms. "I can sit wherever I want to sit. And today? I'm sitting with Hixon here. You got a problem with that?"

Angus backed up one step, his hands raised. "No ma'am. No problem at all. And you know why? Because I can see right through you, Em. I know who you really are. I've seen you strung out. I know you can't stay away from it, or me, for that matter."

Emory felt his words like knives piercing her desire for a new life. But she took a step toward him. "I'm not who I was back then, Angus."

Hixon gasped.

She looked at him, wondering what it was that made him gasp like that. She couldn't read his eyes.

Hixon stood. "You heard the girl. She's not what she used to be. God has a different plan for her. And anyone who truly loved her would welcome the change."

"Love," Angus spat. "Love? Oh, I see how this is going down. You love her. Is that it?"

Hixon reached for Emory's hand, and she gave it to him. It felt right there, like God had made her hand to fit into his like a perfectly matched puzzle piece. Hixon's hand was his way of saying he loved her, she knew that now. Maybe she'd always known it, the way he fixed her sidewalk, her doors, protecting her, covering her. But how could he after all she'd done to him?

Big Earl paced over to the gathering of three. "Angus, I see it's time you left. Don't worry about the pie. It's on the house."

Angus laughed. "This is downright comical—your ridiculous lovefest. Em, come on. You know I've loved you ever since I laid eyes on you. I've loved you longer than this burned-out old man."

Emory found her voice; it seemed to have traveled through Hixon's warm hand into her heart. "I don't love you," she told Angus. "Never did. You told the truth, you know. About me. I was all those things. But I'm not anymore. At least I hope not. So if you'd kindly leave me be, I'd like to have pie with Hixon. In peace."

Angus wagged his head, rolled his eyes, swore. "You'll be back, Em. You'll crawl back to me, begging." He left. She could hear his motorcycle roar to life. And then silence.

Big Earl excused himself while she and Hixon sat opposite each other in booth number seven.

Hixon didn't reach for her hand again; he kept both hands under the table. But he looked into her eyes. She left his gaze, preferring the table.

"You can't look at me," Hixon said.

Her head shot up. She saw his eyes, how pained they looked.

"I am not a handsome man." Hixon cleared his throat.

She waited in silence for him to speak, but he said nothing. She wanted to run out of the diner and nurse her humiliation with the coffee can of dope and papers. But she stayed put, waiting.

"I need to tell you something," he said finally. "God loves you. He must. Because he told me a long time ago that you were beautiful. Only you just didn't know it yet. And my job was to help you see it."

"I've made a terrible mess of things."

"We all do. Lord knows I did. But that's where Jesus comes in. And if we let him, he takes us, turning us from orphans to adopted, loved children, taking our regrets and sadness and giving us unexplained joy. Kind of like the joy I feel right now." Hixon, teary-eyed, fumbled with something in his pockets, then smiled. He got out of the booth, then knelt before her.

Emory's heart throbbed through her. She didn't deserve any of this. She put her hand up to protest, but Hixon held her eyes steady.

"Missy, I love you. I'm a broken man who doesn't deserve a first chance at love. But if you'll have me, I'll spend my life making sure the last half of your life is one million times better than the first half. It'll be my privilege to see you grow in God's love. Will you marry me?"

She pulled him to his feet, then stood face-to-face with the man who covered her with his coat, who slept across her threshold. He put a simple gold ring around her finger. She stared at it, wondered at how right it felt there. For a moment, she lost herself in his eyes. How much love lived there? How much forgiveness? Miles and miles of love and forgiveness, she knew. But the road to loving her was much longer. It ended beyond the outstretch of Hixon's love.

She pulled the ring off her left ring finger, opened Hixon's palm. She traced his suicide lines with her eyes, then placed the ring in Hixon's hand, closing brown fingers around it. "I can't," she said, devastating his eyes.

When a heaving cry burst from her, she ran out into the afternoon.

Sixty-Five

Emory ran breathless toward home, passed it, then turned left toward the rendering plant. Muriel's mural called her, had something to say to a woman who refused a marriage proposal from a man with such eyes.

She saw Hixon in the painting, walking on a path toward a horizon—one that didn't include her. She cried, touching the one-dimensional man, noting how the brown paint of his skin contrasted hers even as the sun dipped behind a tree. It was her left hand she pressed to the cement wall, a naked, ringless hand.

She felt unusually hot. She remembered her mama's words about Texas weather—yet another warning. "If you don't like it now, just wait a few minutes; it'll change." Change it had. Where yesterday had been a chilly, cloudy, bone-cold day, today felt like spring. Far away a rumble of thunder echoed.

While the smell of dead animals assaulted her, she walked the length of the long cement mural, noting its colors, the pictures, the joy that danced on the wall—a joy she'd never really known. Three people painted that mural—one dead, one bent on marrying her, and one she still blamed for Daisy's death. And yet, here they all were, their brush strokes testifying that life still went on. Muriel's images were still bright today, living beyond her years on earth.

Emory left the mural behind, cutting through the woods.

Sweat dampened her underarms. A strangely beautiful day to pilgrimage to the place Daisy went missing. Behind her, she heard a twig snap. She turned but saw nothing. She spun around. "Listen," she shouted. "I don't know where you get off trying to scare the bejeebers out of me, but you can just knock it off, you hear me? I'm sick of you trying to scare me. So quit!"

Her words bounced off pine trees, going nowhere really. Emory felt her heart thump in her ears. She spun around again. Nothing. No waving branches. No noise. Just the stillness of a Sunday forest. She breathed in the pine scent. She placed one foot in front of the other, slowly making her way through the trees. She came to a clearing—Jed and Daisy's sky chapel—and sat on their log. She looked up at the sky. The sunny day created a circle of pure blue above. Thunder growled on the earth again, but she couldn't see any thunderheads from her vantage point.

The sun seemed to follow her as she pressed through the woods. A winter sun, living low in the sky, elongated the trees in front of her into giant shadow redwoods. Beneath the sun's angle, Emory looked like a willowy tree-woman, long-limbed and breezy. She walked with her shadow until she broke into the semi-circle of pasture surrounding the old church. At the sight of the church, she gasped.

There it stood, quietly, like it held secrets it wouldn't tell. But her head bombarded her with words nonetheless, as if to fill in the blanks the silent church wouldn't say.

If you hadn't been stoned, this wouldn't have happened.

Neglectful mothers have their kids taken from them.

You are your mother, Emory.

You deserve every terrible thing that's happened to you.

You don't deserve Hixon.

Why not rid the world of you? No one would care.

She didn't fight the thoughts, the thieves bent on stealing from her. She welcomed them like long-lost friends bringing a picnic, letting each morsel settle in, poisoning her mind because she deserved that. Ouisie had said she needed to resist the Hap-like voices, but standing in front of Daisy's last-known free place on earth, Emory knew that was all hogwash. This was her fire in the forest, her deserved punishment.

She mounted the crooked stairs, feeling them give under each step. She turned and faced the field and forest, scanning both for the tattooed man, almost hoping he'd show himself once and for all. She saw nothing. She turned, then entered the church. Thunder boomed outside, but it didn't make her jump. A winter storm was rare but not unheard of.

She walked down the center aisle, remembering hearing about folks who walked the aisle repentant of their sins. She didn't walk that way right now. Oh, she knew her sins well enough, but there was no hope to get them taken care of. They were hers and hers alone. Not even Jesus himself could take those from her. Certainly not Hixon. And as she remembered him again, walking the aisle seemed even more painful. She would not walk it toward Hixon, a white dress covering her nakedness.

Emory made her way to the front pew, then sat there. The church smelled of mildew and neglect, much like she felt in her heart. In a moment, she remembered one of the last times—besides Daisy's funeral—she sat in a pew like this.

It was Mama's funeral. Emory sat in the front row, the casket draped in flowers in front. Mama's face looked peaceful, finally, now that she couldn't spew words Emory's way. Death had beautified Mama in a strange, unsettling way. Emory was called on to say a few words. She clutched a piece of paper and made her way to the pulpit. She smoothed the page while Mama faced the ceiling, expressionless. Emory read the words, not looking at anyone in the congregation.

"Some folks leave their marks on the world in a thousand ways. Good marks, important marks. I can't say I know enough of my mama to say that's true. I'm not even real sure she loved me."

Emory heard gasps around the small chapel, but she read on.

"But she gave me life, and for that I'm grateful. Thank you."

She didn't go back to her seat. Instead she left out a side door, never to return. She said her piece and left, no doubt electrifying folks with her words. The rumor mill would churn and spit out all sorts of tasty morsels about the ungrateful single mom who probably poisoned her mother.

Her funeral words blistered her mind: *But she gave me life, and for that I'm grateful.* Had the situation been reversed, and Emory were kidnapped instead, leaving Daisy on this earth to grieve, would Daisy have said the same at her funeral? That all Emory was good for was giving Daisy life—and nothing more?

Emory felt her insides shudder. Felt her heart fold in on itself, collapsing under the grief of who she was. Who she'd become. Who she probably would always be. She'd never be the woman Hixon thought she'd be.

Thunder rocked and rolled outside; lightning flashed through a broken stained glass window to her left. She waited for the familiar sound of rain on a rooftop, but none came. She'd heard of dry lightning before, but hadn't experienced such a thing, certainly not in December. Thunder clapped again, shaking the floorboards beneath her.

In a flash, lightning argued back—a single, nearly blinding strike through the opened roof above the pulpit. Flames erupted just feet in front of her.

But Emory didn't have the will to run away. Her punishment. Just in time.

Sixty-Six

Home wasn't where Hixon was supposed to be, though he wanted it to be. With the ring in his pocket and his intentions out there on the stage of Little Myrtle's, his humiliation was complete. He'd done what God asked, and she'd said no. Simple as that. Time to nurse a lifetime of loneliness, shutter the house, and live a reclusive life.

When he pulled in behind his house, he knew he wasn't supposed to cocoon there, just like he knew Jesus died for his sins. That kind of knowing. Idling in the driveway, he sat there, wondering what it all meant. Was he supposed to grit his teeth and make his way back to Missy's house for another rejection? Was there unfinished business with Jed? Were Jed, Sissy, and Ouisie in danger? Was someone breaking into Muriel's home? He felt doom in his chest, but had no idea of the nature of the doom. This made him antsy.

He drummed his fingers on the steering wheel. "Where to, Lord? You're telling me something. I feel it in my gut. Where to?"

Nothing dropped into his head. Not a thought, impression, and certainly not God Almighty's audible voice. Just the silence of idling. The only thing he knew to do was to drive. So he backed out of the driveway and drove. Nowhere and everywhere.

Sixty-Seven

So hot. So terribly hot. The heat sizzled Emory's face, the flame's strength igniting the church like it was dried up kindling. She choked and coughed while billowing smoke churned in front and around her.

Though relieved that dying greeted her, she hated suffering through its handshake. She ducked under the pew, lying prostrate on the floor. Thoughts smoldered through her head, particularly the irony that here she was finally, at the altar of a church, flat on her face, and yet she wasn't turning from her sin, really. Because she was sin. All of her. In a way, she was laying her sorry, sin-stained life before the God who seemed so distant, the God who stole Daisy. She had nowhere else to turn. For a time he didn't snuff her out as he should. She watched as panels of the ceiling fell overhead, crackling, then flaming all around her. With the pew above her as shelter, it was as if God created a little fire-safe haven, keeping her from the increasingly taunting licks of flame.

"Oh, come on, you can do better than that!" Fire absorbed her voice. In hollering her words, her throat scorched.

God answered back by consuming her—the smoke from his nostrils choking out every bit of life she once had. She'd hoped that dying would finally give her peace, but in the effort of pulling in sooty breaths, she felt nothing but panic and despair. The final judgment was no comfort—it was pure, raging agony. She could feel the claws of hell pulling her closer.

Sixty-Eight

After driving circles through the neighborhoods of Sunday-afternoon Defiance, Hixon resigned himself to the painful inevitability: Missy's house. He parked his car out front, opened the door, and smelled smoke. The white house looked as it always looked, but the deadness of the air and the rumbling of the thunderhead high in the sky puzzled him. From very far away, he heard sirens.

He ran to her door and knocked. Nothing. He tried the handle. Locked.

He looked to his right, then his left. Hovering over the forest beyond the rendering plant, he saw smoke. And in that instant he knew. She was there. In that smoke.

Hixon leapt off the porch, abandoned his car, and hightailed himself through the forest, screaming Missy's name. She didn't answer back.

Behind him, he heard the grunts of someone trying to run hard, but not able to. He turned. In a flash, he saw a man dashing through the underbrush. The man stopped, stared right at Hixon. His eyes were lighter than a morning sky—and they held Hixon hostage. Those eyes. "Why, it's you," Hixon said.

The man startled at the words. "You know?"

"Yes," Hixon said. But nothing made sense.

The man pointed to the clearing. "She's in the church." His

voice sounded garbled, almost husky. "But" — he smiled — "it's too late. Flames from the sky do that, you know? Kill the enemy beneath." The man slowly turned and walked toward town, as if that's what he did every day on this earth — prowling and haunting and never getting caught.

Hixon hollered, "You will be found!" but by the time he finished his sentence, the man was gone.

Hixon ran to the church, his breath coming in hesitant gasps. The smoke choked through his lungs, singed his breath. Flames circled around and through the church, roaring, licking, cracking, searing.

"Missy!"

No one answered.

In a heaving roar, the roof collapsed. Without thinking, Hixon bolted through the church's still-intact door, praying that the good Lord would wrap his cool hand around him, protecting him from the fiery furnace.

Sixty-Nine

It felt like a trip, this smoke-induced high. Emory saw Mama laughing—a sight she hadn't seen before. Mama pointed at her, made a face, then burst out laughing again. "You think dying will make it right?" More laughter. "You're a sorry excuse, you know? Dying only makes it worse. Because there ain't nothing you can do to fix the past. You rehash it over and over again like moldy leftovers."

"Go away, Mama," Emory felt herself say.

"Suit yourself, child. But mark my words. Your dying won't do a thing. Won't right the wrongs."

David floated into her dream. He walked this time, no wheelchair holding him down. "Go back," he said. "The world needs you, Emory. Don't buy into the lie that death's the way to escape. Believe me, I know. I wanted to die too. But I didn't, and I'm so glad."

He flew on butterfly wings into the bluest sky she'd ever seen. She wanted to fly that way too, loved the way David looked so free.

Muriel stood in front of her now, no longer bald. She smiled broadly, but a tear crept down her face. "Not yet, dear one. Not your time. You can't move God's hand to take your life when it isn't time. Take a breath, you hear me? Right now. One, two, three." She held up three fingers. But Emory couldn't obey.

Couldn't take a breath. "Here, let me help you, okay?" She bent close, so close Emory could feel Muriel's cool breath. She blew life into Emory, and she gulped Muriel's air, suddenly hungry for more.

"I can't fight it," she said.

"You can and you will." Muriel shook her head. "The world needs you, dear one. Problem is you don't know that. A single life leaves an indelible mark. By leaving, you erase it forever."

"But my mistakes. My sins."

"Fiddlesticks. Nothing's too big for the hands and feet of God, baby. He went through the flames for you. You let those rest there." Muriel nodded again, smiling with pure white teeth. She hunkered close and breathed another cooling breath into Emory's lungs. And then she left, singing "Amazing Grace" on key.

Seventy

Hixon heard "Amazing Grace" clear as a waterfall as he fought passing out. Now on his hands and knees, he crawled toward the song, praying that Missy wasn't in this church but worried that she was. Whose voice was that? Why so clear? So beautiful?

He ducked under the pews as the roof continued to splinter and collapse above him. He hesitated under each pew, then leapt into the space between them, praying nothing would fall on him in the middle. The voice came clearer and louder, even in the melee of snapping, sizzling, roaring, and consuming. Hixon grabbed ashy breaths as low to the ground as he could crawl, but each gasp became more and more needy and desperate. His lungs begged him to leave that place. He disobeyed, feeling hell all around him.

"When we've been there ten thousand years, bright shining as the sun."

Hixon shook his head. Was that Muriel? How could it be?

For what seemed like an hour, he crawled toward Muriel's voice until he collapsed, flat to the floor.

I can't go on, Jesus. I pursued Missy like you said. I did. And though I'm a confused man on the inside, I think I've done right with my life. He thought of Muriel's last breaths, how she choked and sputtered and died. He wanted to die with dignity, as she did—even through the struggle, he'd seen light and beauty in her eyes. Would anyone see his? Would a soul know he died well? Hixon remembered repairing his relationship with Jed just hours before. A fitting end, he thought. Perhaps this was the Almighty's plan all along, to bring him to Mama Muriel sooner rather than later, after he'd spent a life well lived.

I lay my life down, Jesus.

Oh. No. You. Don't. The voice circled through and around him, shooting a blast of cool, wet air his way. Hixon opened his burning eyes.

"Amazing grace, how sweet the sound, that saved a wretch like me."

Muriel's sweet voice, but Missy's face.

Hixon pushed toward her. He crawled on burning embers, under another pew, until he lay next to Missy, calling her name over and over again. But all she did was sing like an angel a hymn he'd never heard her sing. With every ounce of life left in him, he pulled her. She didn't crawl, didn't stir, gave him no leverage. She stopped singing.

He pulled her dead weight, painstaking inch by inch to the side of the church, praying God would send water onto the flames rearing their ugly heads. In an instant, he saw the forest outside through a thick firewall. He grabbed Missy around the waist, heaved in another heavy breath, and stood, flopping her limp form over his body.

From deep inside a holy roar burst from his lips. As his voice pulled through his lungs, his feet seemed to sense the call to war. He ran Missy through the flames like a kid would run his finger through a lit candle—his face feeling the lick of heat with each step. He collapsed on the grass outside, his face burning. He looked up at the sky then, prayed God would save Missy's life.

He felt his pocket, gasped, and pulled himself back up. He had to return. The ring was gone.

Hixon heaved himself back into the inferno, crawling, touching, burning, scraping his way through the dying church. His breath burned whether he inhaled or exhaled. His eyes were on fire. He could smell his hair burning. In the middle of the church, while timbers creaked and fell, he prayed that Jesus would give him this one last request: the ring. It was a maddening request, he knew—an impossible one. But being so close to the Almighty's breath, Hixon wanted to finish the marriage race God had set before him, and he couldn't do that without a ring. He closed his eyes, groping along the raging floorboards. In a holy second, he felt the circle of gold. He closed his burning fingers around it and tried to retrace his crawling, but he found his lungs and legs and arms uncooperative. "Please," he said to the fire. "Please."

He drifted toward eternity, toward a warm, unburning light, wavering, wanting so much to see Jesus but agonizing over a job not completed. From behind him something closed on his ankles—someone's grip. It pulled him through the fire with such strength, he knew it was Jesus.

Under the canopy of a smoky sky, Hixon labored to catch air into his lungs. He only needed a little to say something. And he needed Jesus to do one last job. But instead of Jesus' face above him, Jed appeared, his face ashen.

"What were you doing running back in there like that?" Jed's voice sounded like Hap's and Ouisie's mixed together—fury and fear.

Hixon tried to speak but couldn't.

"They're coming—the paramedics." Hixon noticed tears in Jed's eyes, though his eyebrows had been scorched.

"Missy," he said. Jed's face warbled out of focus, replaced by Jesus, shiny and beckoning. Hixon shook his head. "No." Jed returned.

"Miss Emory?"

Hixon nodded.

"I don't know. They're working on her now."

Hixon breathed in a jagged breath, his lungs howling inside. He unfolded his hand and motioned to it with his eyes. "Please."

Jed took the ring. "What, Hixon? What is this for?"

"Put it," he wheezed, "on her." Jed morphed into Jesus again, then returned. "Her ring finger. We're married."

"What? Miss Emory and you are married? Since when?"

"Since now." Jed's face faded away as Hixon closed his eyes, longing for sweet sleep. "It is finished," left his burning, smiling lips.

Seventy-One

Emory's eyes fluttered open. The light overhead burned, so she shut them again. She heard voices so far away. Mama? Hixon? Muriel? Daisy? She couldn't tell. Couldn't make out the words, only that the voices sounded serious. She smelled the hospital, the medicine, the stale antiseptic. And in that moment, eyes closed like coffin lids, she smelled death. Was it her own? She'd heard enough about it to know she'd be floating above her body, hovering like a curious angel above herself while a big, bright light would entice her to a happier place as her duties to earth clawed her back down. But none of that was true in this instant. No floating. Hovering either. Just burning eyes and a belly full of anger that she was still messing with earth.

And yet, a part of her felt relief. She didn't have to face reckoning—no final judgments.

She heard a man's voice.

All she really wanted to do was sleep. And then sleep some more. And maybe she'd end up dancing with the angels. Or jigging with the devils. Hard to say. So very hard to say.

Someone touched her face. This made her angry. Who would do such a thing? Only Daisy would touch her face, sometimes to wake her, but never anyone else. Not even Angus would do such a thing.

There it was again. A brush of a hand against her cheek. She nearly crawled out of her skin at the thought of it. This called for some eye time, but not adoring eyes—angry eyes. She willed her lids to open, but she felt like each lid was covered in liquid lead. Finally, she opened both, only to see shapes, not people. She tried to talk, but her mouth wouldn't work. And all of a sudden, her mouth felt like she'd been chewing cotton balls. She shut her eyes again, then opened them—a little faster this time. Now she could see but still could not talk. The first blurred face she saw was Ouisie's.

She wanted to ask where Hixon was, but she couldn't.

"There you are. We've been worried sick about you. What in tarnation were you doing in that church? I swear. If Hixon hadn't—"

A shush shot from Emory's left. She rotated her eyes toward the shushing, her eyeballs slow to respond. Jed Pepper. He wore the most serious expression she'd ever seen on him. More serious than the night they discovered Daisy was missing. His mouth did not move, but his eyes said something terrible. She hated him all over again. Hated the sight of him. Hated that Ouisie wanted her to offer forgiveness. How could she do such a thing? If she forgave Jed, then she'd have to face her own part in Daisy's death. And that was simply too much for a mama to bear.

Emory tried to make a noise, but only a painful grunt came out, searing through her throat, which felt like it was a dime store ashtray receiving the butt ends of one thousand joints. How could she tell Ouisie to make Jed leave? Her eyes closed with the pain. Emory felt tears wet her eyes, but could do nothing about them. Her hands and arms, if they were still attached, felt very far away from her torso. All while Jed looked on.

"What I mean to say is," Ouisie cleared her throat, "I've been worried about you. Jed too. We've been by your side ever since the fire."

She opened her eyes again, adjusting to the light. "Where am I?"

"Tyler General. They're watching you for smoke inhalation." Ouisie smiled down at her with those haunted blue eyes, a thick smear of makeup covering up a bruise on her left cheekbone.

"You're hurt."

"She didn't have to be," Jed said.

Ouisie shushed him. "Jed, honey, why don't you go get me a cup of tea in the cafeteria. I need a little time."

Thankfully, Jed obliged her. Once the door opened and shut—she could feel the air in the room change and hear the whoosh of the door—Emory saw the old Ouisie again. Not the confident Ouisie who forgave her or the fiery one who confronted her. Just the Ouisie who dodged fists. "Is he up to his old tricks?"

"Oh, you know me. Clumsy as all get out. I hit my face on a tree branch."

"Really."

"Listen, there's something I need to tell you, Emory." She smiled.

Emory saw right through Ouisie's expression. It was her there's-something-wrong-but-I'm-not-going-to-tell-you smile. "You leaving Hap?"

Ouisie's smiled erased. "It's Hixon."

Emory tried to shake her head no, but she couldn't. Somewhere inside she knew how she escaped the fire. It had to be Hixon's doing—Hixon who always rescued, even when she didn't deserve it. Hixon who fixed her walkway, who fitted her door with locks. Hixon who covered her with his coat while she gazed at the dull sky. Hixon who made sure she was safe. Hixon who loved her when she never bothered to return the favor. Hixon who wanted to marry her.

Ouisie sat on the corner of Emory's bed and took her faraway hand. She could feel Ouisie's warmth on her fingers but could not squeeze. She could not pull away, but right now she had no desire to let go of Ouisie's warmth.

"He... Well, he..." She sniffed in tears, then wiped her face with the back of her free hand. "That man is more like Jesus than anyone I ever met." She shook her head.

Emory needed to hear more, wanted to, but in an instant, her eyes felt leaden again, and she drifted into a darkening sleep and a terrifying dream where Hixon no longer walked the earth.

Seventy-Two

Ouisie still held her hand. She could feel its warmth on hers. But this time Ouisie didn't speak. She just held on—not too tight but not too loose either. Emory relaxed her hand into her friend's, trying to figure out how to pray. She wanted to thank God for something simple like that—a hand in hers—but wasn't sure how to do it. Did you just say thanks? Or was there more to it?

She drifted into the last moments she remembered, circling around to David's note. He'd told her to go back to Crooked Creek. The page, typewritten and neat, flashed before her, then stayed floating in front of her. She read the words again, eyes still closed, while Ouisie hung on to her hand.

> Dearest, sweetest Jesus,
>
> Your Emory is in the fight for her life.
>
> She needs to know you love her, Jesus.
>
> But she can't seem to feel it.
>
> Bring her back to Crooked Creek Church—the place where it all started.
>
> And find her there.
>
> And love her there.
>
> Dear, dear Jesus, hear my prayer. Will you?
>
> Rescue her. From herself.

But if her inkling was right, it wasn't God who found her there in Crooked Creek Church as it burned under a winter sky; it was Hixon. It wasn't God who rescued her; Hixon did. And paid a terrible price. She remembered Ouisie's words, how Hixon was more like Jesus than anyone Ouisie'd met. Emory connected all the dots, all wildly far apart, until they figured into a picture of Hixon and Jesus all mixed together. Jesus in a black man's skin. Only now, both of them had died in their sacrifice, and only one resurrected.

Seventy-Three

That same warm hand. Hap must've really changed to let Ouisie go to Tyler so much. She told her eyes to open, but they wouldn't budge. She tried to speak again, but could only growl until her throat burned and spittle leaked out of one corner of her mouth. The hand let go, then wiped her mouth. Indistinct voices swirled around, but she couldn't focus on one. Then sleep overtook her again, and she floated away on a cloud of black sadness.

It came to her quite unexpectedly, the word that rustled her from her long, dark sleep. She'd seen Ouisie that one day, then couldn't rile herself until just now when the melody of a voice meandered through her head. Was it real? Or another dream?

It came after one thousand dreams about her life. She saw it all plain as day played on the movie-house screen of her mind. Her mama. All those terrible words and shanty houses. Her love affairs. The anger that boiled way down deep. The thirteen years of Daisy's walking the earth, Emory not paying enough attention, not caring enough, not cherishing enough, not celebrating small things like Daisy's first word—Mama—or the multitude of flower pictures Daisy painted for her that ended up in the trashcan in the kitchen when Daisy wasn't looking, not holding her hand as they walked to town, not stooping low to blow out a dandelion, not skipping alongside Daisy as she sung her way down the street, not paying any mind when Daisy went wandering, not quitting her pot-smoking habit even though Daisy begged her. All these regrets felt like links in a heavy chain Emory now wore as a painful necklace around her neck. It coiled around her like a metal snake, tightening its grip on her throat.

It was precisely in the midst of that despair that the voice came, low and sweet, like the best coffee you've ever had paired with a vine-ripened cantaloupe that tasted of heaven.

"Missy."

What? She told her eyes to open, but they stayed shut. She tried again. She felt her lids lift, then shut again. Another "Missy." This time Emory prayed, not in high-church language with all those *thee*s and *thou*s, but with her own honesty. God, her mind said, please let me open my eyes. At that, they finally obeyed. And when she opened them, she saw the most beautiful Jesus in the world. But when she closed her eyes and opened them again, Hixon was gone, only an empty ceiling where he'd been.

Seventy-Four

He squeezed Emory's left hand, then let go. She felt the heat leave her fingers, wishing again for the warmth of Hixon's hand. She would say yes this time, the moment she saw his face. His beautiful face. In that shimmer of memory, she concentrated on his eyes. The rest of his face was crisscrossed in fire welts, his scars for saving her life. But it was his eyes that captivated her. Hixon cleared his throat. She begged again to see him. Prayed yet another prayer. God answered, gave her back her eyes.

But only Jed stood above her, his eyes red.

She swallowed. Her throat felt scorched.

"Mama sent me in," Jed said. He shook his head. "No, that's not right. I sent myself."

"Hixon." Her voice soothed at the mention of his name.

"He went in after you." Jed sat in the chair next to her bed.

She wished he'd leave. She didn't like having to go through this boy to get information about Hixon's whereabouts. Maybe Ouisie did send him in, to silently encourage Emory to forgive the boy. She shook her head. "I know that. And I saw him."

"But he went into the fire again."

That made sense, after seeing his scars like that. She felt the guilt hover over her like a cloud of fire-air, choking her. She'd done that to him. Her. All because she wanted to die, and he was bent on saving her. The sorrow of that suffocated her.

"And he gave me a job."

Emory shook her head. A job?

Jed took a long breath, then let it out. He looked older than fourteen now, more like a man. It made her wonder how Daisy would look today. Would she have the look of a woman? Would her slender frame have started to fill out? Would she have Jed's look of weariness?

"Hixon's ring." He briefly touched her hand, pointing to her ring finger. There, shining golden, was Hixon's ring on her finger—the one she had folded back into his hands the day of the fire.

She smiled. So he'd given her the ring. Did she already say yes? "I saw him. Where is he?"

Jed coughed. Looked away. Said nothing.

"Oh, come on. He was just here, standing right over there." She pointed her ring finger in the direction of Hixon's memory.

Jed stood. "I pulled him from the fire. He dragged you out, then ran back in. Lucky thing I saw him. He'd dropped the ring, I'm guessing, because when I pulled him out of Crooked Creek, he had it in his hand." Jed's voice sounded choked, as if smoke swirled in the room hovering near his lungs.

"So why are you telling me this story and not him? Are you trying to prove how brave you are?" Emory coughed.

"No ma'am. He can't tell his story, which is why I'm telling it."

She didn't remember much about Hixon, but she distinctly remembered him saying her nickname. "Missy," she said.

"Yes, that's the name he said after I pulled him out. He gave me the ring. Said you were married. Told me to put it on your finger."

"He didn't put it there?"

Jed paced to the end of her bed. "Miss Emory. I'm sorry. Mama wanted to tell you, but I felt it best that she didn't have to do such a thing. Believe me, it's not like I wanted to be here. With you."

Emory remembered her affair with Hap in that instant, and wildly colored dreams danced across her mind. She didn't want Jed here either, considering. "Just tell me what you need to say and leave."

"Hixon is dead."

Seventy-Five

Emory twisted the ring in her hand with every tear. Alone in her room, she tried to picture Hixon's face again, but her memory failed her. He couldn't be dead.

But he was.

The nurse confirmed it, gave her a sedative she didn't take, and quietly left.

When Hixon whispered her name in the hospital room, she had felt the voice of God behind it, and now she understood why. Tears watered her face, but she didn't wail. A strange peace burned inside, a slight knowing, a hint of Daisy and Hixon and paradise all mixed together. At least in heaven Daisy'd have a father. And Hixon would dote on a daughter. She touched the ring again, wondering at its story, trying to figure exactly when it was she had fallen in love with Hixon.

It was his kindness toward others that flashed through her mind. How he scraped and painted her home, easing Jed's task. The way he cared for Muriel, tenderly nursing her as death came near. How he loved Emory enough to confront her about those pills. How he'd let go of pretense, showing his scarred wrists, desperately trying to show her Jesus. How he brought her yard flowers. How he chose not to expose her to Officer Spellman. How he covered her with his coat even after she'd betrayed him in every way, leaving a shivering man. When he covered her like that, she tasted grace, felt its weight on her chest. And now all that grace wrapped in Hixon was gone. Love too.

It was Ouisie who bore her weight as she walked to the hospital's morgue. It hadn't been long since she'd last ghosted the halls of Tyler General's underbelly. With each step, her lungs hurt, but it was her heart that threatened to explode with grief's shrapnel. "I need to rest a moment," she told Ouisie.

They sat on plastic chairs. "Are you sure you want to do this? We'll be remembering Hixon soon—in a nice memorial service. Why don't you wait until then?"

"I have to see him. Have to say something."

They waited in silence while hospital personnel rushed past. When Emory stood again, her stomach felt like morning sickness. Ouisie steadied her. Kept her on her feet. "It's this way."

A white-coated man met them in the waiting area. "I'm sorry," he told Emory, "but only next of kin are allowed to see the body."

She thrust her left hand his way. "He's my husband," she said.

Ouisie nodded. "It's the truth."

And it was the truth, in a way. He'd given her the ring. They'd been together in a church. And God performed the ceremony, Jed the unlikely ring bearer.

"Right this way." He pushed through several swinging doors, so much like the trek to see Daisy's lifeless eyes. "It's in here." He pointed to one last door in the whitewashed hallway.

"His name is Hixon Jones," Emory said.

"Very well, Mrs. Jones. We've pulled him from the morgue and de-bagged him. He's covered in a sheet." He paused. "I need to warn you, the burns were bad." He turned, padding down the echoing hallway.

"Let me go in with you," Ouisie said. Her eyes were already filled with tears. "You'll need my help."

Emory pulled in a breath, let it out into the antiseptic hallway. "No," she said. "This is something I need to do alone."

"I'll be right outside the door."

Emory nodded.

She pushed through the door, reliving the same memory. Except this gurney was much longer, and the person beneath it taller, stronger—at least in life. Emory watched the sheet for a long time. Ouisie called through the door to see if she was all right, and she said she was, but she really wasn't. Mama had been right to warn her. She looked at her palms, railroaded by trouble lines. And then she settled her eyes on her wrists. Trouble intersected her life on every front, in every way.

She neared Hixon, placed her hand on the white sheet and pulled it back. There he was, his skin gray-brown, crisscrossed by licks of flame. His eyes were closed, sunken a bit, and his mouth formed no smile. This was the man who had saved her. This dear, dear, Jesus-loving, flower-giving man. She wept over him every regret, every time she turned him away, every time she cursed him silently. All he'd wanted to do was love her, and now he laid here with no breath, his air stolen by the fire he saved her from.

No. It wasn't right.

Heaving in a wail, she told God as much. "You should've taken me. Reunited me with Daisy. This world doesn't need me. It needs him." She touched his face, ran her hands over its burnt contours. So cold, so very cold for someone who surged with life. She pulled back the sheet, exposing his left hand. She bent to kiss his wrist—the wrist that echoed her own. "You should've taken me." She intertwined her fingers with his, wishing they'd grip hers one last time.

It was then she noticed the ring. Scorched over his wedding ring finger was a crude scar, circling. "Oh, Hixon. God did marry us, didn't he?"

Holding his hand, Emory said, "I love you, Hixon. And I'm

sorry. I'll spend my lifetime being sorry. Because besides Daisy, you were the best thing that ever happened to me." She let go of his hand. It fell to the side of the metal table with a thud. She turned away, nursing tears.

She almost left the room with him exposed like that, the raw ache in her chest compelling her to leave. She turned instead, faced Hixon again. Standing next to him, Emory removed her robe and covered Hixon with it. Returning the favor.

Seventy-Six

Officer Spellman paced her hospital room, back and forth, like if he did it enough, he'd solve every Defiance mystery.

"I need to tell you something."

"Is it something about the investigation?" She shifted in her bed, thankful she'd be leaving soon. Tyler General had become more like a prison. She wanted her bed. And she even wanted Mary Jane—the cat, not the can.

Officer Spellman sucked in a long breath. "It's Clyde Van Tassell. He's taking back your house. He's asked me to tell you to pack your things."

"What?"

"Says you're way behind on your rent."

She nodded. What would she do now? Where would she go?

"Do you have someplace to go?"

"No." Her denial sounded hollow.

"Wherever it is, it needs to be a safe place. We haven't found the killer yet, Miss Emory, and I'm worried about your safety." His hand nearly settled on hers, but he withdrew it. "I wish I knew how to protect you."

"What does it matter, Officer Spellman?"

"Please." He held up both hands like she was arresting him. "It's Hank."

"I know."

"But you won't call me that."

"It doesn't seem proper, is all."

Officer Spellman stood, paced some more. "This whole thing has me puzzled. The detectives too. Daisy's gravestone is still missing. Her picture too."

"Actually, her picture is on the mantel again."

He spun around. "What?"

Emory's voice felt raw. She took a drink. "It came back. I found it on the mantel, then saw Daisy's open window."

"I'll need to take that picture in. And have a look at her window."

"Do you have to?"

"That's how I'll keep you safe, by catching this guy. I'm sorry. I know the picture must mean the world to you."

"It does." Emory told herself not to cry. Her house meant the world to her too. All those Daisy memories. And now Hixon's too. They'd be erased forever when the house was packed. "Did you find anything from all that dusting at my house?"

"Just a lot of your fingerprints."

She remembered how she'd been the vandal the first time, but with the real intrusion, she hoped there'd be something left behind. "The shoe?"

"Nothing. And believe me, this case keeps me up at night. Keeps me walking through Defiance's outskirts on my time off looking for this man. He's like a ghost—no fingerprints, no clothing shreds, nothing left behind."

"Why are you doing this? Seems like you're going beyond the call of duty."

"No one deserves to have their child taken."

She wanted to scream, I do, but her throat ached, and her will drained out of her.

She touched her ring. "Or her husband."

"I'm sorry for your loss. Hixon was a good man."

"He was."

This time, he covered her hand in his. "Sometimes folks need mercy."

She pulled her hand away. "You?"

He retreated to the doorway.

She sat up. "It was you, wasn't it?"

"I'm not sure what you're getting at. I need to get going. It's clear I've riled you, and you need your rest."

"I'm only riled when I meet a hero—someone who pays for a little girl's funeral." She nearly choked out the words.

"It was nothing," Officer Spellman said. "Just a collection I took up at the station."

"It was everything to me. How can I repay you?"

"By staying safe, you hear me? That's the only payment I'll accept." He looked at his shoes. "I best be going, Ms. Chance."

"Call me Emory, Hank."

As he left, she saw him smile.

Seventy-Seven

Emory called David the day she got out of the hospital, finally able to keep talking without a scorched, fiery throat. Her house was full of banana and canned tomato boxes—all waiting to be filled and transferred to nowhere.

Alone in her house, she reached for the phone and dialed David.

"Hello?"

"It's Emory."

"I heard the news. You okay?"

"Yeah, very funny. I'm fine. Those were some notes you've been sending. Practically got me killed and all. Tell me, was this all a part of your evil plan to win me back? Because it didn't work so well."

"What?" David's voice sounded genuinely surprised.

She'd have to spell it out. "The notes. You know, the typewritten ones, addressed from Burl. With all those prayers in them?"

"I have no idea what you're talking about."

"You didn't send me typed prayers in the mail?" Now she was the surprised one.

"No ma'am. But I've been praying for you just the same."

Emory sat at her kitchen table, then looked at the phone. "You sure you haven't been sending me typed prayers?"

"Sure as anything in this life."

"Then who sent them to me?"

"How would I know?"

She hung up the phone. She'd been so sure. If it wasn't David, then who could it be? She remembered the church, the lightning, the story Hixon told of how he pulled her out of the church. He knew where she was. He said God told him.

Emory stood in Joe Ed Thornton's office. He told her to sit, but she kept standing. "I don't understand."

"It's right here in Muriel's will. Her house is yours now."

"But it was Hixon's, wasn't it? Didn't Muriel give it to him?"

"Yes, but she gave it to you, too, equally. Thankfully, I have an extra key. Hixon had the other one." He handed her a key. "She lived out in the country. I can drive you there if you'd like."

She nodded, holding back tears. She'd priced little apartments this week—all out of her price range. Big Earl told her she could live at Little Myrtle's—there was a small room behind the kitchen—but she couldn't imagine smelling like chicken fried steak, nor could she figure out where all her stuff would fit. And now this. A house. In her name. It felt too good to be true.

Emory walked through the house, smelling Muriel and must while Joe Ed waited in the car. She wanted to fling open every window, let in the winter air to blow in some life, but she told herself to wait until she moved her things within its cozy walls. She could mourn here. The wide-open fields flanking the house gave her the space she needed to do it—her own Swan Field surrounding the house like a citadel. She sat on the brown couch, marveled at the wood floors, touched the fireplace's stone. A home. She had a home.

Emory returned to the white clapboard house to find Ethrea Ree on the porch, swinging gently, saying nothing.

"Ethrea Ree," Emory said.

But the woman rocked back and forth, humming. She pointed to the doorway, where a pan sat covered in wrinkled, flattened tin foil.

Emory picked it up, pulled back the foil, and spied more chicken and dumplings.

Ethrea Ree cleared her throat and stood. She put thin, veined hands on her wiry hips. She huffed in a breath, then let it out slow, like a decompressing tire. "I made it for you," she finally said.

"Thanks. You're a great cook."

"What do you mean, cook?"

Emory set the pan down to unlock the door. "Won't you come in?"

"No."

"Well, I don't know quite how to thank you other than offering you some tea."

Ethrea Ree backed up, put her hands out in front of her as if an offer of tea were an invitation to drink poison. "I love needles."

"Okay. That's good. Maybe I'll just be going inside." Emory

wondered if Ethrea Ree meant she'd put needles in the chicken. With all the scariness around these parts, it wouldn't surprise her anymore.

"No. Not yet. I gotta 'fess."

"'Fess to what?"

She sat again on the porch swing, running her left hand through her thinning gray hair. "Needles and thread and verses of dread."

"I'm sorry," Emory said, this time leaning against the porch railing. "I don't really understand."

"The needlepoint. I made it."

The old lady could've said she used to be governor of Texas, and Emory would've believed it over this. "You?"

"I ain't proud."

"Why did you do that?"

Ethrea Ree rocked. But she didn't answer.

The creak of the porch swing sounded like birds in pain, squawking back and forth under the old woman's slight weight. She folded her hands on her lap and said nothing.

"I'm not sure what to say. Thanks?"

Ethrea stood abruptly, pushing the swing behind her. She crossed the porch, then stood in front of Emory, her eyes aflame. "Responsibility is a sketchy thing, Miss Emory Chance. We're all responsible for someone's downfall. Every last one of us." She skittered down the stairs, down the path, and opened the gate, letting it shut on itself. She said no more words, but Emory heard the word *responsibility* in the wind and felt despair settle in over her heart once again. Guilt too.

Seventy-Nine

Emory, alone in the boxed-up house after Ethrea Ree left, longed for Daisy's framed picture again, suddenly needing to hold it. Now in her bedroom, she picked up Daisy doll, deciding her to be the perfect substitute for what she needed to do. Maybe someday she'd have the guts to confess the rest.

Hixon's sacrifice birthed two desires, both conflicting inside. One was to believe life was a big, fat nothing so she could throw it away with pills and pot aplenty. The other surprised her. For the first time this desire grew stronger than the need to escape. It was simply this: she wanted to make things right. Needed to. And she had to start with Daisy.

Mama never did say she was sorry. Not even when death snuck in and pulled her toward the afterlife. She fought saying sorry like she battled death—like a ninth-grade girl fight with scratching and biting and hollering. Maybe, Emory thought, doing this one thing would free her from becoming Mama.

She sat on her bed and held Daisy doll in front of her. Inanimate eyes stared back. Emory remembered seeing her own sweet Daisy with eyes like that, looking blankly at the coroner's ceiling. She remembered how cold Daisy's normally warm hands were. Remembered how death felt in her chest, like a vacuum cleaner sucked out all her breath. And since Daisy's death, she'd been walking this earth like that, breathless and longing for air.

"I'm sorry," she told the doll. "Oh, God." As soon as *God* left her lips, a bowling ball settled on her chest. She felt it physically, but she couldn't roll it off, and Daisy doll did nothing to help her. Tears flooded her cheeks, draining into her mouth. Deep sobs erupted from places inside her she didn't know she had. Memories speared her on every side. Mama this. Mama that. She wept some more, remembering all those times she begged Mama to hold her, to tell her she loved Emory, only to feel nothing and hear silence. The grief stayed heavy upon her chest, until her own motherhood memories slipped around her neck.

She watched in slow motion as Daisy clung to her. What was she, five years old? Blonde hair like plucked weeds made her look like a wild hippy child. "Mama," her sweet voice sang. "Do you love me? Tell me you love me."

"I gotta get ready for work," Emory heard herself say in the memory. The noose around her neck tightened.

"Hug me. Please?"

She watched as she pulled each tiny finger away from her waist, unleashing Daisy's hold. "Listen, I need to work. Do you understand me? If I don't work, you don't eat. That's what I'm put on this earth to do. Feed you. Put a roof over your head."

"Just one hug." Daisy pleaded with those blue eyes.

In one quick motion, Emory hugged her daughter, less than a split second, and left the room, leaving Daisy alone. Giving Daisy the same bowling-ball-memories. "Oh, God," she said again. With history repeating itself like that, there was no hope.

Mama did wrong by her, and she did wrong by Daisy. And nothing could stop the heavy memories or the choking ones.

"Oh, God, I'm sorry. I'm sorry. I'm sorry." More sobs consumed her, heaving her breath in and out while Daisy doll watched. "I've made a mess of things. Of everything. I wasn't a good mama." She turned to the doll. "Daisy, I don't deserve your forgiveness, but I'm asking. Please forgive me. Please forgive me.

Please forgive me. I wasn't what I wanted to be. I turned into what I didn't want to become. I left you alone." Emory rolled onto her face, her body splayed on the bed. Both the bowling ball weight on her chest and the noose around her neck lessened while she cried a lifetime of pain—pain given by others, and pain she gave to folks.

How long did she cry there? She didn't know. But with each tear cried and each confession, her grief leaked out and a little bit of light crept in until she was able to roll over and sit upright again. The sun shone brighter in her room after the cry, like Defiance after a thunderstorm rumbled through and gave the sun back. She noticed how the dust caught the light, how it danced like Daisy used to say. Maybe it was that she had Daisy's eyes now—full of life and imagination and possibilities. She'd told God how sorry she was, how neglectful she'd been, how she wanted to be someone different. Maybe he answered even if Daisy couldn't.

She stood, picked up Daisy doll, and placed her in a box for safekeeping. She'd wake up in Muriel's place. Emory pulled on her uniform, then went to the kitchen to get a drink. She passed the can of pot on her way. A little hitch in her heart told her to throw it away now, but she didn't do it. Not just yet. After a long drink of water, she went to the bathroom and splashed water on her splotchy face. Instead of Mama staring back, she saw Daisy there.

Why would God do such a kind thing? Why would he listen to her, let her cry away so much regret and grief, and then let her see her precious daughter in the mirror like that? Emory smiled, and then she sat on the toilet and wept some more.

Eighty

The letter slipped through the slot in Emory's door. She was there to witness the simple white envelope hit the wood floor of her living room. She'd wondered when the seventh letter would come, and here it was. She never thought a plain white envelope could be more beautiful.

> Dear, dear Jesus,
>
> Author of everything beautiful,
>
> Thank you for showing Emory your undying love.
>
> Thank you for changing her, for making her a woman who loves again.
>
> And now I pray you'd show her what remains.
>
> In the joy of her new life, reveal the untied threads.
>
> Oh, how I pray that every single day,
>
> Emory would know she's treasured.
>
> That she'd receive and give your love.
>
> That she'd receive and give your forgiveness.
>
> You take care of her, Jesus, because I can't.
>
> Amen.

She held the note in her hands a long time, relishing each word, wishing there would be more prayers coming. But the amen said it all. Or did it? She noticed writing on the other side. She turned the paper over.

Dear Missy,

I'm not one to deceive or pull the wool over, so I added this note to the last letter Muriel typed. These letters were her last acts of grace on this earth. She finished them all, then instructed me to have her friend Denim send them to you from Burl. I didn't know when each letter would be sent; I was to leave it up to Denim, who, according to Muriel, is a God-fearing, praying man. Hopefully by now, you know that my intention is to marry you. The good Lord hushed your name into my ear awhile back, so I've been praying and hoping and trying since then. I figured writing this would keep me accountable, and I hope that by the time you've received this, you'll have my ring around your finger. And if not, it'll be pretty embarrassing for me. But either way, you'll know my intentions. I love you, Missy. God gave me the love slow-like, a smolder of a fire igniting into a blaze over days and days. And now it can't be stopped. So as you read this, I pray you'll know how much I love you, that I will always love you, and that it will be my supreme privilege to call you my wife.

With love, Hixon

She touched the sentences he'd penned, then turned the paper over and admired Muriel's words, her typing. Both messages from heaven now. She tried to picture Muriel typing, one finger at a time, while her breath came in spurts. That kind of love knocked Emory flat. To risk discomfort like that. To spend her last moments on earth on words meant for a rebellious woman. It was too much. Too much. She cried as she reread Hixon's love letter. His wife. Her husband. Their love. She'd spend her life living up to outrageous love like that.

She spent the last night in the white house with Muriel's word *forgiveness* moving in and through her. Forgiveness. She'd been forgiven a city dump of wrongs. And yet, one person remained that she held a dump-heap against. Jed. All evening, while the sun slept and the moon rose and she turned on every light in her house, she thought of Jed. How he left Daisy in that church that now half-stood, charred against Defiance's grass. How he ran home to Hap, more worried about eating dinner than Daisy's safety. She pictured the tattooed man, still lurking somewhere in the shadows, grabbing Daisy, dragging her, stealing her life. She heard Daisy scream, but couldn't comfort. All because of Jed.

She sat in the living room. Looked at the half-hidden can behind *War and Peace*. She grabbed the book off the shelf instead, understanding the irony of the title. It was like Hixon said. The first half of her life was not so good, but maybe the last half would be beautiful even without Hixon. Like war, then peace. She'd never read the book, had always intended to after picking it up in a thrift store years ago. As she opened it, she noticed a bookmark partway through. She flipped to it and saw the book had been marked up. She scanned the underlined sentences then sucked in a breath.

To understand all is to forgive all, it read. Then scrawled in the margin next to the sentence was a name: Elliot. Emory knew Jed's name should be there. Right behind hers. She understood the world all too well. Understood how she messed up her own. Understood that Jed was only fourteen years old and already nursed an Emory-sized regret. Understood the painful truth that she slept half naked on the floor while Daisy went wandering off to Crooked Creek Church, that if the holy spotlight of truth were swiveled here and there throughout the earth, it would land on her, not Jed. She was Daisy's mama. She took pills and escaped her responsibility, and Jed took it on far more times she could count. And now he believed he was to blame.

Forgiving him meant watching herself sleep under God's light while the tattooed man stole her daughter. It meant bearing the weight of her own sins, her neglect, her desire for escape larger than her desire to mother her baby. In the light of her home, she saw all this, how Jed became her scapegoat when she should've been pointing the finger at herself.

She set the book back on the shelf, hiding the can, and went to a pile of boxes in the corner. Rummaging around for a few dark minutes, she found what she was looking for. She sat on the paisley coach, placing the contraption on her lap. One finger at a time, she typed a letter.

Dear Jed,

I forgive you.

I'm sorry. The whole thing was really my fault.

I hope you can forgive me.

Miss Emory

Emory folded the paper into threes and placed the note in an envelope, writing Jed's name in red ink on its face. She didn't know when she'd deliver it. But she knew she would. Maybe after Hixon's funeral.

Emory looked at her wedding ring, remembering Hixon's face when he hovered above her in the hospital room, the word *Missy* on his lips. Even from heaven he would protect her somehow; that she knew. Even as the tattooed man lurked and shot worry through her veins. Having the love of a man like Hixon made her feel settled, peaceful.

In the emptiness of the brightly lit house, she could almost hear Daisy's laughter echo off the stark white walls. Could almost smell Daisy's hair. Could almost see her dance.

"I love you, Daisy," she said to the quiet night. "And if I could, I'd give you ten million hugs to make up for the ones I never gave." She turned off the kitchen light, felt the power of letting go of light, of letting go of her fear. "Hixon's there now. He'll give you the hugs I never gave. I know he will."

"Good-bye," she said when she turned off the living room light. Emory walked through the house, switching off every light. With every pool of darkness, she said another good-bye—to fear, to Daisy, to who she used to be, to Mama, to the man who dragged her into the woods, to Muriel, to Ethrea Ree's cross-stitch, to Angus, to the can behind *War and Peace*, to Hixon.

Emory didn't like good-byes much, but this time saying them in the darkness felt right. Because she couldn't say hello to Missy Jones until she turned the page on Emory Chance.

It was Daisy's room she kept lit a long, long moment, while the rest of the house slept in darkness for the very first time. She scanned the room, pulling out every precious memory her mind could hold, cradling each like a newborn baby.

"Good-bye, Daisy," she said as she turned out her light.

Acknowledgments

To my sweet Daisies, Sophie, Aidan, and Julia, I so appreciate your grace as I wrote in the mornings of your summer break. I pray I am more and more like Hixon in your lives. Patrick, you embody the beauty of Hixon, even when I'm Emorying. You've shown me the heart of Jesus in ways I can't communicate. And I believe you'll be showing the world his beauty again in due time.

To Leslie Wilson and D'Ann Mateer, we're in this for life. I'm so blessed to call you friends. Wow. God's really been up to some cool stuff, hasn't he? I can't wait to hold your books in my hands.

Andy Meisenheimer, thanks for pulling from me that which I didn't feel possible. I've needed to dig deeper, and you've given me a backhoe to do so.

Beth Jusino, you've kept me on the path, reminding me why I do what I do. You've cheerleaded in the best possible way.

Wendie, thanks for giving me proper and beautiful insight to Emory's heart.

Thank you, prayer team, who prayed me through this book: Ashley and George, Kevin and Renee, Carla, Caroline, Cheramy, Colleen, Jeanne, D'Ann, Darren and Holly, Dena, Dorian, Elaine, Erin, Ginger and JR, Helen, Katy, Denise, Anita, Diane, Cyndi, Lesley, Leslie, Lilli, Liz, Marcia, Marcus,

Marilyn, Marion, Mary, MaryBeth, Michael and Renee, Pam, Don, Paula, Rae, Rebekah, Becky, Sandi, Sarah, Shawna, Sue, Susan, Tiffany, Tim, Tina, TJ, Tracy, Twilla, and Heidi. You've lifted my arms in the air when they fell to my sides. You've blessed me in every possible way, tangibly and intangibly. And you've stormed the gates of hell on my behalf. Thank you.

Jesus, you saw miserable me, how much like Emory I could've been, and you rescued me from the fire.

Read an excerpt from the final book in the Defiance Texas Trilogy!

DEFIANCE, TEXAS, DECEMBER 1977

When Hap swift-kicks me in my stomach, the last flash I see is the retreat of one well-polished pastor shoe. Mama always said you could tell the value of a man by the shine of his shoes. How he treated them reflected on how he treated his women, she believed.

"If you can find a man with polished shoes, Louise," she told me, "then you'll find the world."

The world I find today is dirt embedded into a yellow linoleum floor. No rushing kids preparing for school reverberate the kitchen—Jed and Sissy are gone now. I can't even remember what brought on the kick, what inciting words I said to deserve Hap's rage. I try to stand, but the world twirls around me, nearly the same feeling I get when I drink a little too much, though not nearly as sweet, not as beautiful an escape.

I re-taste my breakfast, then swallow it again. I'm terribly good at swallowing things these days—particularly secrets. Sissy and Jed gulp down their share too. If the church body would dethrone Hap from his pulpited pedestal and truly look him square in the eyes, they'd see these secrets, but no one bothers—not even the elders and deacons who know more than they let on.

So we ingest secrets like gravel, our stomachs distended in the effort, never really feeling fed. Or alive.

But his is not my only secret. A few months ago, someone killed Jed's best friend, Daisy Chance. She was a waif of a girl, thirteen and gangly. The love of Jed's life, though he wouldn't say such things. And as sure as I've memorized the streets of Defiance, Texas, I know who killed her. Hap believes I'm slow;

he doesn't understand the real Ouisie Pepper. When I'm holding my head in our curtained bedroom, convulsing under the spasm of another headache, I think.

And remember the man in the woods.

You want to know, don't you? You want to know what kind of person would strangle a sweet teenaged girl. Isn't it ironic that a woman people pass on the street, nod politely to, gossip about, actually knows Defiance's most horrible secret? But I'm not telling. Not yet.

Don't fret yourself, though. I'm pretty sure Daisy will be the only one taken.

I steady myself at the kitchen sink, placing cereal bowls in the sink, washing them one by one. I scrub in circles, round and round until they squeak beneath my sponge. And I watch the winter from my window.

It's not a cruel winter, not terribly chilly as you might expect this season. But this is Texas after all, prone to doing its own thing. As I settle myself into the day's plain mediocrity, the wind musters strength, bending trees, ripping browning leaves from stark branches. There are no clouds shifting in the wind, no birds protesting. It's a silent torrent, threatening to unhinge everything anchored down. Leaves tornado to the ground, but I can't hear them. And even if I could, I couldn't stop their demise.

In the quiet of my afternoon, a knock at my front door ends the day's silence.

I open it to Emory Chance, face afluster, eyes telling a story I cannot understand.

"Can you be married to a dead man?" she asks.

"Let's sit on the porch," I tell her.

She slides slender hands down her blue jean thighs. "He was fixin' to marry me. He asked me once." She reveals a simple gold ring, the ring she's shown me several times this week—a symbol of her confusion, a testimony to her grief.

I look at Emory, noting her blonde hair, so much like Daisy's.

Yet grief has nearly old-womaned her. Tiny lines crease around her downturned mouth. She smells of smoke, but her eyes don't hold fire anymore. It's a strange thing to me, and perhaps to you, that Emory has recently become my closest friend on this earth. But standing in our midst is that terrible out-in-the-open secret of her affair with my husband. I wonder if Hap still loves her, still sees the beauty beneath the lines, behind the smoke. Or maybe it was plain, undecorated lust.

"I said no." She sighs then, like she's letting out every hurt she's ever felt into the cool Defiance air. She owes her beating heart, her respiration to a man named Hixon who rescued her from herself, hauling her from a burning church, though I'm sure she scratched and scraped at the earth as he pulled her from the fire's destruction. She wanted to die. And he, saint that he was, wanted to marry her.

"You said no. Now you regret it. I say give it to Jesus. He keeps our grief. Holds it." But the words feel like sandpaper on my tongue, the abrasion shaving my taste buds.

Head in her hands, she grapples her skull with thin fingers. "He loved Jesus so much. Me? I'm a caged animal, a restless girl. Loving folks, Jesus in particular, doesn't come easily for me. Religion feels more like a trap."

"Jesus said the truth will set you free." The word truth slips out of my mouth like preferred vocabulary, like I'm accustomed to telling the truth with every sentence. But me saying truth is its own lie.

"Freedom." She says the word like it's Moon Pies on a high unreachable shelf.

"He will bring it, but it's never easy to grasp. Or understand. God gives his freedom and love like a mystery."

Emory hushes in and out. I know because I see her breath turn to mist. She looks at me. "Do you ever feel you deserve love like that?"

"No," I say. I don't deserve anything but rage. Certainly not affection. They say folks define their relationship to God by how their daddy treated them. My daddy was benevolent, but it's Hap I see in the Trinity now.

She stares at me, examines my face. "Has he been at you again?"

I shake my head, hoping tears won't bother my eyelids. Hap is adept at hurting me so it doesn't show, now that the elders and deacons got a sneak peek into his "home issues." He kicks me in the gut like he did this morning, below my ribcage, and I crumple on the kitchen floor, grabbing at breath.

"Ouisie?"

I shake my head. "I'm sorry."

"I'm not the marrying type." Emory holds herself. She shivers too. She pets her gold ring. "I loved him," she whispers—the quietest declaration of love I've heard, but the loudest too. "But I never told him. And now he'll be scattered atop the earth with so many unspoken words hovering above the ground."

With those hopeless words filling the space between us, Hap pulls into the driveway. My heart grows colder than the December afternoon. Emory shoots me a frightened look. Hap opens the door to his Chevy, a smile etched into his pastor face. "Well," he says. "Look here."

"I'll see you later." Emory haunts each stair, barely touching the risers.

Hap approaches her, puts up his hand. "What's that?" He points at the gold ring on her left index finger.

"Emory said Hixon asked her to marry him." I raise my voice when I say it, then cough, hoping he won't notice.

Hap stiffens. His teeth leave his smile, replaced by a tight-lipped grin. He sighs. "That's one I never pictured, to tell you the truth. Coffee and cream mixed together in Defiance, Texas? It's not the Almighty's plan."

Emory stops, turns, and looks Hap square in the face. "I always thought cream tendered the coffee. The coffee's the better for it, wouldn't you say? Or do you like yours black?"

Hap keeps his smile, shoves his hands into his dress pants pockets. "You know folks around here don't like the races mixing."

"Since when have I cared about what Defiance thinks, Hap Pepper?"

Words that only a woman not married to Hap could say. I wonder if he's enamored with her sass. Oh dear Lord, I hope not.

"There are norms, Emory. Societal standards that keep a town running smoothly. I'm just saying you and Hixon would've been in for some ugly behavior."

Emory laughs. "I'm touched by your concern. Really."

"What's that supposed to mean?" His biceps twitch beneath his white pressed shirt. I suck in my worry. I want to say something, anything, to diffuse Hap, but the fuse has been lit, and I hear its crackling spark. The sizzling burns my voice clear away.

"I best be going." Emory turns, seemingly unaware of what she's ignited.

Hap grabs her arm.

She jerks it away. "You make your point well."

She brisks away before I can beg her to stay.

We are left to stand on the cold porch, anger roaring between us like a campfire baptized with gasoline. Sissy will be home soon. Hap won't have time to take his fury out on me in the next seven minutes, so he looks at me with those secret-holding eyes. I capture a snapshot of his gaze for later examination in my memory, for one of those days the headache plagues me, because for a moment I see the hint of the man I first married, the reason I stay and don't run one thousand miles away.

"I'm hungry." He swallows.

"I'll make us a snack." I open the door, feel the warmth of our house, and thank God for Hap's hunger and Sissy's imminent arrival. That's enough grace for me today. And I guess I don't deserve much more.